No Such Thing as Home

by Ciaron Fox

Copyright © 2014 Ciaron Fox

The right of Ciaron Fox to be identified as the Author of the Work has been asserted by him in accordance with the Copyright, Designs and Patents Act 1988.

All characters in this publication are fictitious and any resemblance to real persons, living or dead, is purely coincidental.

for Charlotte

Chapter 1

It was dark and the village was still asleep as the old lady picked her way down the narrow lane to the edge of the path which led along the cliff top. Only when she was safely outside the village did she light the small lantern she carried. Then, using the dim light from the lantern she carefully picked her way along the rocky path round the headland.

When she neared the cliff tops above the narrow entrance to the bay she stopped and straightened up, she was growing old and rather stooped. She looked out over the open sea, squinting against the freshening breeze. Dawn was just breaking and the young sun stretched its grey fingers out along the horizon.

A gust of wind tugged at the thick silver hair which was pulled back from her face and tied with a length of dark green ribbon, the finest piece of cloth she owned these days. Her hair had once been her finest feature black as a crow's wing with a sheen of deepest blue when it caught the light, but all that was a distant memory now.

For a brief moment there was hope. But as usual this quickly faded as she scanned the empty sea.

Once, on the boy's fifth birthday, she was sure she had seen something, a face perhaps, for the briefest of seconds in the rolling surf. But then it was gone swallowed by white foam and spray as the waves crashed onto the rocks. She had seen nothing since, if she had indeed seen anything in the first place.

She stared out at the sea for ten minutes or more before she reached into the large pocket in the front of her heavy skirts and took out a white shell. It was a dog-whelk shell, spiral in shape, chalky white on the outside, pearly pink inside and about the size of her fist. She brought the shell up to her mouth and softly whispered into the open end. "Your son is sixteen years old today. He is a fine, handsome lad, the very image of his father, you would both be very proud."

She then gave the shell a small kiss before throwing it, as high and hard as she could. She watched as the shell went tumbling down into the foaming surf breaking on the jagged rocks below.

She waited for a short time, as if for some kind of reply. Then after a moment or two she heard a low *"kraa!"*

She turned toward the dark raven which had perched itself on the whin bushes growing along the cliff top "Don't you dare laugh at me; I've no time for your sarcasm this morning!"

Then wiping the merest hint of a tear from her eye she sighed, her errand done for another year, she headed home.

***

Finn woke to the smell of pancakes, he loved his birthday. Every other day of the year meant porridge for breakfast but on his birthday Granny made pancakes, what a treat.

He pulled back the rough-spun drape that separated his bed in the alcove, from the rest of the small dark cottage and leaped out. His feet barely touched the beaten earth floor before he was on his stool at the rickety wooden table by the hearth. "Good morning Granny!" He said cheerfully.

"Happy Birthday my boy" she replied and leaning down with a platter of steaming pancakes she kissed him on the forehead, before depositing the plate in front of him on the table.

Finn tucked in to the pancakes, he wanted to eat them while they were still warm and the butter was melting on them. They were delicious, made with the gull's eggs he had gathered from the cliffs the previous day, dangerous work but well worth the effort.

"I've been chatting with old Norman the watchman" said Granny, reaching over to the hearth and lifting the pot off the hook hanging over the fire. She poured a little hot water over the dry herbs she had been braking up in a small earthen bowl.

"Since your sixteen now and all grown up you need to be doing something productive with yourself. Norman's not getting any younger and he's finding it hard keeping watch on the firth. Cold nights and old bones don't really go well together" she stopped to take a sip of the tea she had just poured. It was made to her own secret recipe from various herbs she had gathered. "I've managed to persuade him that you're just the lad he needs."

Finn coughed, almost choking on the pancake he was chewing. "But... but I'm supposed to be apprentice deck hand with Dougal, it's all sorted!"

"Being a fisherman's just too dangerous" said Granny. "I've decided, and I've explained it all to Dougal, so that's that. Now finish your breakfast, you can help me in the garden today, till its time to go with old Norman" she said stirring her tea with a small bone spoon.

Finn knew it was pointless to continue the argument, when Granny had made her mind up there was nothing would change it. He finished his breakfast, washed the sleep off his face and put on his clothes. He pulled the rough woollen tunic over his head and fastened the leather belt around his waist. His shoes were made of leather soft soled and gathered up around his toes. It was spring, so his legs were bare, in the winter he would wear a pair of loose fitting woollen britches.

Finn spent the rest of the day working in the garden, stopping around midday for a bite of lunch. Granny kept a fine garden; it provided most of the vegetables for their plate. One corner however was set aside, it was where Granny grew some of the herbs and other plants that she used to make cures for the villagers ailments.

After a dinner of fresh fish poached in milk with fresh greens, Finn sat on his small stool by the front door of the cottage. The spring evening was drawing to an end and the light was just starting to fade. He looked round the curve of the bay, watching the rest of the village settling for the night. The cottages were gathered together deep in the bowl of the bay, small and squat, thick dry-stone walls topped by heavy heather thatched roofs. The walls were made from rocks gathered from the cliffs long ago; they had small shuttered windows and low doorways, the better to keep out the harsh winter winds that blew in off the cold northern sea.

Down on the beach the fishermen were checking over their boats which had been pulled up high onto the sand well out of the reach of the tide. Their wives were collecting the fish baskets and chatting, some with children perched on their heavy skirted hips or running around, getting under their feet.

Why couldn't she just let him be a fisherman like the other boys in the village? He knew that when his father had been lost at sea, it had broken her heart, but it was just so unfair. The day he had come into the world had been the worst of days; he had been burdened from the start.

He had killed his mother that day.

It didn't matter how many times Granny told him that it wasn't his fault he knew in his heart that it was. Her labour had been long, exhausting and she had lost so much blood, even Granny with all her skills couldn't save her. She had breathed her last the very moment he had drawn his first breath. The babies blue breathless cry becoming a lament for the mother he would never know.

His father had been at sea at the time, gone since first light; he knew nothing of his son's birth. The child had been expected any day, but he needed to take advantage of the lengthening spring days to provide for his growing family and besides, the silver herring had started to run.

When the boat returned Granny had been waiting on the beach, braced to deliver the terrible news. But Rae had not been on board.

Once his traumatised, grey faced crewmates had been helped out of the boat, they told a tale of a white maiden, who appeared from the very sea and had stood upon the waves calling for them to join her.

They had tried so hard to stop him, but Rae had gone with the maiden. He had dived over the side and was quickly lost in the mist.

That was that then, the boy was bad luck, and nothing would convince the villagers otherwise. Many women died in childbirth, that was just an unfortunate fact of life, but to loose both parents like that, it was just too much for the superstitious villagers. The boy was cursed and that was all there was to it.

All Finn ever wanted was to be normal, to go to sea and fish with the other men, settle down and raise a family of his own one day. He just wanted to fit in, it had taken months to persuade Dougal to even entertain the idea of taking him to sea with him, and now that hope was gone too. Night watchman! That was a job for the old men, injured or too weak to go out to sea, he was only sixteen.

"Are you ready then young Marwick?"

Finn looked round startled, "Oh! Yes. Yes, I'm ready"

He ran into the house to get the blanket Granny had looked out, leaving old Norman standing by the garden gate. Picking up the lantern and packed supper that Granny had wrapped in a piece of cloth he followed the old fella down the lane.

Barely a word passed between them as they walked along the path around the cliffs in the setting sun, the tip of the old mans stick clicking rhythmically on the stones.

The village of Bruann, was tucked deep in a sheltered cove, the rocky arms of which wrapped the village in a warm embrace and sheltered it from the worst of the storms that were common in the seas of the north.

Sheltered by the cliffs, the entrance to the bay was so narrow, that the low lying village was all but invisible from the sea. The safe harbour could only be accessed by those who knew how to approach and negotiate the treacherous fingers of jagged rock that guarded the narrow entrance to the bay.

By the time they reached the cliff top above the gap the light was fading, Finn lit his lantern and carefully followed old Norman down a winding set of steps that had been carved into the bare rock.

The steps were well worn and hollowed out with the passage of feet, wind and rain over the years. Finn was just wondering how many sets of feet had used the steps, when they reached the bottom.

There at the bottom of the steps, was a flat ledge of rock about four feet wide which formed a path between the bottom of the steps and the entrance to a cave which was really little more than a wide crack in the cliff face. On the wall of the cliff about halfway along the ledge was a rusty metal ring set into the rock and there, hanging from the ring was a large green bell.

"Here we are!" said Norman, as he led Finn inside. The caves narrow entrance, widened out considerably once inside and there was room for a small wooden table and a stool which stood in the corner.

Old Norman put his lantern down on the table and sat heavily on the rather flimsy looking stool. "You can store your food and such like in here, the cave's only to be used in the worst of weather mind, you spend all your time in here you might miss something out there" he waggled his walking stick out towards the ledge.

"You keep careful watch over the sea from out on the ledge there, course it's not so easy at night but you'll get used to it."

"Well, I'll be off then" said Norman. He leaned heavily on the table and grunted as he got to his feet. "Remember to ring the bell if any unknown ship approaches the bay. We'll need plenty warning if we're to get everyone safely to the top of the cliffs."

Finn watched the light from the old man's lantern fade as he trudged back up the steps and headed home. It was going to be a long night.

He went back inside the cave and put his supper onto the table. Then pulling the blanket a bit higher up his neck to ward off the cold sea breeze and leaving his lantern inside the cave he stepped out onto the ledge to begin his watch.

It took a few minutes but his eyes soon became accustomed to the dim light and he found, with the help of the moonlight, he could see reasonably clearly over the wide empty sea. It really would be a long time till dawn.

Chapter 2

Dawn eventually arrived and Finn was relieved to see big Billy Ogg, whose turn it was to keep watch during the day, lumbering heavily down the worn steps.

To put it mildly Billy was a hefty fella with the ruddy weather beaten complexion of a man who spent most of his days at sea, or drinking ale which was his secondary occupation. He was in his forties and a father of six.

The two eldest boys helped their father crew his fishing boat while the eldest girl helped her mother in the house. The other children were still too young to be anything more than a hindrance to their parents as yet.

The local men all took their turn as day watchman; the rota was drawn up by the village elders at the beginning of each month. The men all undertook to keep watch for a week, during which time the other fishermen provided for their family.

There was no such respite for the night watchman; his was a permanent post, with only four nights off per year by prior arrangement with the council of elders who would nominate the necessary replacement for the nights in question.

"Hullo there young Finn, I didn't expect to see you here this morning. Where's old Norman?" Billy said as he reached the bottom of the stone steps.

Finn stifled a yawn with his hand. "I'm the new night watchman, apparently. Granny spoke to Norman about it and that was that."

"Well there's no use in arguing with your Granny, you get off home now and get some sleep, you look dead on your feet" said Billy, squeezing himself through the narrow entrance to the cave carrying what looked like enough food to feed Finn for the rest of the week.

He didn't need to be told twice, he gathered up his things and trudged wearily back up the steps and along the path towards home. It was a good job his weary legs knew the path well, he was almost completely asleep by the time he got home.

That had been the longest and most boring night of his still too short life. The thought that this might be his lot until he reached the same ripe old age as old Norman filled him with despair. Or it would have done if he had the energy for despair right now.

Once he got home, he shrugged off his blanket and dropped it over his stool, scuffed his feet across the room and toppled into bed, asleep almost before his head hit the pillow.

Granny crossed the room and sat lightly on the edge of his bed. She reached out and stroked the boys smooth hairless cheek with the back of her hand.

He was such a handsome young man; it was a pity that none of the village girls would take a shine to him; he'd make a fine husband. Stupid girls, don't they know that you make your own luck in this life. They should make their own minds up rather than listening to the idle tittle-tattle of their idiot parents.

As she sat there looking at the lad she had brought up from a baby, she found herself whispering a lullaby. When the song was finished she took off his shoes and gently pulled the woollen blanket up over his shoulders, then she stood and carefully pulled the heavy drape across the front of the bed.

***

The next few boring nights passed much as the first had. Finn, who had always been a bit of a dreamer, now found that he had as much time as he wanted to let his imagination run free. There was nothing better to do while watching the empty sea for hours on end.

He dreamed that he was one of the crew on a large ship skimming over the waves towards the distant horizon and far off fantastic lands, lands he had heard the older fishermen telling tall tales about while they mended their nets.

There was a place apparently where the sea was as warm as broth, and blue as the sky. You could swim for hours without getting cold. He had also heard of other places where it was so cold that the very sea itself froze into large jagged blocks of ice and huge grey whales swam in between. How he longed to see those places, stuck there on the rocky cliff.

As he kept watch he also found that, just as old Norman had said, his ability to see in the dark got better with each passing night. There was just so little to see out there, nothing but miles and miles of grey gloomy sea. He could just make out the shadowy peaks of the mountains far off across the wide firth and the white iridescent foam down below, where the dark waves broke themselves onto even darker rocks.

Well the monotonous nights all too quickly turned to weeks and the weeks turned to months. Finn was becoming incredibly weary of the watch, how could old Norman have endured it for so long, thirty years and more, according to Granny, who was always right when it came to such matters.

He had spoken to the other watchmen. Nothing of any note had happened for the past two years, except for what looked like a few merchant ships passing by, far out on the horizon.

Something exciting may well have happened sometime before that but no one he spoke to could remember that far back. Nothing exciting ever happened here.

He scarcely even got to see daylight since starting on the watch, by the time he had wakened and eaten, the sun was already falling in the sky and night was fast approaching. He would have to find some way of persuading Granny to change her mind and let him go to sea.

He finished his soup and mopped up the remnants in the bowl with a thick crust of bread. It was already beginning to get dark, time to go to the cliffs again.

"You wrap up warm tonight Finn" said Granny who had already finished her meal and was clearing the table. "There's a chill in the air, wouldn't be at all surprised if we get fog."

"Yes Granny" he said wearily. What was the point of standing there all night watching a sea which was most likely going to be covered in thick fog? It all just seemed so pointless.

"Granny, I was thinking. I don't think this watchman thing is really for me. Maybe if I did it for just a few more weeks whilst you and the rest of the elders found a replacement? There must be one of the older fishermen who's tired of going to sea or….. or injured even?"

Granny barely looked up from the bucket where she was washing the dinner things. "The watchman's job is a very important one Finn; you should be pleased to have been chosen."

She stood up from the bucket and walked over to where Finn still sat at the table. "There's been a watchman on those cliffs for over a hundred years, keeping us safe. I won't hear another word about it. Now let's get your things, it's getting dark. I've packed some bread and cheese for your supper."

With that she helped Finn with his blanket, wrapping it tight round his neck, handed him his lantern and bundled him out of the door.

The old woman watched from the doorway as he rounded the low stone dyke and walked off down the lane.

Why couldn't he just be happy with his lot? The boy's a dreamer, far too much like his mother, thought Granny. She shivered and pulled her shawl tighter round her shoulders; there was a definite chill in the air tonight. "Time for a cup of tea" she muttered and she closed the door on the cold night.

The early part of the night passed just as the previous ones had, Finn stood on the ledge scanning the sea, trying to keep himself from tucking into the bread and cheese Granny had packed. If he ate it too early he would have nothing else to occupy himself with later. The trick he found; was in timing supper just right.

About midnight just as Granny had predicted, a thick fog rolled in from out at sea, he watched it silently approaching like a thick grey woollen blanket being pulled over the world.

That was that then. No point, standing there in the cold looking out when he could barely see his hand in front of his face. The fog was so thick that the entire fleet of Yoric Harkansen could sail right past him and into the bay and he'd be none the wiser.

Finn went back into the cave and sat wearily on the stool. He picked up the bag with his supper in it. "A wee bite to eat will help pass the time." He had resisted the urge to speak to himself at first, but after a while he found it helped to fill the silence and there was no one else about to hear him anyway.

"What was that?"...............

At first he thought it was the wind, the faintest of notes, high pitched but soft. Like the sea breeze whispering between the rocks. Then there was another note, slightly lower than the first but just as sweet.

He stood up and tiptoed to the cave entrance, to see if someone from the village had come out to play a trick on him. The fog was thick outside and he could see very little, but on checking the rocky ledge and walking up the steps to where it joined the path at the top of the cliff there seemed to be no one there at all.

He walked back down the steps to the entrance to the cave and was coming round to the idea that it had been his imagination, when he heard the sound again.

It was clearer now that he had left the cave, it was a soft note and it seemed to float on the mist. Then there was another note and another and another. Each note seemed more beautiful than the last as they swirled and curled intertwining with each other in a melody like none he had ever heard. He stood there motionless, entranced by the heavenly music, letting it wash over him in wave after wave.

Time seemed to stand still as he stood there in the mist listening intently. Then the music stopped, the last note slowly fading in the air. He stood there suddenly feeling empty inside, the warmth that he had felt only moments ago was gone and he suddenly felt very foolish.

He tugged on his collar and quickly went back inside the cave, where he slumped back down onto the stool.

It had all been a dream; obviously. He was tired, exhausted even. He had fallen asleep standing up. That was the only explanation. He slapped himself hard on the cheek, then again on the other cheek, just to make doubly sure that he was definitely awake.

He opened the bag again and ate the bread and cheese that Granny had packed for him as slowly as he could, waiting for dawn and the end of his watch.

The fog lifted just as dawn was breaking and the rising sun lit the fast retreating shreds of mist in delicate shades of pink and red.

He had worked out his report for the day watchman. "Cold night, thick fog, nothing of interest to report."

Yes, he was quite sure, there had definitely been nothing of interest to report at all.

Chapter 3

The next day Finn woke much earlier than he had done for the past few weeks. In truth he had not slept much at all that day, he had been tossing and turning feverishly in his bed, his mind racing. Strangely despite his lack of sleep he felt more awake and full of energy than he had done for weeks.

He could not stop thinking about the sound he had heard in the fog. The more he thought about it the more he was sure that he couldn't have imagined or dreamed such a magical sound. Even if he had been asleep; he had never dreamed something so vivid before and doubted if he would even have the imagination to dream up something so fantastical.

Especially when it came to something so beautifully musical, he could barely whistle a simple tune. As for his singing voice the last time he remembered trying to sing Granny had ordered him to stop immediately as she feared that his voice would curdle the milk.

He got out of bed and immediately saw that Granny was out and about. He had a quick breakfast of tea and cold porridge which had been left at the side of the hearth for him, before pulling on his tunic and heading down to the shore. It was a bright spring afternoon; the sun was shining between puffy white clouds which were scudding across the sky, pushed along by a brisk westerly wind.

Finn took a deep breath, filling his lungs with the salty tang of sea air and smiled as he felt the warm sun on his face. He immediately resolved to get up a little earlier from now on and go for a stroll. He had almost forgotten how pretty the village was on bright sunny days like this.

Before he knew it, he had reached the track by the beach. The track was rough, just wide enough for a cart to pass and scribed a rough semicircle the length of the beach. The beach itself was almost empty, as the fishermen were still at sea, squeezing every last minute out of the lengthening spring days in order to maximise their catch. It had been a long lean winter after all.

The only boat left on the beach was "The Harvester" owned by Billy Ogg who was still working out his week's duty as day watchman. Finn saw Billy's eldest son Donald hard at work on the boat, he was using a flat wide metal blade to scrape the accumulated barnacles and weed off the hull, huffing and puffing as his chubby hands pushed the heavy metal scraper across the wood.

Donald Ogg had never been a thin boy but now as he reached manhood it was increasingly obvious to all that he was destined to become the very image of his father. His already ample gut was fast approaching the girth of his fathers' prodigious stomach.

Finn nodded over at Donald by way of a greeting, but if Donald saw him, he ignored him and carried on with his work,

This was nothing unusual, Donald and Finn had never been the best of friends, especially since the day that Finn had blackened Donald's eye and embarrassed him in front of the other kids. But that had all happened years ago; they had only been children, about ten or thereabouts.

Well if Donald wanted to bear a grudge that was his problem. None of the other boys ever called Finn "a Jinx" again after that. Well at least not to his face anyway.

Looking past where Donald worked on his father's boat, Finn saw old Norman sitting on an upturned basket. The old man was leaning forward, with both hands heavy on his stick, stubbly chin resting on his knuckles. His thick grey bushy brows shaded his eyes from the sun and from where he was standing Finn could barely tell if Norman was asleep or awake. He decided to go over anyway.

Finn gave Donald a wide berth, a bit too wide as he nearly got his feet wet in the little waves that tickled the sandy shore, and walked over to where old Norman was sitting, motionless, like a statue or one of those dragons he had heard of on the front of a ship which stared out over the sea.

"Good afternoon Norman" Finn said brightly.

Nothing, Norman didn't move a muscle, not even a twitch.

"I said good afternoon Norman" Finn said a little louder, he didn't want to give the old fella a fright after all.

Still nothing.

Finn reached out and gave Norman a light shake on the shoulder. That did the trick; Norman grunted, spluttered and almost fell off his seat. He regained his balance and wiped a little spittle from the corner of his mouth with the back of his hand as he sat back and squinted up at Finn, "Oh, it's yourself; how are you young lad?"

"I'm grand Norman, just grand" said Finn in his most carefree, nothing is worrying me at all, honest, voice.

"What's that about the sand? You'll have to speak up I'm getting a bit deaf! Sorry about being asleep and all that, been sleeping during the day for as long back as I can remember, it's a hard habit to break. Take a seat lad" and he gestured to another discarded basket a few feet away.

Finn sat down alongside Norman and decided to just ask the old man outright, after all none of the village wanted anything to do with him anyway. Nothing would change if they thought he was mad as a March hare, as well as unlucky.

"Norman you were keeping watch for years out there on the cliff. Did you ever hear anything strange out there?"

Norman looked closely at Finn, he seemed to be struggling with his memory, he puckered up his face and then……

"It's no use boy, you'll have to speak up, didn't get a word of that."

"In all the time that you were watchman, did you ever hear strange sounds out there on the cliffs, weird music; like singing almost?" Finn was almost shouting as he leaned towards the old mans ear.

"So, hearing voices now; are you Finn?" It was Donald; he was walking towards them from where he had been cleaning the boat. The grin on his face was almost wider than his waistline. "Couldn't help overhearing; now what's all this about singing?"

Great, that was all Finn needed, before nightfall the whole village would have something new to laugh at him for. He fought the urge to wipe the stupid grin off Donald's fat face with a good right hook. It was a stupid idea anyway; if Donald punched anywhere near his weight Finn had no chance.

Norman seemed oblivious to Finn's plight and was still scratching his stubbly old chin as he wracked his memory. "Nope, never heard anything out there for years, mind I have been a little hard of hearing, the past ten years or so."

"Thanks for your time Norman, sorry to be a pest." Finn got to his feet and walked smartly away from the beach.

"What does this song go like then Finn, sing us a few notes!" Shouted Donald at the rapidly departing night watchman.

Just wait till the rest of the fishermen got back, thought Donald, they would love this story. He could hardly wait.

Finn trudged back up the hill towards home as fast as he could. He wanted to be well out of the way by the time the fishermen got back to port. When he got home he picked up his hoe and busied himself weeding between the vegetables.

He had been tending the garden for about an hour or so when Granny arrived back at the house, she had her big basket with her and Finn could see the wide gaping mouths of two large cod sticking out of one side.

That could only mean that she had been down to the shore, she must surely have heard about his conversation with old Norman. Donald was sure to have told almost the whole village by now.

"Good afternoon my boy, you're up and about early today" said Granny as she swung the gate shut and bustled up the short path.

"Yes, I had trouble sleeping. Its a bright day, seemed a shame to be asleep on such a nice day."

A flicker of worry crossed the old ladies face as she met Finn's gaze. "I suppose so. Well you finish what you're doing and wash up; dinner will be ready in a wee while."

Finn stood there watching her back as she went into the cottage. He had never seen Granny look even remotely concerned about anything before. What was wrong? She never usually cared for the village gossip.

Finn did as he was told and having pulled the last weed from a row of young cabbage shoots, he propped his hoe against the back wall of the cottage and went inside.

The interior of the cottage was dark as usual, and it took a few moments for Finn's eyes to become accustomed to the gloom. He could smell the steam from the vegetables boiling in the black pot over the fire, then there was the smell of the fish which he could now see frying in the flat griddle Granny was holding wrapped in a thick cloth in her hand. His stomach suddenly growled loudly.

"You sound hungry Finn. Dinner is nearly ready, just wash your hands and take a seat." Said Granny as she turned over one of the now golden filets of fish in the hot griddle.

He quickly popped back out into the garden where he rinsed his hands in the bucket next to the path. Once he had shaken the water off and given his hands a quick rub on his tunic he was back in the house and sitting down expectantly.

He was hungry. He had forgotten about food as he worked in the garden, but now having smelled dinner his empty stomach was making its' presence felt as well as heard.

There was another feeling in his stomach however, like he had swallowed something heavy and cold, he was dreading having to sit there at the table and speak to Granny.

She would no doubt want to speak about what she had heard down at the beach when she was picking up the fish, he could lie to the other folk in the village but with Granny it was different, she was a hard person to lie to. It was as if she could see right through him, through the most calm, expressionless face he could manage; straight to the worry, and self doubt which was lurking just underneath.

Well there was no escaping it; he would have to face the interrogation. "That smells wonderful Granny" he said as she eased herself down at the table.

"Yes, its fresh caught today. I got it from Murdo, as payment for that tincture I made to treat the rash his wife had last week. Its amazing what a little witch-hazel will do if it's prepared right" she said as she broke off a rather large piece of fish with her spoon, and sucked it into her mouth with a loud slurp.

He decided to try to take control of the conversation. He couldn't bear this slow build up, best to just get it over with.

"You'll have heard what happened down at the shore this afternoon then?" He said, looking her straight in the eye.

Granny didn't look up from her plate as she prepared another spoonful. "Yes, I did as a matter of fact. Why can't you and Donald just drop all this sillyness? You're both grown men now after all."

"Och! Donald Ogg has always been a neep, you've said as much yourself Granny!" Finn was deflated, he had built himself up for an argument, a confrontation with her on even terms at last and there he was again, feeling like a wee boy being told off for fighting by his Granny.

They ate in silence, other than the scraping of spoon on bowl, until both had finished their meal. Then just as Finn was about to get up to wash the bowls Granny broke the silence. "So, tell me about this singing then?"

Finn sat heavily back in his chair. He sighed deeply and was about to protest when he saw the look in Granny's eye. He took another deep breath and tried to explain what he had heard to her.

It was difficult; he had been listening as if in a dream and couldn't begin to try to recreate the sounds he had heard. Likewise his mind did not quite posses the words to describe the wonderful sound.

He tried hard to explain to Granny the feeling of warmth which had spread through him while he listened, how he had forgotten what a cold night it was. How he seemed to be warmed from within, or at least ignorant of the cold.

Granny listened intently, not daring to interrupt Finns' rambling except to provide an occasional encouraging nod of the head or grunt.

While Finn talked she sat there as calmly as she could, trying desperately to suppress the panic she felt building up inside her and holding back the tears she could feel welling in the corner of her eyes.

It was exactly as she had feared when she first heard the fishermen talking down at the shore. Finn her darling boy was as good as lost to her, it was inevitable. Or was it?

She had an idea. There must be something in the book about this, some guidance or advice to protect him from this.

That was it, she would wait until Finn had gone out to the cliffs for the night and she would slip out to the village meeting house and go down to where the village records were kept.

Yes there definitely must be something about this in the book.

Granny suddenly realised that Finn had stopped talking. He was looking at her expectantly, waiting for her reaction to his revelation. She smiled at him, the same warm smile that calmed his fears when he was a wee lad.

"You must have been dreaming Finn, it's not surprising really. It takes some time for your mind to get used to staying up at night. I remember when Norman took on the job all those years ago, for the first six months or so the poor man didn't know if he were coming or going."

She looked carefully at his face, waiting to see any signs of doubt in his eyes. There were none, thankfully.

Finn gathered up the dinner things and took them over to the bucket by the hearth. He picked up the cloth and started scrubbing.

Did she think he was stupid, still just a boy that could be calmed and placated with a few wise words and a sympathetic smile. Well let her think that. He was certainly not stupid or mad, he had heard what he had heard and that was that.

As he scrubbed he remembered the beautiful music. He smiled, not long till he had to go to work, he could hardly wait.

Chapter 4

Once Finn had finished the washing up he got ready to go to work. He pulled on the heavy blanket like a cloak, it may be spring but it was still quite cold at night. He picked up the lantern, packed supper and stepped out into the night.

Granny watched from the window as always, as Finn strode off down the lane towards the cliffs. Once he was safely out of sight Granny closed the heavy wooden shutters which were fitted to the cottage window. She then went to the other window and tightly closed the shutters there too, before pulling across the curtain which hung on the tiny window at the top of the door.

The inside of the cottage was now black as pitch, illuminated only by the flame of the small candle she held in her hand. Granny walked carefully across the cottage to her bed, in the opposite corner from the alcove where Finn slept.

The old lady reached under the bed and pulled out a heavy wooden chest. It was just over a foot long, very old and made from dense heavy wood with a deep red lustre the edges of which had been polished by countless fingers over the years.

The corners of the chest were capped with dull golden metal which was inscribed with strange spiral patterns. The same patterns covered the straps which bound the chest together and the semicircular handles which hung from either side. The lock was carved into the head of a great wolf with the mouth held wide open as a keyhole.

Granny reached into the neck of her blouse and pulled out a small golden key tied to a length of leather cord which hung loosely round her neck. She took the small key and slid it into the mouth of the wolf. The key turned smoothly in the lock, there was a tiny click and she slowly opened the chest.

The glow from within the open chest lit up the smile on the old ladies face and cast her shadow onto the ceiling above. She gazed at the contents for only a second before reaching inside and pulling out a large heavy iron key. Putting the key down on the floor she turned her attention back to the interior of the chest.

Granny stared into the chest for few more moments, she dared not look any longer than that, before she shut the lid and plunged the room back into darkness. She quickly secured the lock, slipped the key around her neck and pushed the chest back to its hiding place under the bed.

She picked up the heavy key and stuffed it into the large pocket of her apron, leaning heavily on the edge of the bed as she pushed herself back onto her feet with a groan. The old lady then pulled on her shawl and quickly slid out of the cottage door and down the lane making barely a sound.

She slipped quietly through the village like a shadow, on surprisingly nimble feet for someone of her age. Only when she reached the village meeting-house did she stop. She took a quick look round to check that she had not been watched and then quickly went in through the unlocked door.

Once inside she stopped and let her eyes adjust to the dim light. She didn't want to risk lighting a candle just yet, it was best no one saw that she was there.

She walked across the room to a spot on the southern wall she knew well. She felt along the tightly woven, willow screen lining the rear wall, her deft fingers searching for the crease she knew was there. Having found the right spot she took the heavy key from within her pocket and slid it into the odd shaped gap in the lattice. The key turned smoothly with a soft thud as the lock mechanism slid a heavy bolt back. She gave the wall a sharp push.

There was a click and the door sprung outwards about an inch with a dank waft of air. Granny grabbed the edge of the door with her finger tips and pulled it open, exposing the entrance to a dark narrow passage within.

Short as she was, even she was obliged to stoop low as she entered the tunnel. The passage had been carved out of the bedrock behind the building and it led slightly downhill, deep into the cliffs behind the village. The walls were green with slime, the roof dripped and the bare stone floor was treacherously slippery as she knew from bitter experience.

Once she had closed the secret door behind her, she took a candle from within her apron pocket and lit it. Using the flickering candle to light her way, she walked further and further down into the gloom.

She remembered when she had first been shown this passageway many years ago; she thought that it must lead to the very depths of the earth itself. Or at least be the hiding place of some fell beast. It was a place she was still very uneasy about, she avoided coming down here unless she really had to. Shivering slightly she clutched at the shawl about her neck.

As the passageway ended Granny entered a large cavern. The sound of her footsteps echoed off the cavern walls and reverberated around the cave.

The wan light of the candle was not quite strong enough to reach the outer walls of the cave and it left dark menacing shadows at the edges which appeared to move quite independently of the flickering light.

Granny walked across the cavern floor towards the centre of the cave where there stood a thick raised pillar of milk white rock. The pillar reached up towards another identical pillar of stone which was growing downwards out of the roof. The two pillars reached out towards each other, unable to close the gap. The gap was wide and it would take two grown men standing on each others shoulders to bridge it.

At the base of the pillar was a huge flat stone which had fallen from the roof sometime in the dim and distant past. The stone formed a long low table, slightly off kilter, on which, flanked by two tall candlesticks, lay a large leather-bound book.

Granny lit both the huge candles on the table with her own before snuffing her candle out with a pinch of her fingers and putting it down on the table next to the book.

She then opened the book and began to read. The great book contained the accumulated knowledge of the village elders. It charted the history of the world from the dark beginnings to the time when the village of Bruaan had been founded. It documented the various family trees of the village. Every villager past and present was named within the book and it also contained various accounts and tales of historical importance to the village.

Of most interest to Granny was the section at the back of the book. This portion dealt mainly with magic.

She shook her head to clear her thoughts and returned her mind to the task at hand. She began leafing through the pages. She had heard several accounts of people hearing strange singing voices in the past and knew from bitter experience that it seldom ended well.

She knew of seafarers tales where the crew of a ship had apparently heard beautiful singing voices in the night. The voices had drawn the crews closer and closer, until it was too late to turn away and the ships had been dashed on jagged rocks. The sailors on board were generally drowned in the dark waters or ripped apart on the rocks.

The source of the singing was generally unknown but was usually attributed to lonely mermaids or sirens. She had even heard some of the older sea-dogs claim that the singing was made by the poor dammed souls of drowned sailors who were desperate for company in the deep.

Granny didn't care what or who was responsible for making the music; she just knew that she needed to protect her boy from it.

So the old lady stayed there in the middle of the dark cavern reading and searching until the candles on the table had burned quite low.

In the end the only advice she could find was just an ancient protection spell which was apparently of use in warding off all bewitchments and magical beasts.

The method depended upon the use of a specially prepared piece of stone which was to be worn on the neck much like an amulet and would afford protection to the wearer.

The stone used must be no bigger than a thumbnail, red in colour and was to be prepared by heating until white hot in a fire. Various incantations were then to be spoken or preferably sung over the hot stone which would absorb the magic as it cooled.

Granny took out a small scrap of parchment and an even smaller shard of charcoal and licking the tip, she quickly transcribed the necessary incantation; it was not one she was familiar with. She then stuffed the charcoal and note into her pocket and quickly closed the great book.

Far too quickly, she immediately realised, as she found herself coughing in a large cloud of dust with her ears ringing from the slam of the hastily closed book, the sound of which continued to echo round the walls of the dark cavern.

She coughed a bit more and then patted the dust off her clothes with her hands. Granny then lit her small candle from one of the large candles on the table before blowing the large candles out and making her way back across the cavern to the passageway which led to the village.

As she reached the steps up to the entrance of the tunnel she saw something, just for a fleeting second, out of the corner of her eye, creeping back into the deep shadows on spindly legs.

She turned quickly, but whatever it was, it was already gone.

She really did hate this place. It was far too creepy and she was far too old to be skulking about in a cave at this time of night. Oh for the life of a normal old lady, tucked up in a warm bed with her knitting. The days of intrigue and adventure were long past thankfully; she was getting too tired for all that in any case.

The old lady sighed and made her way quickly up the tunnel back towards the village. She really hoped it would be a long, long time until she had to go back into that cavern alone again. It was so much easier during the annual ceremony when all of the other elders were with her. Safety in numbers.

When she got back to the meeting hall she saw that it was almost dawn. The first grey light of day was creeping into the hall through the small windows. She had been reading the book much longer than she had intended. She quickly closed the secret door checked that it was secure and remained almost invisible and slipped out of the hall.

Granny passed quickly through the village to her cottage making barely a sound. As she went she could hear the sound of the waking villagers from within their houses. Mothers were already shouting at their naughty children and informing their husbands that breakfast was on the table and they had better get their lazy arses out of bed.

From the occasional house she could still hear the occupants snoring. "Lucky clots" she muttered under her breath as she passed.

She had just enough time to take off her shawl, stoke the embers of the fire into life and put the kettle on to boil before Finn arrived home.

"Good morning Granny" he said stifling a yawn with the back of his hand. "Did you sleep well?"

The old woman smiled back at him. "Yes, I slept very well indeed my boy" she said brightly, just before turning back towards the hearth and letting out a yawn so huge that it made her eyes water.

Once Finn had eaten some breakfast and was safely tucked up in bed asleep. Granny laid herself down on top of the covers of her bed and was also quickly asleep.

She had left the curtains in the window at her side of the cottage open and knew that at about midday the sun would shine in through the window onto her face and wake her. She had never been a very heavy sleeper in any case.

That would give her the rest of the afternoon to prepare Finns amulet.

Chapter 5

Granny had spent the better part of the afternoon at the far end of the beach sifting through the pebbles which had been washed up by the surf.

The current that passed through the mouth of the bay was quite strong and as it rushed through the rocky gap it picked up stones and pebbles from the sea bed and carried them along to the beach. The larger pebbles were dumped first onto the beach; they were just too heavy to be carried very far.

The smaller pebbles were carried a little further along the beach and so it went on and on, smaller and smaller, until up at the end of the beach where Granny was looking, where the pebbles were no bigger than the nail on the end of your thumb.

There were millions of little pebbles there at that part of the beach, laid into a gentle arc by the waves, which washed over them again and again. Granny watched the waves, looking for the slightest glint of red as the pebbles were dragged up the beach and then back down again by the surf.

Once or twice she had reached into the water to grab one of the little stones only to retrieve it from the water and find that it was not quite as red as she required. The closest she had got so far was a dark orange colour, which she had set aside just in case it was the reddest the sea could provide. She would give it another half hour or so and then give up for the day. Finn would be awake soon and she needed to make sure she had time to prepare dinner.

Her mind was just wandering back to that strange singing that Finn had been hearing, when she saw it.

It was definitely red, just the merest glimpse of scarlet as the wave passed. The water started to retreat and there it was again! She reached quickly into the water and grabbed a handful of pebbles.

Granny slowly opened her hand and saw there in the centre of her palm a small stone so red it appeared for all the world like a round droplet of blood. She brushed away the other pebbles and sand and picked out the pebble, it was almost perfectly round and slightly flattened like a broad bean. It was completely red, its only blemish being a thin line of black which appeared like a crack running from top to bottom.

"Just the job" she said with a little chuckle. She gave the pebble a quick wash in the sea and then taking a scrap of cloth she wrapped the stone carefully and put it in her pocket. "Time to go home" and she trotted off along the beach towards the village and home.

As she got nearer she suddenly remembered to slow her pace a little and stoop over. It was so difficult remembering to play the tired little old lady all the time but it did avoid all the tricky questions.

As Granny made her way through the village she was asked the usual questions by the usual people. She handed out several pouches of herbs for making teas, very good for the treatment of coughs and colds and she gave old Norman his usual liniment, made mostly from ground ginger root and lard, which he swore eased his rheumatics.

When she was almost home she met her neighbour Jenny. She was less than twenty five but already had two youngsters running around at her feet and another who was still only a babe in arms. The poor girl looked exhausted. "Hello Jenny, how are you today?" Granny said.

Jenny smiled at the old woman, but her eyes appeared drawn with dark circles underneath. "Hi Granny, I'm fine, just fine. Isn't it a lovely day?"

"I take it the little one is still not sleeping too well?" Granny asked as she reached out and cupped the babies head with her hand, he felt a little hot to the touch.

Jenny looked down at her child. "Oh, he's a good boy most of the time, but he just seems so restless at night. I'll be glad when he is big enough to sleep with the other children."

Granny reached into her apron and pulled out a small package, which was wrapped in a green dock leaf and tied with a length of string. "Here take this; it's a mix of dried herbs and the like. I want you to drop a small pinch of the mixture into some hot water just before you put him to bed at night. Give him a spoonful and then drink the rest yourself, it's mostly camomile with some other bits and bobs, it should give both of you a better nights sleep."

"Thank you Granny" said Jenny tucking the package into her pocket. "How's young Finn getting on as night watchman? Is he settling into the routine?"

The old woman sighed. "Oh, he'll be fine, it takes a while for the body to get accustomed to being awake all night. But I'm sure he'll be fine when he settles into the job. Anyway, must get on. I hope you sleep better tonight Jenny" and with that Granny bustled off up the path towards her cottage.

When she stepped into the dark cottage she could hear Finn snoring. Good, good she thought as she went to the hearth and stirred the dying embers of the fire with the metal poker. She added two small logs of wood and watched as the flames took hold of the dry wood; there was a crackle and then a small pop from one of the logs. She had a quick look round but luckily Finn hadn't stirred, she could still hear him fast asleep snoring behind the heavy curtain.

When the fire was strong enough, Granny carefully took out the package from her apron. She unfolded the cloth and stopping to inspect the pebble once more she picked it up using the iron tongs she used to put coals on the fire. Granny then thrust the tongs into the hottest part of the flames and deposited the pebble there in the centre.

She watched and waited until she could see the little stone glowing like the pupil of a dragon's eye, there in the very centre of the blaze. Then she picked the pebble up with the tongs and carefully set it down on the stone hearth in front of the fire.

She quickly got down onto her hands and knees and leaning her face as close as she dared to the still white hot pebble, she began to sing.

"Vala huurst vhikla, khor aamisk ne.

Vala huurst vhikla, khor aamisk ne.

Vala huurst vhikla, khor aamisk ne."

She sang in a whisper for fear of waking Finn and having to answer far too many awkward questions. She did hate awkward questions.

She then sat back on her heels and reached her hand down towards the stone to see if it had cooled. It was still warm to the touch but the combination of Granny's whispered breath and the cold stone floor had drawn most of the heat.

Granny picked up the small pebble and placed it carefully onto the table. She then went over to the back wall of the cottage where she carefully took Finns' tunic down off the peg.

She knew that there was no way she would be able to convince Finn to wear the pebble on a cord round his neck. He was far too sceptical and would ask far too many of those awkward questions again. She had come up with a plan however. The book simply stated that the person must wear the amulet around their neck; it didn't dictate exactly how it should be worn.

Granny sat down with the tunic and taking a small knife she began unpicking the stitching where the fabric of the neck had been rolled round to form a collar. When she had opened it just far enough, she pushed the little red pebble in through the seam. She checked and could only just feel the pebble through the thick wool. She then took a needle and thread and quickly sewed up the small hole in the collar.

When she had finished she sat back in the seat and inspected her work. It was perfect, Finn would never notice and whenever he wore his tunic he would be protected. She took the tunic and placed it back onto the peg exactly as Finn had hung it up that morning.

***

A short time later Finn was wakened from his slumber by the smell of eggs sizzling in the skillet Granny held over the hearth. He rolled himself up, throwing his legs out the side of the bed and sat on the edge for a few seconds letting his eyes adjust to the late afternoon sunlight which filtered through the small cottage windows.

Finn scratched his head and getting to his feet with a groan he lumbered across the floor towards the table where he flopped down in his chair.

"Good…….morning" he yawned, "or good afternoon or whatever, you know what I mean."

Granny turned round from the hearth "did you sleep well today Finn?"

"Yes, yes I slept fine, it's the waking up that's the problem. Did you have a busy day today? Looks as if it was a nice one" he said looking out through the window at the bright blue sky.

Granny returned her attention to the eggs which were almost ready. "Oh not really, just the usual. I saw Jenny from down the lane; she's exhausted, what with all of those children of hers. Dinner is almost ready so go and put some clothes on young man, I don't want to have to eat while looking at those hairy legs of yours."

Once dinner was over it was almost time for Finn to walk out to the cliffs to take over the watch, the sun was already sinking toward the horizon and the sky was getting darker by the minute.

"Well I suppose it's that time again" he said with a sigh as he pushed back the chair and stood up. He went and sat down on the edge of his bed reaching a hand underneath to retrieve his shoes.

Whilst Finn was tying his shoes Granny packed some food into his sack. She wondered if the singing would return to the cliffs again tonight. She hoped not, but part of her, just a small part of her hoped that it would. It would be a good test of her skills to see if the amulet she had made would work. What did she mean if of course it would work, the old wisdom always worked.

Finn was also thinking of the singing voice. It occupied most of his waking thoughts these days, it was very distracting. Even when he slept he could hear the song weaving itself amongst his dreams. He hoped to hear it again, and soon. He felt sure he had already forgotten parts of the song and feared that as time passed he would be robbed of fragment after fragment of the wonderful music, until it became only a vague and distant memory.

He clumped wearily across the floor, pulling on his cloak before grabbing his supper and lantern. He remembered to mutter a quick goodnight to Granny as he opened the door and walked out into the twilight of the evening.

Granny watched him as he strode off into the night, down the lane towards the cliff path. Well he was wearing the tunic; that was good, he was protected.

She had done her best all of his life to protect him, first from the cold and wind, then from the more cruel children of the village, who liked to pick on anyone who seemed in any way different from themselves. She had even tried to protect him from himself, when he had that silly idea of going to sea like his father.

She tried hard to remember at what point she had agreed to this duty. It was hard work, far too hard for someone of her age, she giggled softly to herself at the thought.

Well he was protected now. "Time for bed." She said, it's been a very busy day. She yawned loudly as she shut the heavy old door on the world with a thud.

Chapter 6

As Finn got to the edge of the village he stopped and turned around on the path. The night was drawing in as the sun sank; lower and lower on the western horizon. The village had a calm air in the hazy dusk light, the warm glow of lanterns and candles flickered invitingly in the house windows and he could see one or two of the villagers preparing for bed.

Some of the women were taking in the washing from sagging lines strung across the narrow lanes and passageways like the meandering of some huge spider web. The women bustled about desperate to save the clean clothes from the perils of night-time showers and damp early morning mists.

As he looked down to the beach he saw some of the fishermen pulling the last of the boats out of the glittering water, dragging them up high onto the safety of the beach. He strained his eyes to see if he could make out which of the crews it was, but they were just too far away and the sun was growing too dim.

He opened the door of his small lantern and lit the wick, letting the flame settle into a steady bright flame, before closing the door and continuing down the rock strewn path towards the cliffs.

When he had got to the bottom of the steps by the watchman's cave he met Linus Dane. He was waiting there impatiently at the cave entrance, tapping his foot, all packed up and ready to scarper.

"Bout bloody time Finn! Thought you were never going to pitch up!" He said as he bent over to pick up his small leather bag from the ground.

Finn scowled at the back of Linus' head and quickly stuck out his tongue, changing instantly to an apologetic smile as Linus straightened back up to face him. "Sorry Linus, just lost track of time a little, won't happen again."

Linus shoved him out of the way, pushing past on his way to the steps. "You see that it doesnae happen again Finn or you'll be sorry!" And with that he was gone, striding up the stone steps on those lanky legs of his. He always reminded Finn of a heron, all legs and beak.

He did have a very beaky nose indeed, thought Finn with a smile.

Linus was about two years older than Finn, but he was a deckhand on one of the fishing boats and he was going out with Elspeth Wordie. One of the prettiest girls in the village; and she knew it! Well Linus and Elspeth were just made for each other as far as Finn was concerned both had a nasty selfish streak a mile wide.

He put down the small bag containing his supper, laid down the lantern on the table and with a heavy sigh, went back out onto the ledge to start his watch.

When he got to the ledge he took up his favourite seat on the large boulder with the shallow depression on top, it could have been made for the very purpose of sitting on.

There he sat, legs dangling over the edge looking out to sea as usual. He yanked up his cloak against the cold sea breeze and watched as the very last glimmers of light from the setting sun danced on the peaks of the distant mountains making them appear as if they were on fire.

The effect lasted only a few more moments before the sun set completely, plunging Finn's world into darkness, apart from the thin strip of dark blue sky just above the western horizon. There in the middle of the deep blue ribbon twinkled the first star of the evening. Granny had told him the name of the star once but he had never been particularly good with names so it was long forgotten.

He sat there almost motionless scanning the empty sea, he had spent so much time there that he almost felt like one of the rocks, doomed to stay there for all time listening to the waves crash over and over again at the foot of the cliff. He watched as the stars began to appear one by one across the sky, he really should have paid more attention to Granny, she seemed to know the name of every star in the night sky. He wished he could name them all now, at the very least it might help pass the time.

Finn lay back on the rock, the sea can take care of itself for a few minutes he thought. The sky was studded with bright pinpricks of light, some appeared much brighter than the others, or maybe they were just bigger. Finn lay there wondering what they were; the old tales claimed that they were just holes in an old blanket which the gods had draped over the world every night since the world began, he wasn't quite convinced.

He lay there lost in thought when he heard it. Yes! He heard it again.

His heart leapt in his chest in surprise and delight. He froze, frightened that the slightest rustle of his clothes might drown out the sound and strained every fibre in his body, listening to the beautiful music once more.

The notes were no more than a whisper faintly blown in on the sea breeze. But the sound was unmistakable, so delicate and sweet that the very air itself seemed scented with lavender. The notes were just as clear and so much more beautiful than he remembered.

As he lay there he realised that this time he could fully appreciate the singing, he was aware of the slightest change in pitch and tone. Before the melody seemed to dull his senses and overpower him completely. He felt fully awake this time, awake and overwhelmed with curiosity about the source of this fantastic sound.

He slowly and silently pushed himself up from where he was lying on the rock and standing behind the large boulder he peered out over the top searching the sea for the source of the music. His eyes scanned the water moving closer and closer to shore, but he could see nothing. Then as his eyes reached the shoreline he saw something. A small dark shape at the edge of the surf, outlined just for a second as the waves broke on the rocks in a spray of white foam.

When the next wave broke, larger than the last he saw it again, something or someone appeared to be sitting on the rocks. He had to investigate.

Finn shrugged off his cloak and bent down to remove his shoes; he would move more quietly and be much more surefooted on the rocks in bare feet. He clambered over the edge and lowered himself down on his arms, toes feeling for a foothold in the rocks. He made his way slowly and carefully down the rock face to the small strip of beach below.

The lower down the cliff he went the clearer he could hear the music. He felt quite light headed with excitement and fear. Fear of both falling from the cliff to his death or at the very least breaking an arm or leg on the rocks and of what or who might be the source of the music.

As he neared the bottom of the cliff the rocks became damp and seaweed clung to every crevice making the going treacherous. Finn's right foot slipped on some weed and he slid a short distance down the rocks scraping the skin off his knees and toes as he grabbed out with his fingertips searching for purchase on the ragged rock face.

His fingers found a small crack and held, his body weight pulling his arms almost out of their sockets and his injured knees grating on the rock-face once again. He bit his lip and winced in pain as he hung there motionless, afraid that the sound of his fall had revealed his presence but as he listened he found that the sweet singing continued.

The breeze was blowing in from the sea taking the noise he had made away and the breaking surf was much louder down here on the beach drowning out his noisy scrabble down the ragged face of the cliff.

He inched his way down the remainder of the rocks and found his way to the soft sand beneath. Finn felt the cold damp sand pushing its way up between his toes as he carefully slinked towards the edge of the sea using the large fallen boulders and rocks to hide his movements.

When he had gotten as close as he dared, he slowly, very slowly peered around the side of the rock he was hiding behind. There sitting on the top of a small boulder, her feet trailing in the water of a small rock pool was a girl!

She was looking out to sea, lost in thought, singing softly, as she pulled a comb through a section of the long dark hair which tumbled down her back, almost reaching her bottom.

Her naked bottom, Finn suddenly realised. He blushed and ducked back behind the rock.

The singing continued and Finn peeked out again from behind the rock. The girl was still there and having gotten over the initial embarrassment, he was desperate for a better look.

The stars seemed to glitter in the girl's long dark hair and her soft skin appeared almost to glow, iridescent in the moonlight. Her hands, still combing, moved with sinuous grace mirroring the soft roll of the ocean swell out beyond the crashing waves. She sat there blissfully unaware that she had an audience for her recital.

He was completely captivated and before he realised what he was doing he had taken several steps out from behind his hiding place towards the girl. His foot found a tiny branch of driftwood, half buried in the sand but protruding just enough. As the wood split there was a sharp crack, and the spell was broken.

He froze, his heart almost leaping out of his chest through his gaping mouth. The girl looked round, startled, fixing the boy with deep sea-green eyes. She grabbed what appeared to be a shadow from on top of the rock and throwing it around her shoulders like a cloak she was gone with small splash, as she slipped into the surf.

"No! Don't go! I didn't mean to frighten you!" Finn called as he ran blindly into the waves. "Come back, please, I'm sorry!" He peered out past the waves, searching, searching the dark water.

If his eyes had been just a little better or the moon just a little brighter, he might have seen the black head, bobbing on the waves as the dark eyes of the seal stared back at the beach, curious about the boy.

Chapter 7

He had no idea how long he had stood there staring out to sea, but he awoke from his reverie with a sudden fright as a wave washed over his bare feet.

He hopped back falling over clumsily; backside landing on the sand with a thump, then quickly stood up and brushed the sand off his bum with his hands.

Finn then walked slowly over to the rock where he had just seen the selkie, or seal maiden as some called them. He had heard several tales of selkies from the older more superstitious fishermen, but he had dismissed the stories as just, more old tosh.

As he reached the rock his eye caught a faint glimmer in the moonlight. He looked down and saw a comb, half submerged in the small rock-pool. As he picked it up he noted how light and fragile it was. It seemed to weigh almost nothing in his hand and he immediately felt very clumsy, holding such a delicate thing. As he turned it over in his hand the moonlight glinted off the pearlescent surface of the comb.

Finn took out the piece of cloth he used as a handkerchief and carefully wrapped the comb before tucking it safely inside his tunic.

He cast his eye out to sea once again but could see little in the dark water out past the breakers. It was no use; he had better get back to the watch.

It took him over half an hour to climb back up the rock face to the watchman's cave. When he got there he was tired and sore, climbing back up with cut knees and fingertips had not been easy. He had already decided to bring a length of rope with him when he came back out for the next watch.

When he got back to the ledge outside the cave he quickly scanned the sea to check that nothing had changed whilst he had been gone. Then he sat down on his boulder, exhausted, to wait for sunrise.

***

Finn spent most of the next morning tossing and turning in bed, unable to sleep at all, as he replayed his encounter with the selkie over and over again in his head.

He had hidden the comb, still wrapped in the hanky, under his pillow. He had resisted the temptation to unwrap it, mainly through fear that by handling it he would almost certainly break it.

When sleep eventually found him the sun was already high in the sky. As Finn slept he dreamt of the sea and the seal maiden. He was swimming with her under the waves, holding tight to her hand. They swam between waving fronds of kelp and seaweed watching the dark fish darting here and there, always just out of reach.

Finn looked at the maiden and she smiled at him warmly, he smiled back, he had never seen a face so beautiful. Then, realising that he had been holding his breath, he started to swim to the surface. The maiden gripped his hand tightly, holding him fast, still smiling.

He kicked and pulled, frantically trying to break free, to swim up, lungs on fire, desperate. The maiden held tight, smiling, smiling sweetly as Finn finally surrendered and breathing in, filled his lungs with cold seawater.

Finn sat bolt upright in bed, breathing in with a loud gasp, startling granny so much she dropped the bowl she was carrying. The bowl smashed on the floor scattering the contents.

He was awake and alive, thankfully. He sat there catching his breath; bedclothes all twisted and soaked with sweat.

Granny sat on the edge of his bed and reached out a hand to his cheek. "Sweaty, but no fever thankfully. That must have been quite a dream?"

"I don't remember much about it" he lied.

"Well suppose I'd better tidy up that mess." She said looking at the broken bowl and scattered barley. "You gave me quite a fright there."

Finn washed himself down in the corner of the room while Granny bustled about picking up the broken pieces of pottery and then sweeping up the barley from the floor. He couldn't shake the image of the selkie's smiling face, watching him as he drew his last breath; it sent shivers down his spine.

When he had washed and eaten Granny began to strip the covers from his bed. "You can't sleep in these again, I'll wash them tonight and hang them out in the morning. There's a good wind just now they will be dry in no time at all."

He nodded absently as he sipped, then suddenly choked on the water. The comb!

He darted across to his bed and grabbed the covers out of her grasp. "It's alright Granny, I'll do this if you put the water on to heat."

"Alright, if you insist, you're really not quite yourself today Finn. That dream has put you all out of sorts." And she picked up the big pot, taking it outside to the water trough.

The second she was gone Finn slipped the wrapped comb out from under the pillow and quickly tucked it inside his shirt.

Once the bed had been stripped, re-made and the dirty sheets soaking in the pot of hot water, the sun was almost setting. "Time I was off!" He said standing up from the table.

"You're a bit early tonight." Granny said looking out of the window. "There's at least half an hour till dark."

"I've a quick errand to run on the way." He said, picking up his lantern. "I'll see you in the morning." With that he was gone slamming the door shut as he went.

Before heading out to the cliff path, Finn went down to the shore, to the place where the fishermen hung out the ropes on racks to dry.

Big Billy was there coiling one of the ropes into a large wicker basket. "Hullo there young fella, isn't it about time you were out on the point?"

"Yes, I'm just on my way now. Can you spare a length of rope? One of the older pieces will do."

Billy put down the rope he was coiling. "The old ropes are over here." He said leading Finn towards the back of the drying racks. "These old ropes aren't much cop, they're almost worn out, but you help yourself, if they're any use to you."

"Thanks Billy, they'll do just fine." Finn spent a few minutes picking out the best of the old ropes. When he had found one that he was fairly confident would hold his weight, and was long enough to reach down to the beach, he carefully coiled it round his forearm and threw it over his shoulder.

By this time it was almost dark and he set off at a trot to the watchman's cave. Once the day watchman had gone Finn took the length of rope and tied it carefully around a rocky crag.

He had considered using the metal ring that the alarm bell hung on as an anchor point but the risk of inadvertently ringing the bell, raising the alarm and sending the villagers fleeing from their beds up into the hills. Well let's just say the rope was better tied to the rocks.

Once the rope was securely tied he tossed the coil over the edge, down towards the beach. It was too dark to see if the rope reached all the way to the bottom of the cliff. He would just have to take a chance and climb down; he could always climb back up again or indeed pick his way carefully down the remainder of the cliff if it was too short.

Grabbing the rope he eased himself over the edge of the cliff. He began to clamber down and discovered that if he held firmly to the rope he could straighten his legs out and walk backwards down the rock-face quite quickly.

When he had reached the end of the rope he was relieved to find that he was only a few feet from the sandy beach. He let go of the rope and landed on the sand with a small thump.

He then crept quietly on all fours, across the beach to the rock where he had seen the maiden. When he got there he stayed crouching low and hid himself behind the rocks within arms reach of the small pool where he had found the comb.

He lay there silent, motionless, listening to his heart pounding in his chest and the waves breaking on the rocks.

He did not have long to wait until he heard footsteps splashing out of the sea. He peered out from behind the rock and saw the maiden as she bent down; laying what appeared to be a heavy black cloak on top of the rocks. As she did so her dark hair fell forward in heavy curls obscuring her face.

Then she crawled forward on her hands and knees, plunging elbow deep into the rock-pools, fingers searching the nooks and crannies. "Where is it, where is it." She whispered to herself as she worked her way methodically from crevice to crevice towards where Finn lay hiding.

When she had got as close to Finn as he dared. He reached into his tunic and taking out the pearly comb, he slowly sat up, afraid that any sudden movement would startle the maiden and send her running straight back to the sea.

"Is this what you are looking for?" He asked in a voice not much more than a whisper.

The maiden looked up, startled and stared open mouthed at the boy through dark tousled curls. She was about to turn and run when she saw that he held her comb in his hand, her precious comb, the only thing she had of her mother's. She swallowed hard, fighting back the fear in her belly and the sudden urge to run back into the surf.

"Yes, yes it is. Give it here." She said impatiently, sweeping her hair back with one hand as she reached out towards Finn with the other.

He pulled back his hand a little. "I will give it back, but only if you'll sit and talk for a bit."

The maiden sighed and slowly sat down on the rock, quite oblivious to her nakedness "If that's all you want I'll stay, but only for a short time. Then you will give me back my comb, won't you?"

"Yes, I promise." Said Finn as he too sat down on top of the rock, taking care not to get too close. He didn't want to frighten her and anyway if he got within arm's reach she might just grab the comb and run.

"Well what shall we talk about, the weather? Or have you something more important in mind?" She said sizing the lad up. He was a little taller than her but still quite skinny. She weighed up the chances of beating him in a fight. Too close to call, so she decided not to risk it for the moment.

Finn was at a loss, not only was he sitting there in front of the most beautiful girl he had ever clapped eyes on, but she was naked. Her dark wavy hair tumbled from her head, cascading over her shoulders and breasts. Only that and the fact it was a dark night protected her modesty.

"My name's Finn!" He managed to blurt. "What's yours?"

"It's Merryn; at least that's what everyone calls me. I doubt that a landling like you could even come close to pronouncing my proper name." She said tossing her head back dismissively.

"I'm very pleased to meet you Merryn. It gets quite lonely out here on the cliffs; it's good to have someone to talk with. I'm supposed to be keeping watch from up there." Said Finn jabbing his thumb up towards the cliff-top and his neglected watch post.

"What are you watching for up there at night, you won't see much in the dark, seems like a proper waste of time to me."

"No, no, it's a very important job. I'm the night watchman, have been for almost four months now. It's my duty to watch out for raiders and raise the alarm to warn the villagers." Finn said, not noticing that he had puffed his chest out a little. After all it was important; Granny and the other elders had said so.

"Well if it's so important, just give me back my comb and I'll be going and you can get back to your watching, or whatever." And she held out her hand towards Finn.

Finn didn't want her to go just yet, she was interesting, she was a creature of magic, he had so many questions to ask and besides, she was very pretty indeed.

"No. Not just yet. As the official watchman of Bruann it's my duty to protect the village from all threats from the sea. You're from the sea, you might be a threat? Or, I don't know, even a scout sent out to prepare the way for an army of selkies."

"I'm not a threat at all! How dare you suggest such a thing. I had no idea there was a village anywhere near this place. If I did I certainly wouldn't have stopped here." She said folding her arms across her chest.

"I'm on my own in any case, it's a traditional of ours, when a maiden or indeed a boy comes of age they must leave their home and family and wander the seas for twelve moons. Only then can they return. That's if they can find their way back of course, there's some can't…………"

Finn wondered how he would feel if he were away from home for so long. He had never been more than an hours walk from Bruann in his life. "How long is it since you left home?" He asked, looking at the maiden who suddenly seemed very young and fragile.

She didn't look up. "Almost four moons now, I've spent the past moon round about here. There's plenty of fish close at hand and……………it reminds me a little of home."

"You must be cold, will I fetch your cloak?" Finn said gesturing at the dark shape draped over the rocks nearby.

"No it's fine; I don't really feel the cold at all." She said wiping the tears which had begun to well up in her eyes with the back of a hand. "I really should continue my journey, especially now that you've found me and if there's a village nearby. I need to go now before I'm discovered. Can I have my comb back?"

Finn handed her the comb. "It's alright, I won't tell anyone about you, I promise. Please don't leave just yet; I know a small cave quite close by, right by the water. It's safe and cosy; no one would find you there. You could come and meet me here tomorrow night, we could talk. You did say this place reminded you of home."

"I'll think about it." She said hopping up from the rock where she sat and grabbing the dark cloak. "Where exactly is this cave?"

"It's along the coast to the west, about half a league or so."

"I hope it's as cosy as you claim." And she pulled the dark skin up around her shoulders as she dived headfirst into the waves and was gone.

Chapter 8

Merryn found the cave quite easily. It was a wide crevice in the flat face of the cliff which had collapsed in on itself at some point flattening out the top and giving it the appearance of an archway. The entrance would be almost completely awash at high water which would make it difficult to approach on foot.

Once she had swum for a distance on either side and had found nothing suspicious she hauled herself out of the water and lumbered up into the entrance of the cave. She didn't want to risk changing back to her maiden form and in any case she was tired, it was always safer to sleep in seal form.

The inside of the cave was just as Finn had described. It was narrow but deep enough so that once in the back she could sleep well away from any draughts from the cave entrance. The bottom of the cave was filled with a thick blanket of soft sand which would make a comfy bed.

She wriggled back and forth hollowing out a small depression in the sand before she closed her large dark eyes and tried to sleep, listening to the waves breaking at the entrance of the cave.

This cave was cosy; it was the cosiest place she had slept since setting out on her wandering. It was so difficult; she had not left her mother and father's side since birth, the thought of spending a whole year away from them, well it was almost more than she could bear.

She had always been independent to an extent when she was growing up, but that independence hinged on the trust she had in her parents. They had always been there casting a watchful eye over her, even if she hadn't always been aware of it.

Father was a great warrior and was often called to serve the king whenever the need arose. Her mother was also called to serve when required; no one could match her skill with the bow.

Still it was no use thinking of them now. They and her homeland were far off, over the western horizon. She had better just buck up, grit her teeth and get on with it; only eight more moons and she could return a woman.

***

When he got home that morning Finn was almost too excited to sleep. He had spoken to a selkie, a real life seal maiden and she was just as beautiful as the the ones in the stories.

He lay there in his bed replaying the night's events over and over in his head before exhaustion finally claimed him and he fell into a deep slumber.

Once she saw that Finn was sleeping soundly Granny picked up her basket and left the cottage. She had a busy day ahead of her. The summer solstice was fast approaching and she and the other elders must see to the preparations for the festival.

It was village tradition that a young maiden be picked to take the lead in the festival. She would be named the sun maiden and then, crowned with yellow flowers she led the day's festivities. She would spend the day being waited on by the whole village carried from event to event on a litter strewn with spring flowers.

The rest of the village would take part in singing and dancing and the young men competed in games. There was a race up the steep cliff path and back, followed by wrestling on the beach and then a swimming race across the bay. The victor would be crowned with a garland of white seashells to represent the moon.

The culmination of the day's events was the marriage of the sun and the moon, the victorious lad and the sun maiden became the centre of a ceremonial wedding. The villagers then danced and made merry well into the night, taking full advantage of the longest day of the year.

When Granny arrived at the meeting-house she found that the other elders were there already. They were all sitting, stools drawn up in a circle in the middle of the wide room.

The elders, seven in all, were representatives of the six prominent families of the village, the Spraggans, the Millers, the Oggs, the Wordies, the Danes and the Vass. Granny was the seventh elder, purely there to serve as their spiritual guide and advisor.

The elders all took turns to lead, each elder taking over the role for the period of one year immediately following the solstice celebrations. As such old Jack Spraggan sat in the only proper chair in the room presiding as chief elder.

"Ah Thora you're here, now we can start the meeting" said Jack gesturing for Granny to sit down on her stool.

The general consensus was that old Jack was about 60 years of age, although it was difficult to calculate anyone's age with any certainty past about twenty.

The village had only begun properly documenting the birth of each child twenty or so years ago. Since then all births had been recorded in the annals by the elders.

The records before that date were rather vague to say the least. There were records of most of the main events of the village which had been recorded as they happened but calculating dates involved a hap hazard reckoning, backwards from one significant event to the next.

Old Jack Spraggan had been born in the summer of the year that Bryn Ogg had been lost overboard, caught in a storm out in the firth. By most folks reckoning that was about 62 years past.

Age had yet to dull any of Jack's sense. He had what most folk called a wee twinkle in his eye and there was little that passed him unnoticed.

He had been a fine looking man in his day almost 6 foot tall and broad shouldered. He was growing a little stooped but he was still an imposing figure of a man, especially when angered. Luckily that happened very little these days.

When Granny had taken her seat Jack got the meeting under way. The main topic for discussion was the impending solstice and the selection of the sun maiden

The favoured girl was Elspeth Wordie. She was indeed fair there was no denying that, my but she knew it too! There was just something quite disagreeable about the girl, spoiled rotten, that's what Granny thought.

Elspeth had been proposed by her great uncle, Edwyn Wordie who sat on the council representing his family. He was the longest sitting member of the council by about 9 years or so, and also the oldest by far.

A couple of other girls had initially been suggested, but in deference to his age and seniority all of the other elders had supported Edwyn's selection.

That made it very difficult for Granny to voice her concerns and though it pained her, she bit her tongue and nodded her ascent to the selection.

The rest of the meeting dealt with the more mundane aspects of the celebration, in all of which Granny had little interest or opinion. She was glad to sit back and listen to the others assigning the villagers their tasks without having to take an active part.

So she sat there, nodding mindfully every how and then, while her mind wandered. As usual, her mind turned to Finn, she did worry about the boy, he was just so restless, why couldn't he be content with the quiet life she had planned for him? He had far too much of his mother in him.

When the meeting was over and most of the planning had been done, Granny picked up her basket and was just making towards the door when she was intercepted by Jack Spraggan. "Have you time for a chat Thora?"

Granny smiled "I always have time for you Jack, you know that."

They walked back to the now empty circle of seats and both sat down. "Is there something on your mind

Jack?" She asked once he had settled himself in his chair.

"I was going to ask you the same question Thora, you seemed miles away for most of the meeting."

"Oh, it's nothing really; you know I'm easily bored. I don't know why they spend such an inordinately long time on such little decisions. As if whether Janet Miller or Joan Gunn make the sun maidens garland holds any interest for me or anyone other that Joan and Janet!"

"I know, I know. Truth be told I have very little interest in the matter either, but it's more than that Thora. I could see you were miles away there, you seem troubled. Is there anything I can do to help?" He reached out and took the old ladies hand gently in his.

Granny smiled "It's just Finn; I do worry about the lad. He's apparently been hearing music, out on the cliffs. The whole bloody village knows about it. When I suggested he take the watchman's post it seemed like the best way to protect him, stop him from going to sea and keep him here in the village where we could protect the lad. Now I'm not so sure."

"Try not to worry Thora; I'm sure the lad'll be fine. The watchman's post always was a lonely one; he's probably just letting his imagination get the better of him. You were right to suggest he take the post. You had my backing and that of the other elders remember. The lad'll settle in time, just you wait and see."

Granny looked up into Jack's deep blue eyes. "You're a good friend Jack and still a handsome devil. It's a good thing you're a married man."

"I could never have tamed the likes of you Thora; you're still far too much for most men. Now talking of wives, I'd best be getting back to mine she'll be wondering where I've gotten to."

Jack and Granny got to their feet and walked to the door where, after a small hug they parted and walked off in opposite directions.

She made her round of the village distributing various lotions and potions and picking up the fish and vegetables she was offered in exchange.

Once her errands were done Granny walked up the steep cliff path and spent the sunny afternoon on the rolling hills behind the village. It was the best time of year to harvest herbs. The early spring growth had hardened off and the herbs were reaching full potency in the warm summer sun.

***

When Finn awoke it was to the smell of the fresh-cut thyme which Granny was in the process of hanging from the roof beams. The old lady was balancing precariously on a three legged stool, reaching up to hang the last bunch of herbs onto a wooden peg.

"Good morning Granny." He said as he sat up and rubbed the sleep from his eyes.

"Good afternoon, you mean. It's a lovely day Finn, why don't you take a walk down to the bay and wake yourself up with a nice swim. That's what most of the other lads have been doing this afternoon." She said as she carefully stepped down from the wobbly stool.

"They're probably practicing for the race. Don't know if I'll bother taking part this year Granny. I'll have to be on duty that night in any case."

Granny picked up the small stool. "Nonsense, I was speaking to Norman this afternoon and he was offering to keep watch on the solstice in your place.

He doesn't want a young lad like you missing out on the celebrations. You're a good swimmer Finn you could do well in the contest."

Finn got out of his bed stretching his arms as high above his head as the low roof would allow. "I don't know why I would even bother entering the contest, its common knowledge that Elspeth is going to be the sun maiden. Why anyone would want to compete for that snooty cow's affections is beyond me?"

"It's only a ceremonial wedding Finn, you know that."

"Even so!" he said as he picked up the soft linen towel Granny had laid out for him and walked out of the door into the warm summer sun. "Your right though, it is a good day for a swim."

As he walked down to the beach Finn weighed up his options for the coming solstice. There was no way he wanted anything to do with wedding Elspeth, ceremonially or otherwise, Linus was welcome to her. Still it might be worth the effort just for the chance to wipe the smile off Linus' face.

But if he allowed Norman to do the watch that night he wouldn't be able to see Merryn, assuming of course that she was still around. She would make the perfect sun maiden, he thought. Now that would be a prize worth competing for!

Finn sat down on the sand and pulled of his shoes and tunic. Then laying them in a neat pile on the beach he stepped into the cold water. He walked a few steps out, feeling the chill water in the pit of his stomach and then he dived, slipping effortlessly into the water.

After a few seconds he surfaced and taking a deep breath he struck out for the opposite shore, swimming in long powerful strokes.

When he reached the middle of the bay he stopped and turned, looking back at the village. He was lost in thought taking in the peaceful scene when he found himself suddenly plunged under the water. He felt strong hands on top of his shoulders pushing down, as he gasped desperately for breath. Then just as suddenly, he was released.

Finn bobbed quickly back to the surface, arms flailing, coughing, spluttering and gasping for air. When he wiped the salt water from his eyes he saw Linus' laughing face close by.

"Ha ha! Did that wake you up Finn? You'll have to swim better than that if you plan to beat me in the contest. Or will you be out on the cliff-top with all of your friends as usual?"

Finn fought the impulse to wipe the smile off Linus' face there and then and smiled. "That was actually surprisingly refreshing; thanks! Oh, and yes; I will be taking part in the contest, would be a shame to miss it."

With that Finn turned and struck out for the shore, nice and slow, so as not to give Linus the satisfaction of racing him.

When he got to the beach he suddenly felt very hungry indeed. He quickly pushed most of the water off his body and legs with his hands and rubbed himself with the linen towel. Then throwing the towel around his shoulders, he picked up his clothes and boots and trotted off up the hill for dinner.

Chapter 9

She stayed there, out past the breaking waves, her head just breaking the surface of the water, large dark eyes watching, waiting.

She had to be sure it was safe. She had spent the better part of the evening mulling things over in her head, could she trust this landling boy? Something told her that she could but it went against her better judgment.

So she stayed where she was, just watching and waiting until she was quite sure that there was nothing suspicious afoot.

She watched the boy, firstly in the fading light as he took over his post on the cliff. At that point the other man left, she saw him walking away along the cliff-top. It was just as he had said; he was all alone up there at the watch-post.

He stayed there for some time before she saw him step into the cave and return a few moments later with a length of rope which she watched him tie securely then toss down the cliff side. She continued to watch as he clambered down the cliff, alone again thankfully.

She left him standing there at the edge of the surf for almost a half hour. She watched the boy looking out to sea, scanning the dark water with eyes that were so much poorer than her own in the dim light.

She watched him getting more and more agitated, he began to pace up and down the sand stopping every now and then to turn and look back out to sea.

When she was quite sure that the boy was alone and that no others watched from the cliffs above she submerged and slipped silently to the shore.

She reached the beach a stones throw downwind from the boy; shrugged the seal skin off her shoulders and wriggled out onto the sand. This was when she was most vulnerable and she didn't trust the boy well enough to allow him to be too close at hand.

Then she quickly stood up, picked up her skin and walked along the beach towards the boy. "Looking for someone?" She called out over the noise of the surf.

Finn turned round startled, then immediately relieved, his heart beating in his chest like it might burst. "I was beginning to think that you had left; or worse......"

She sat down on the edge of the rocks with her back to the sea and laid her precious skin down next to her on the rock.

Finn sat down awkwardly. He suddenly felt very self conscious and clumsy. "Did you find the cave?"

"Yes it was just as you described, very cosy. I don't know what I'm doing here? I should have turned and ran as soon as you gave my comb back."

Finn smiled. "I'm glad you stayed, the more I think of you out there all alone, it's just terrible, very dangerous."

It was Merryn's turn to smile. "Oh, it's not so bad really; my people have been practicing the wandering for hundreds of years. It what makes us strong and self reliant. It's part of who we are." She stopped herself, suddenly shocked at how much like her father she sounded.

Finn felt her awkwardness. "Are you hungry? I brought some food with me for supper; you can share it if you like?"

He got up and walked over to where he had left his bag. When he returned he opened the little sack and laid out the food on top of the rock between them.

"What's this?" Said Merryn holding up the small wedge of cheese he had brought with him.

"It's just cheese. Don't you have cheese where you come from? You take cows milk and then heat it gently over a fire until the curds separate from the whey. Then you drain off the runny whey and pack the curds in a cloth squeezing out all of the water. Then you put it aside for a few months till it dries out."

Merryn screwed up her face in disgust. "What on earth do you do with it then?"

"You eat it of course; it's really nice with bread."

She quickly put the cheese back down and picked up an apple, at least she recognised that. "Do you mind if I have this? We have an apple tree near our house at home, I haven't tasted one since I left."

"Yes, go ahead." Finn took out a knife from his pocket and used it to cut a small sliver of the cheese which he then laid on top of a crust of bread. Merryn tried not to look as disgusted as she felt when he bit into the bread and cheese, she could smell the sour odour on his breath.

When he had finished the first mouthful he asked. "So what do you eat when you're travelling?"

"Mostly fish, it's easier to eat when I'm in seal form, there are plenty around here. Some types of sea weed are delicious and there are mussels and whelks on the rocks." She stopped and took a large bite out of the apple.

Finn took another bite of the bread and cheese. "We sometimes eat mussels too, they're nice cooked on the open fire until the shells open up."

"Yes that's exactly how I cook them. They taste almost smoky from the fire, delicious!"

Once he had finished the bread Finn offered her some of the elderflower water he had brought with him in a small clay jar. "Tell me about your home, is it far away?"

"Yes it is quite a distance from here, far away over the western horizon. It's taken me almost 4 moons to get this far, although I could probably get back quicker than that if I took a more direct route."

Finn was amazed that she had travelled so far, he had never met someone from that far away. "What is it like over the horizon Merryn? Some of the older men in the village have travelled a bit, but none as far as that. Is it true that to the north the sea is so cold that the very water itself freezes into solid lumps of ice?"

"I wouldn't know about that I've never been that far north. My father did travel to the north during his wandering, he saw great towering cliffs of blue ice that he says creak and groan as if they are alive and moving."

Finn shivered at the very thought of all that ice. "I've never been anywhere. I've lived here in Bruann all my life, just me and Granny."

"So you live with your Grandmother? Did something happen to your mother and father?" She asked.

"My mother died when I was born. Granny says she was exhausted and had lost far too much blood. My father was lost to the sea on the very same day." He noticed the look of pity on Merryn's face and quickly changed the subject. "Anyway, you were telling me about your home?"

"Yes. Yes I was, wasn't I. It's really quite beautiful you know. We have long beaches of white sand and lush green rolling hills leading to the high mountains. Most of my people live at the edge of the sea; it's where we're happiest." As she spoke she turned her head, eyes gazing out past the surf.

"It sounds beautiful. Maybe I'll go there some day?"

"Don't be absurd!" she scolded. "No landling has ever set foot on Tir-nan-og!" She turned back and saw the crestfallen look in the boy's eyes.

"I'm sorry; I didn't mean to be rude. It's just that it's forbidden, you see? Can I have a little more of that drink?" Finn passed the jar to her and watched as she lifted it to her soft lips.

"Why is it forbidden?"

Merryn put down the small jar. "Don't know really, I think it was one of the laws set down by the Fae. They were the first people to live there so most of the rules and laws were set down by them years and years ago."

Finn had never heard of the Fae, but as he didn't want to look foolish he just nodded his head in agreement. "So who else lives in this land then?"

"Well let's see, there's the Fae obviously, then there's us the Seilkin and there's the Duegar who live deep under the mountains." She said counting each one off on the fingers of her left hand. "The Fae live in villages and towns built around great castles, each family chief has his own castle and lands and such, it's all very well organised you know."

Finn nodded thoughtfully again. "Where do your people live?"

"Well, we live mostly in villages and small towns on the shore; we don't really like to be out of sight of the sea."

"And the Due…?"

"The Duegar, they live in great halls hollowed out far under the mountains." She shivered a little at the thought of life in the dark caves.

"You must really miss your family being away from home for so long?"

"I do, I wish I could have stayed with them, but after my wandering I can return a woman and spend the rest of my time there, and I'll marry and have lots of beautiful children there by the sea."

Their conversation went on long after all the food was eaten. Both Finn and Merryn quite lost in each others company, until the eastern horizon began to glow with the faint glimmer of the coming dawn. "It will soon be light, I must get back to my post and you should be well hidden before the men put out to sea!" Finn said gathering up the remnants of their meal into his bag.

Merryn picked up her skin and stepped to the edge of the surf. "Will I see you again tonight landling?"

Finn looked up from tidying, the grey light of dawn glinted in her eyes. "How could I refuse an invite like that? Of course, I'll see you tonight. Now get going while it's still dark!"

She stepped into the glistening skin, pulling it up over her shoulders and was gone with a small splash into the waves.

Finn watched as a dark head bobbed to the surface a few seconds later out past the breaking waves. He raised his hand, waved and then grabbed his bag and ran across the sand to the rope.

He had only just managed to hide the coiled rope and was trying to calm his breathing when he heard the scuff of feet on the steps leading down to the watchman's cave.

One last quick look round and he popped his head out of the cave. "Hello Will!" He called as the man reached the bottom of the steps.

"Morning Finn; anything to report?" Will said as he barely stifled a huge yawn with the back of his hand.

"Nah! Boring night as usual Will. Time for bed, I'll be off. Have a good day." And with that he picked up his bag and trotted off up the stairs.

Chapter 10

It was the week before the solstice and the days passed quickly as all the villagers of Bruaan busied themselves with preparations for the festival.

The womenfolk braided long lengths of brightly coloured yarn into garlands to hang around the necks of the revellers. The newly green boughs of the trees were cut and intertwined to decorate the lintels above every doorway in the village.

The fishermen had been working hard for the past week so as to bring enough fish in to port to feed the hungry villagers with a little left over, set aside for the feast.

Big Billy Ogg had tapped one of the barrels of his legendary brew *Billy's bonce blower*. "Just to taste it for quality mind" he assured his glowering wife. She found him several hours later asleep on top of the leeks in her small vegetable patch. You can bet it wasn't just the ale that accounted for his sore head the next morning.

Granny and the other elders had dutifully overseen the preparations, it was a busy time for the whole village as they all worked tirelessly to prepare. Not a soul complained about the hard work as they all looked forward to a day spent with family and friends eating drinking and making merry. It was times like this that tied people together and gave them something to look forward to during the long hard winter months.

Finn had had little to do with the preparations at all, what with keeping watch all night and having to sleep most of the day. By the time he was up and about, the villagers were mostly all packing up at the end of their days work.

He had spent every night for the past two weeks and more, down on the beach with Merryn.

The time passed so quickly when they were together that he almost wished that the dawn would never arrive each day and when he woke in the afternoons he almost scolded the sun for not sinking quickly enough in the sky.

His heart longed for the night, the sound of the surf in his ears and the happy hours spent with his beautiful Merryn down on the sands.

***

Linus Dane had set out for the days fishing just after dawn, he and his two crewmen, Jon and Ian Vass. They were brothers separated by only a year.

Linus had wanted an early start. He had been skipper of his own boat for less than a month and was the youngest man in the village ever to skipper his own boat, mostly due to his father James' influence and wealth and as such he felt he had something to prove to the other men.

He had not shared his plan with Jon and Ian as yet. He knew that they were far more experienced fishermen than him, not to mention older by a year or two and he didn't want to face the shame of an argument with his crew in front of the other skippers.

When the little boat had been launched and had navigated the treacherous rocks at the mouth of the bay, Linus set course due north. The wind was with them and as the morning drew on; the summer sun rose high in the sky warming their backs.

Linus leaned back against the stern of the boat, right arm draped over the tiller, feeling the swell through the boards of the little boat. He tilted his head back letting the sun warm his face as he listened to the sail crackle in the wind. What a perfect day, he thought.

"Linus!" It was Jon's voice. Linus opened his eyes and looked over to where Jon sat against the starboard gunwale, mending a small tear in one of the nets.

"What?" Linus said impatiently.

"I'm just a little confused; we've been at full sail for almost two hours now. We're quite a way out from shore and we've still not set any nets. We'll be lucky to catch anthing this far out."

Linus grinned. "We won't be setting any nets today boys." He reached down and pulled out what appeared to be a long thin pole wrapped in sack cloth.

He smiled at the confused look in the brothers eyes, pulled back the sackcloth uncovering one end of the pole and revealed the tip of a wickedly barbed harpoon. The sun glistened on the oiled iron. "I thought we'd bag ourselves a sunfish."

Jon and Ian looked at each other; they knew full well that their skipper was a little young and lacked experience but this? This was pure folly.

Ian spoke up. "We can't land a sunfish, not on our own. That's a job for at least three boats. Have you ever been out for sunfish before?"

"No, but I've seen one before; they're huge and they do taste good. Wouldn't it be fantastic to land one for the festival? Just think of it, we'd be heroes, landing a sunfish on our own, the other men would be green with envy and the girls, oh just imagine how impressed all the girls would be?"

Linus' last comment had been aimed at Jon. He had been trying to catch the eye of Rosie Miller for months now but she just didn't seem to be interested.

Jon mulled it over, this mad plan of Linus' might work he thought. "We might be able to do it Ian. I'm not saying it won't be difficult but we have a good strong boat and if we try not to harpoon too large a fish......"

Ian couldn't believe what his brother was saying; he was obviously just as mad as Linus. He was about to object when he looked up and saw the pleading look in his younger brother's eyes. The whole village knew how Jon felt about Rosie, he obviously felt that this was his big opportunity to impress her.

Ian shook his head and sighed. "Alright then we'll try, but if it all goes wrong and we live to tell the tale, I'll take great pleasure in reminding you both that I was dead set against it."

Linus smiled, relieved that he had won this little battle. He had known he could make good use of Jon's feelings for Rosie, it was pathetic really. He followed her about like some lost puppy when she obviously had no interest in him at all.

Still she was pretty, he might try it on with her himself when they got back, just for the fun of it. "Right then! Ian tie this line fast to the bowsprit; I'll tie the other end to the harpoon. Jon; keep your eyes peeled for a fin."

When the harpoon was tied fast Jon and Ian took in the sail a little, slowing the boat and allowing Linus to change heading to the east as they began the hunt.

Several hours passed with the little boat scribing a zig-zag course on an easterly heading. Linus was beginning to think that this was not one of his better ideas when Ian suddenly shouted "Fin! Fin!"

Linus sprang to his feet harpoon in hand "Where away?"

"Over there!" Shouted Ian, pointing to the large black triangle of the huge shark's dorsal fin, jutting out of the water about ten boat lengths to the north.

"Jon, take the tiller and head for the fin!" Shouted Linus as he scrabbled his way to the bow of the boat, almost tripping himself on the coiled line attached to the harpoon.

Linus took up position standing at the bow of the boat, left foot jammed against the bowsprit right foot braced backwards. He stood there for a moment slowing his breathing and listened to the blood pumping in his ears. He raised the harpoon and hefted it feeling the reassuring weight of it in his hand.

As they drew closer he could see the tail of the large fish, just breaking the surface of the water, swishing lazily behind it as it propelled the beast slowly through the sea. He could see the dark outline of the body of the fish and just make out the huge mouth gaping open, it looked wide enough to swallow the boat whole.

"That one's a bit big" said Ian taking a firm grip of the harpoon in Linus' hand. "If he dives he'll take us down with him!"

Linus was just about to argue back when Ian pointed just off the starboard bow, at a second black dorsal fin. "That one's a better bet I think."

"A starboard!" called Linus and Jon having already seen the second fish duly obliged.

As they drew near Linus had to agree with Ian, the second fish was smaller than the first but still a hugely impressive catch.

He braced himself again, steadied his breathing and hefted the harpoon back until the point was level with his right cheek. He took careful aim at a point just a hands width below the dorsal fin and with a loud grunt he launched the harpoon forward, almost tumbling over the gunwale as the momentum of the throw carried his right foot forward.

Linus quickly caught his balance and stepped aside as the line rapidly un-coiled, shooting out over the side. He looked out to the fish and saw that the harpoon was safely lodged in the fishes back, there was a long dark stain forming in the water from the wound he had made.

Then suddenly the line went taught, and the small boat lurched forward, timbers groaning as the huge wounded fish pulled ferociously to break free of the harpoon that was lodged in its side.

Linus stumbled, tumbling backwards, cracking his head against the mast as he fell.

Jon and Ian barely noticed their skipper as they struggled to take in the sail and tie it securely. Then grabbing an oar each they thrust them quickly into the oarlocks and dipped the blades into the water in an effort to slow the boats progress as it was dragged through the water by the massive wounded fish.

Linus got to his feet and seeing that the brothers had the oars well in hand he clambered over and grabbed the tiller which was swinging wildly as Jon and Ian hauled on the oars.

"Just try to keep the boat in a straight line!" Shouted Ian over the din of rushing water and groaning boat. "If the fish turns us broadsides he'll flip us over."

"Alright!" Linus shouted, barely hearing his own voice over the roar of the water rushing past the boat as it carved through the water. "Let's just hope it tires before we do!"

But the fish did not tire. Linus' aim had been true but being just a lad; his long spindly arms lacked the strength of the older skippers. The harpoon had safely lodged in the sharks' flesh but had not penetrated deeply enough to mortally wound the large beast.

The initial flow of blood from the wound had quickly stemmed and the large fish swam on, pulling the boat behind it much as a horse does a cart, barely noticing its weight.

The brothers had quickly become exhausted, their hands blistered and their shoulders ached pulling on the oars and so they had drawn them back into the boat. They all sat there, huddled at the stern of the groaning boat, their weight keeping the bow up, safely proud of the water.

Ian was the first to shout against the roaring water. "It's no use Linus, we can't land this fish, it's just too strong. We should cut it loose and make for home."

Linus stared at the black fin in the water, as he had been for the past hour or more, he tried to hide the desperation he felt. "The beast will tire soon, it will, I can feel it in my bones."

Jon took hold of Linus' hand on the tiller and knelt in front of him. "Ian's right Linus, it's only a fish. It's dragged us north for a league and more, we have to cut it loose and make for home now, while it's still light and we can see the land."

Linus ripped his eyes from the fish and looked up at the sky, Jon was right the sun was already well on its way to the western horizon. The fish had dragged them far off course and they would have to sail through the night to hopefully make it back to Bruann by midday the next day.

He shook his head and stood up letting Jon take the tiller. He clambered uphill to the bow of the boat where he grabbed the gunwale and slid his knife out of the sheath on his belt.

"You would have been quite a catch." He took one last look at the huge beast as it swam relentlessly forward and bent down, cutting through the taught line where it was tied to the top of the bowsprit.

The boat slowed suddenly casting a huge wave of cold, salt water high over the deck, soaking them. Jon and Ian stood and all three watched exhausted, as the huge fish that had been leading them a merry dance over the sea all afternoon disappeared into the twighlight with a swish of its mighty tail.

The three boys didn't notice the dark ship as it slid almost silently to rest, looming like a thunder cloud at their stern. It dwarfed the little fishing boat which seemed to cower under the menacing stare of the large carved dragon that served as its figure head.

Chapter 11

She stood there alone on the cliff-top watching the sun set over the distant mountains. The world was bathed in a warm ochre glow as the brooding clouds struggled to smother the light.

The sea was a golden flat calm, it had been a fine summer's day but the gathering clouds and the warm humid breeze were heralds of the approaching thunder storm.

Finn felt it too there was a static in the air, he felt as if his nerves were tightened almost to breaking, the hairs on his arms seemed to tingle with every passing wisp of warm air.

As he walked along the path towards the watchpost he saw granny standing there looking out to sea. The breeze had loosened several strands of hair which whipped around her head as if alive. She seemed taller somehow, larger than he remembered.

As he got nearer she heard his footsteps on the rocky path and turned to greet him. "Good evening my boy, just thought I'd take a wee walk up to the cliffs and take the air. I can't seem to relax tonight."

"Yes I know what you mean, I feel quite restless too."

The old woman smiled her most reassuring smile. "It just the weather, there's a storm coming I think, look at those clouds gathering over in the west. A good storm will clear the air, it should be more settled when it passes."

"If you say so Granny, you know better than me. I hear Linus Dane and his crew haven't come back in yet tonight. Big Billy was saying that he saw them set out just after first light this morning."

"Yes, I did hear that. Still the weathers good, maybe they decided to take advantage of the fine day to try the fishing round the point to the east, the sea round here has been pretty heavily fished for the past few weeks what with the festival preparations."

Finn nodded, but was not convinced. "Yes, your probably right granny, just hope they've made landfall for the night, especially if you're right about that storm. Not that I care what happens to Linus you understand, Jon and Ian are nice lads though. Anyway I'd better be getting down to my post while there's still light enough to see the path. Don't be out too long."

She watched him round the corner and disappear down the steps to the watchmans cave. Then turned and headed for home pulling her shawl up around her shoulders to ward off the chill she suddenly felt. There was definitely a storm coming.

***

Finn and Merryn met on the sand again that night. When he had climbed down the rope he found her sitting, on what he had begun to regard as her rock, waiting for him to arrive.

His heart leapt just a little when he saw her, as it always did. He had begun to dread the thought that some night she might not be there waiting for him.

He knew she must continue her travels soon, if only to return to her homeland. But tonight she was here that was all that mattered, better to live life for the moment and let the future take care of itself. "Here we are again then, we must stop meeting like this, people will talk."

Merryn gave a little laugh. "Then let them talk, all good people should be tucked up safely in bed asleep at this hour in any case."

"I suppose that makes us very very bad then. Are you hungry?" said Finn laying down his lunch sack on the rock as he sat.

"No not really, I managed to catch a good sized salmon today. I had to swim quite a distance for it though, good fish are getting a bit scarce around here just now what with all the fishing your precious villagers are doing."

"It'll be over soon, the solstice is in a couple of days and then things should get back to normal. Do you want half my apple?" He said holding the fruit out for inspection.

"Oh go on then, you know how much I like apples."

Finn cut the apple in half and passed one half to her. "One of the fishing boats didn't come back in tonight. Probably went round the east point for better fishing."

"I think that's where I got my salmon this afternoon, didn't see any boats there though. If I did I wouldn't have stuck around, you know what they're like, they hate seals stealing their fish."

"Yes I know, I know, we think we own the sea don't we? Odd though, I wonder where Linus and the boys have got to. It's a worry, especially with this storm brewing."

No sooner had the words escaped his mouth than the heavens opened. Finn jumped up and stuffed his lunch back into the sack. "Quick let's get out of the rain!"

They grabbed their things and ran across the beach to the foot of the cliffs, where there was a shallow niche in the rock that would shelter them from the worst of the rain.

When they were in, he took off his cloak and shook the rain off it, before laying it on the ground for Merryn to sit on.

He was just settling himself squatting on the sand nearby when she shuffled up a little making room for him. "Sit over here Finn its warmer." She said patting the coat.

"Thanks." He sat down awkwardly trying to keep a gap between them. "Looks like it will be quite a storm; we haven't had rain like this for months."

Merryn sat with her chin on her knees, arms wrapped round her legs looking out nervously at the storm. "Just as long as there's no thunder, I've never liked thunder, when I was little I used to run to mother and father's bed during a storm. Father said it was just an angry god using his hammer. I think that scared me even more." He felt her shiver a little at the thought.

"I don't know what makes the noise at all; maybe it's just the storm clouds clattering into each other. They must blow about a lot in the wind."

"Maybe……." she said staring wide eyed out at the building storm.

BARUUUUUUUUM!!!!!!

The sudden roar of the thunder made her jump and she grabbed out at Finn, wrapping her arms around him, burrowing her face into his shoulder to hide her eyes from the bright flash of lighting.

Finn froze, shocked by the sudden contact, but as he felt Merryn's sobs he wrapped his arms around the girl drawing her to him, feeling her warm body next to his.

She felt safe; she had been alone now for so long, just a girl adrift in the wide world. She hadn't realised how lonely she had been until she met Finn. She knew she didn't feel the cold as such but now, as she sat there in his arms she was warmer than she could remember, and safe.

She lifted her head from his shoulder and drew back a little, looking up at him. Feeling the movement he drew his gaze away from the storm and looked down at her, their eyes met and a few seconds later so did their lips.

***

Granny awoke with a start to find the bed sheets twisted and tied around her legs. She sat up, shook her head and tried to make sense of the dream that had so disturbed her slumber.

Oh if only she had more skill as a seer, but that had never been her gift. Even so, she should have paid more attention to old Brahan when he had tried to school her in such things in her youth.

In her dream Linus Dane had stood like a giant astride the lifeless bodies of his crewmen Jon and Ian while the storm blew and raged around his head. He opened his right hand and she saw that he was holding the whole village of Bruaan in his palm, the waters of the bay trickling out between his fingers.

Then he laughed as he closed his fingers around the village, tendons pulling tight crushing it, destroying it before the fingers opened allowing the raging wind of the storm to scatter the village like dust.

Well whatever the dream meant she knew it wasn't good. She had better be prepared. She got out of bed and pulled on some clothes. Then she quickly reached under her bed and pulled out the wooden chest, resisting the urge to open it and check the contents that she knew hadn't changed from when she'd last looked.

She wrapped the chest in a blanket and tucking it under her right arm and bracing it against her hip, she stepped out into the night.

Granny made her way quickly and silently through the village, her footfalls drowned out by the raging winds and heavy rain that the storm had brought. She reached the meeting hall in no time at all. A quick look round and she was in through the door and out of the rain.

She quickly opened the secret doorway and braced herself for the slippery decent to the cavern. It didn't matter how many times she came and went down this passage it was never pleasant. Her way was lit by the small candle she had brought with her and the wan light it provided did little to calm her misgivings.

When she reached the flat dry stone of the cavern floor she crossed quickly to the large stone altar, she had no time to consult the book and try to decipher her dream. It would soon be dawn and she couldn't risk being seen returning home.

She walked around the huge stone and across the cave to a large wooden chest which lay in a corner on the ground to the right. It was completely hidden in the shadows from any casual observation, but she knew exactly where it lay. Granny put down the candle and her small bundle and opened the large chest which was not locked.

Carefully laid inside the chest were various items of armour, all were fashioned from plates of a dull golden coloured metal bound together with blood red leather.

The most impressive thing in the box was a helmet also made of the golden metal, it covered the wearers head fully to the nape of the neck, the face was covered in an ornate mask decorated with intricate swirling designs and small red gemstones.

Granny picked the helmet up carefully in her two hands and turned it slightly watching the light from the candle flicker back from the gemstones. She then carefully placed the helmet on top of the chest and picking up the bundle she had brought she unfolded the blanket from her little box, she opened the lid and then picking up the beautiful helmet she lowered it slowly into the small box. Physically the helmet was far too large to fit inside the small box, but the physical world had never been much of an issue to the craftsman who had fashioned this particular chest. She remembered him explaining with a wink that the trick of the thing was just to make the inside of the box much larger than the outside of the box. She smiled at the memory, slowly shut the lid and locked it.

Once she'd lowered the little chest into the larger one and shut the lid, she picked up the candle and quickly crossed the cavern to the passageway, and then she was gone, plunging the cavern back into complete darkness.

Chapter 12

It was two days after the storm and the villagers had had their work cut out repairing the damage that the tempest had wreaked.

Several of the thickly thatched roofs had to be repaired and two of the boats on the beach had been damaged. One boat had been overturned by the wind, bringing the mast down on the one beached immediately beside it. The mast had torn a large gash in the side of the vessel before it snapped in two.

They had timber to repair the side of the damaged boat, but the other required a new mast which would entail a long trip inland to the forest and then a time consuming hunt for the correct tree to provide a sturdy serviceable mast. That was a job best left until after the festival.

The afternoon was growing late, when out on the cliffs, the watchman saw a sail approaching from the north. He watched and waited as the vessel approached, he needed to be perfectly sure about its size and course before he raised the alarm.

As it drew nearer he saw with some relief that it was a small craft very similar to the ones used by the local fishermen. It was listing heavily; the sail was poorly set, flapping wildly in the breeze and there appeared to be no one on board.

He continued to watch the boat as it drew closer and then suddenly he recognised the boat; it was Linus Dane's. The watchman ran quickly from his post along the cliff and down to the beach below, where breathing heavily, he quickly told the fishermen what he had seen.

The men immediately stopped their repairs and quickly launched two of their boats. Pulling hard on the oars they crossed the bay and were soon out through the mouth into the open sea.

By that time Linus' boat was approaching the shore some way west of the mouth of the bay and was drawing dangerously close to a large shoal of jagged rocks. The men, seeing the danger pulled for all they were worth crossing the gap before the vessel floundered on the rocks.

As they drew near they could see a lone figure slumped over the tiller at the stern of the boat. They called and called but it was no use, there was no response. A line and grapple was thrown to the boat. The grapple thumped onto the deck of the small boat and then scrabbling across the boards it found purchase on the gunwale just forward of the oarlocks.

The line went taught and Linus' boat slewed violently around to point away from the rocks. The second boat took their opportunity and also managed to secure a line to the stricken craft. Then both boats pulled for the entrance to the bay towing the damaged vessel behind them.

It was a relief for both crews when they had safely made it back into the sheltered waters of the bay. A large crowd had gathered and once the men had beached their own craft there were many hands to take to the lines and quickly pull the stricken boat to safety up on the sands.

They found only one person on board; it was Linus, unconscious and bound to the tiller with ropes. When the bonds had been cut he was lifted out and onto a makeshift stretcher.

Granny bustled over to the stretcher and kneeling down she examined the lad. She could barely feel the slight tickle of breath on her cheek and on placing her head to his chest she detected a faint heart beat. "He's alive, but only just. Quickly get him to my house and light the fire!" Four of the men took the corners of the plank he had been laid on and made for the old woman's cottage as ordered.

Jack Spraggan laid a hand on Granny's shoulder halting her for a second. "Will he live Thora?"

"I think so Jack, he's very cold but he's young and strong. I'll be more optimistic if he makes it through the night."

At that moment Laura Vass, Jon and Ian's mother, ran onto the beach, she saw the boat and looked hopefully at the crowd, searching for the two familiar faces she longed to see. Jack reached her side just as her worst fears were realised. "My boys Jack, where are my boys?"

As he looked at her the comforting words he longed to say stuck in his throat, he softly shook his head and brought her world crashing down around her.

***

Finn was rudely awakened as the door of the cottage burst open and the men carried Linus lifeless inside. "What's going on?" He demanded.

Big Billy spoke up. "It's Linus, your Granny told us to bring him here. Don't just sit there fetch us some bedding."

Finn jumped out of his bed, grabbing his blanket he laid it down on the floor in front of the hearth. The men carefully put Linus down on top. "We were told to light the fire."

"It's alright I'll see to the fire you'd better be getting back to the beach, Jon and Ian must need some help too." He said ushering the men out of the door.

"They didn't make it back, Linus was alone."

Finn was shocked. "No, that can't be right they were good seamen, both of them."

Billy scratched his bristly chin as he looked down at the boy in front of the hearth. "It's true Finn, Linus was lucky to make it back himself, their boat's in a bad way, must have got caught in the storm."

At that point Granny arrived at the house "Is the fire set?"

"Not yet Granny, I was just fetching some wood."

"Well be quick about it, we need to get him warm, time is of the essence."

When the fire was well ablaze Granny set about checking Linus over and removing his wet clothes. The skin of his wrists was red and sore, rope marks, but then he had tied himself to the tiller of the boat.

There were also dark bruises on his torso and if she wasn't mistaken several broken ribs, strange that he had no injuries to his legs or head at all. She had just dressed him in one of Finn's night shirts when there was a loud knock at the door.

"Come in!" She called over her shoulder. James and Cath Dane walked in through the door. Cath who had always been a rather feeble woman was clinging to her husband like a limpet. Both were ashen faced with worry.

James spoke up. "Is he alive?"

"Barely, he's very weak and hasn't spoken as yet. If he sleeps well overnight and doesn't take a fever he may pull through."

Cath began to sob quietly into her husbands' chest. "Can I stay with him?"

Granny laid a calming hand on her shoulder. "Of course you can Cath, Finn pull a stool over to the fire."

Finn set the stool down near to Linus' head and James helped his wife to sit down. "Is there anything he needs?"

Granny thought for a moment. "Yes, some freshly picked comfrey, I've run out completely, it's a small plant with wide hairy leaves and pink bell shaped flowers, it's sometimes called knitbone."

James nodded, "I know the plant; I'll be back as quick as I can."

Finn looked at Granny, confused. "Didn't you pick some comfrey only yesterday?" He whispered."

She whispered back. "Yes I did, but it'll keep James occupied for a while. Men are useless at times like this, best to give them something to occupy themselves with. Now put the kettle on will you?"

***

That night Finn left for the watchman's post at as usual, leaving Granny and Cath Dane nursing Linus. He had lain there by the fire motionless all afternoon.

James Dane had returned just before sunset with an arm full of the comfrey he had been sent to fetch, he was quickly put to work boiling the leaves of the plant over the hearth to soften them into a warm pulp.

When it was prepared to Granny's satisfaction she spread the paste over some lengths of linen and then strapped the still warm poultice over the injuries to Linus' ribs. "He has probably cracked a couple of ribs." She explained to his worried parents. "The comfrey will help the bones to heal and bring down the swelling. Now James if you don't mind boiling the kettle, I'll make a tincture to soothe his aches and pains."

When the kettle was boiled Granny broke up some pieces of willow bark, letting them steep in the warm water for a few minutes before she added some leaves of camomile and thyme. Once the herbs had infused the water she passed the liquid through a piece of cloth into a cup.

"Cath, can you help me sit him up?" Once he was upright Granny held the cup of warm liquid to his lips. The scent of the herbs seemed to rouse him slightly and she poured a little into his mouth. She poured the liquid little by little into the lad until the cup was drained. "There, he should sleep soundly now."

Indeed Linus did seem more restful, the pained expression previously on his face had eased and he appeared to be sleeping deeply. "Now you both need to rest too, Cath you can use my bed and James you can use Finns' he won't be needing it till morning."

"But Thora you need your rest too" protested Cath.

"Nonsense, I need to look after my patient. Anyway when you get to my age you don't need so much sleep." She showed them to their beds and then taking the seat that Cath had been using she sat there to watch over her charge until morning.

Linus slept well and by morning Grannys' worries had eased a little. His breathing was nice and deep and his colour was much improved.

Cath and James had slept little during the night and were up and about long before dawn. They both sat by their son silently willing him to get better. The life they all lived at the edge of the sea was often harsh, death was common, but they had poured their hopes into their only son and they could never give up on him.

When Finn arrived home just after first light, Granny sent him to draw water for the kettle, then she made more of the tincture she had used to ease Linus' pains the previous day.

Then as Cath helped Granny to sit Linus up he roused a little, opening his eyes. Almost immediately his face filled with fear and he struggled weakly to break free from his mothers grip, screaming "NO! NO!"

James knelt down and placed a calming hand on Linus' shoulder. "It's alright son, your safe now."

Linus' woke as if out of a nightmare his eyes clearing and focusing on the familiar face of his father. His muscles relaxed and his breath came calm and steady once more.

Granny put the warm liquid to his lips and Linus was able to drink down most of it, before he slipped back into a deep sleep.

Granny saw the worried look on Cath and James' faces. "He's been through a great deal, but he'll be fine, he just needs rest now. Go home and prepare a bed for him near your hearth, he should be well enough for you to take him home this evening."

Once James and Cath had left; Granny and Finn tidied up the cottage a little before he got ready for bed.

"What do you think happened to Jon and Ian?" Finn asked staring at the lad sleeping by the fire.

"Only Linus will be able to tell us that Finn, they did get caught in quite a storm, the boys were most probably swept overboard I expect."

"Yes you're probably right Granny. It's time I was in bed."

"Did you have a good night out on the cliffs?"

"Yes it was fine, same as usual." and with that he climbed into his bed covering his head with the blanket.

He lay there, eyes shut replaying the previous night spent with Merryn. Her soft voice, the moonlight dancing in her hair and the soft warmth of her lips. He was quickly fast asleep.

Chapter 13

When Finn woke he found that Linus was still lying in front of the hearth. He got out of bed and tiptoed quietly out of the front door to relieve himself.

When he came back in he saw that Linus was awake, his eyes were open, staring blankly into the fire. He didn't seem to notice that Finn was there at all. Finn walked quietly over and sat down on the floor next to him.

"How are you Linus?" He asked in a voice just above a whisper.

Linus' head snapped round startled, he struggled to focus on Finn and then the panicked look left his eyes "Oh, it's you Finn, didn't hear you there, sorry" he said in a weak voice.

Finn smiled, Linus must be in a bad way, it was the first time he had ever heard him apologise for anything. "It's fine Linus, I just asked how you were feeling that's all."

"I've felt better, my chest hurts and my head aches, but other than that" and he smiled a little.

"What happened out there?"

Linus closed his eyes for a moment as if summoning the courage to explain. "We had sailed a bit further north than usual, it was Jon's idea, he had this plan to hunt a sunfish and bring it back for the festival. I was against it but he insisted and Ian sided with him as usual."

Finn nodded his head to encourage Linus to go on. "We harpooned one of them but it was too strong for us and pulled us north for hours. I eventually persuaded Jon to let me cut the beast loose." Linus' gaze returned to the fire.

Finn waited nodding his head, he didn't want to pressure Linus but he was desperate to know what fate had befallen Jon and Ian. "What happened then?"

Linus stared deep into the fire as he spoke. "We struck out for home but the wind wasn't with us, then a storm blew in from the west. The winds tore the sail and we began to take on water."

Finn was growing impatient: he held Linus' head in his hands and pulled his face around; there were tears in his eyes. "What happened to Jon and Ian?"

Linus couldn't meet Finns' gaze and he looked away towards the fire again. "The storm took them Finn, that's all! Once they were gone I tied myself to the tiller, I must have passed out soon after that. That's all I remember."

Linus looked exhausted and Finn helped him to ease himself back down on the pillow. "It's alright Linus, there was nothing you could have done, rest now."

Finn walked over to his bed to put on his clothes. He could hear Linus sobbing softly for a few moments before exhaustion took him again and he was silent, asleep.

As he left the cottage Finn met Granny who was on her way back inside. "Ah your up, good, I need you to run an errand. Can you run over to James Dane's house and check that they're all set for Linus to go home. Once you've done that go down and see Will Dane, he'll be down helping fix the damaged boats, see if he can round up a few of the men, we'll need them to carry Linus home."

Finn just stared back open mouthed, so much for the pleasant stroll down to the shore he had been planning.

"Well, don't just stand there gawping, get on with it!"

"Yes Granny, will there be anything else. I could always take the broom and sweep up as I go."

The old woman scowled at the lad. "Less of the cheek my boy, now get moving or you'll feel my boot on your behind!"

Finn trotted off down the path chuckling to himself, she had threatened him with that boot of hers' for years, he had yet to feel it.

When he got to the Dane's house he knocked loudly on the door. It was quickly answered by Cath Dane, she saw Finn and her first reaction was panic. "Finn it's you! What's wrong? What's happened to Linus?"

He was quick to calm the poor woman. "No no, nothing's wrong. Linus is fine; I was just speaking with him minutes ago, honestly. Granny just sent me to check that you were all set to bring Linus home this afternoon."

Cath grabbed the doorframe, steadying herself. "What a fright you gave me. Yes everything is organised here. I've set up his bed in front of the hearth and James is just down on the beach sorting things out with his crew, he won't be going to sea until Linus is fit and well."

"That's fine. I'll see James down at the beach that's where I'm heading next. Granny wants me to round up a few of the men to help carry Linus home; I don't think he's strong enough to walk just yet."

He turned to walk away but Cath stopped him with a gentle hand on his shoulder. "Did he tell you anything about what happened out there?"

"Yes, a little. Seems that they got caught in the storm like we thought. He's very lucky to have made it back at all."

"Yes you're right, we're very lucky to have him back."

As she watched Finn walking away, down to the beach her thoughts turned to Laura Vass. The poor woman had already lost her husband several years ago. He had been much older than Laura, so it had not been entirely unexpected but all the same, she had doted on those boys of hers'.

When Finn reached the beach he found most of the men gathered round the two damaged boats busy working on the repairs. He searched around for James and saw him a little further down the beach standing by Linus' boat.

As Finn reached James, he turned round, hearing the footsteps. "Finn, what is it lad? Is Linus all right?"

This was becoming a habit thought Finn. "Yes, yes he's fine. Granny sent me down to see you to check that you were all set for taking Linus home. We'll need to gather a few of the men to carry him across the village to your house."

"That sounds just fine I'll round up my crew, they've almost finished work for the day in any case."

Within a half hour Granny heard the men approaching up the hill and was waiting on the door step when they arrived with a large bowl of cold water she had infused with the blossom from an elder bush. She held out some wooden cups for the men to help themselves. "That hill is hard work on a hot day like this."

"It most certainly is Thora" said James as he sat on the garden dyke, he put the cup to his lips and drained the contents in an instant. "That's quite delicious" he said wiping his mouth with the back of his hand.

Granny sat down next to him on the dyke. Finn sensing that Granny wanted a quiet word to James beckoned the men to follow him into the cottage. "We'll check that Linus is ready to go."

When Finn had gone Granny put her hand lightly onto James' shoulder. "Linus should be fine physically in a day or two, but make sure he takes things easy to begin with. He must stand before he can walk and walk before he can run."

"That's fantastic news, I can't thank you enough Thora." James said smiling. Then his face fell a little. "What do you mean physically?"

Granny took him by the hand. "I can't really put my finger on it James. His injuries will heal fine, there'll be no lasting damage but while I've been treating him I've noticed…….. There's a pain in his eyes James, whatever happened out there; it may have injured his mind as well as his body."

"But he will be fine, wont he?"

She gave James a reassuring smile. "All wounds heal given time and some leave scars, we'll just have to wait and see. For now just take good care of your son."

***

The long summer days passed and Linus grew stronger, his appetite had returned and he slept less. He had now returned to sleeping in his own bed. It was a relief for him to be away from the hearth and the constant scrutiny of his parents.

The first night in his bed he allowed himself to weep openly for Ian and Jon. It had been such a terrifying situation. He told himself that there was nothing he could have done about it, only his quick thinking had allowed any of them to return alive.

Still, the decision weighed heavily on him, the guilt sat in his stomach like a rock. It preyed on his every waking moment and haunted him in his dreams. He grew to fear sleep, afraid that he would blurt out something and let slip the terrible truth.

He climbed out of his bed, heavily swinging his legs over the side and standing up with a slight groan as the muscles over his ribs moved to accommodate the change in position.

When he had straightened up as best he could, he walked over from the corner where he slept to the open hearth where a small fire still burned from the night before. He eased himself onto a small stool and picked up the poker, using it to stir the embers back into life.

When he pulled the poker back out the tip glowed dimly red and the smell of burning skin flickered briefly in his nose. He quickly shook his head, clearing the memory from his mind before it fully formed.

"Oh, you're up already!"

Linus turned and saw his father standing at the open doorway. "Yes, it looks like a fine day, seems a pity to waste the morning lying in bed."

James smiled and stretched a little. "Couldn't agree more, I was just heading down to the beach to see how the repairs are going to your boat. Fancy joining me?"

Linus' let his eyes settle back to the hearth where the coals were stirring back to life. "No, thanks, I don't think I'm quite up to walking that far just yet. I'll just take a stroll around here if you don't mind? Maybe in a day or two."

"If you're sure? I'll see you a bit later." And James turned and walked off down the hill towards the beach.

That was a relief, thought Linus. He didn't mind if he never saw that boat again as long as he lived.

Once he had dressed and washed his face he walked out through the door of the house into the bright sunlight. He turned right and walked slowly up the hill away from the beach. The hill was getting easier, every day he made it a little higher before he had to stop and rest.

Today he made it as far as the path leading up the hillside to the road inland. It was a good effort, his legs felt stronger and his breathing was fine, a little laboured perhaps but it was quite a hill after all.

He sat down under one of the birch trees that grew there, roots gripping the rocky soil, the dappled shade was welcome relief from the bright sun.

From his vantage point the whole village lay spread out before him. He watched the villagers busily working; the men on the beach had almost completed the repairs to the damaged boats. The womenfolk had almost finished the preparations for the festival.

Yes, that's right, it was the day before the festival, he had almost forgotten about that. Well never mind, some other poor fool will win the race. It all seemed so pointless now, nothing seemed to give him pleasure any more; even his mothers' home cooked food tasted like dust in his mouth.

He sat there wondering why he had struggled so hard to cling onto this life. His gaze passed over the bay and out to sea, past the small boats fishing close to the shore, past the distant headland at the far coast of the firth to the faint distant line where the sky and sea met.

He shivered in spite of himself and rubbed the back of his neck before quickly getting to his feet and trudging back down the hill towards home.

Chapter 14

The day of the summer solstice arrived. Finn was still down on the beach with Merryn as the rising sun lit the eastern horizon.

"Time I was back up on the cliff top" he said beginning to get up off the beach. Then before he knew it, her arms were around him again, pulling him back down onto the sand.

"Just stay a minute more" she said, stopping any protests with a kiss.

He returned the kiss and thought just how easy it would be to stay there all morning. But no, he must get himself back up the cliff before the day watchman arrived, for both their sakes.

He could only imagine what the villagers would do if they found Merryn, they didn't like outsiders at best but a Seikie, they'd have her in the middle of the village, caged like some kind of wild animal.

He broke free from her lips and pulled his head back just far enough to speak. "Listen, I must go. The day watchman will be here any moment now, if he sees you down here on the beach……"

"Yes, I know, I know. The nights are just not long enough at this time of year."

They both got up and with one final kiss they were off, the boy running to the cliff and the girl splashing into the waves.

Finn got to the watch post, pulled up the rope and quickly stashed it in the cave as he had done every morning. When the day watchman arrived he was sitting on his favourite rock looking out to sea, the very image of the conscientious watchman.

"Morning Finn!" called Will Dane as he reached the bottom of the steps "Much doing?"

"Nah, same old same old. Another boring night on the cliffs. You've been a bit unlucky getting watchman duty on the solstice."

"Your not wrong there Finn. I was really disappointed to be missing out, but then Linus Dane offered to do half my shift. He'll be here after lunch. Recons since he's not well enough to compete in the contest, he'd rather just give the whole thing a miss."

"That's not like Linus." Finn said picking up his bag.

"You're right, but I'm not complaining. See you this afternoon, you still taking part in the contest?"

"Yes, but it won't be the same without Linus. I was sure I'd beat him this year."

"Never mind, I'll see you there. I can almost taste Billy's brew already, supposed to be a very good batch this year."

"See you later Will" and with that Finn ran off up the steps towards home. He needed to get a few hours sleep before the festival started, after all.

***

About an hour before the sun reached its zenith, the boy Granny had sent came panting into the cottage, letting the heavy door swing wide, crashing heavily into the stone wall.

Finn woke with a start and having quickly scanned the room was quite surprised to see the young lad standing there, sheepish, chest still heaving from having run up the hill to get Finn.

"Sorry bout the door Finn, your Granny sent me to fetch you. She said it's time you were up to enjoy the festival."

Finn smiled at the boy. "That's alright Davy, but be a little more careful in future eh? You nearly had the door off its' hinges there!"

"I'll go tell your Granny you're on the way. She's down by the beach with the other elders." And with that he was gone out the door, tripping over a stool on his way.

That boy never stops running, thought Finn as he dragged his tired body out of bed scratching his behind as he crossed the floor to shut the door.

A few minutes later he was dressed and walking down the hill to the beach. It was a truly glorious day for the festival, perfect mid summer with only a light breeze blowing in from the sea.

As he walked through the deserted village towards the beach he could see the entire village gathered there, all along the narrow strip of land between the houses and the sand. Everyone was dressed in their best clothes, walking around chatting and enjoying the fine weather.

There was a raised platform in the middle of the crowd, just high enough to act as a stage and lift the occupants up where they could be seen clearly by the gathered throng. The girls on the stage were dressed brightly in skirts hitched up a little shorter than the norm, all three of them barefoot, dancing to the music being played on a wooden flute.

The three girls danced harder and harder trying to outdo each other in the complexity of their steps and the village watched on with the elders gathered directly in front of the stage watching the contest closely.

Finn wriggled his way through the crowd, hampered by the occasional handshake and "Hello young fella!" as he went. He reached the side of the stage just as the music stopped and the girls gracefully halted and bent low, bowing to their audience.

The crowd erupted with applause, cheers and one or two loud whistles, from the rowdier lads. Then there was hush as the elders gathered in a huddle to decide who had won the contest.

After a few moments the elders sat back and Jack Spraggan slowly climbed the step onto the stage. He gathered the three girls over to him draping his arms across their shoulders.

"Fellow villagers!" his voice boomed out over the crowd. "I'm sure you all agree that the girls have put on a fantastic display of dancing. It really was quite a contest."

He paused riding the wave of cheers and applause, when it had abated he went on "It was a particularly difficult decision for us this year but the winner is................ Jeannie Vass!"

There was a roar of approval from the crowd. She was a popular choice and had danced very well; she was also the cousin of Jon and Ian. It did no harm to give the family something to celebrate thought Jack.

Jeannie was handed a bunch of fresh flowers and she exchanged kisses and hugs with the disappointed competitors, before walking off the stage to the hugs and kisses of her family.

Finn waited until the crowd had cleared a little and crossed over to see Granny. She was chatting with a couple of the other elders as they wandered away from the stage.

"Ah Finn, your up and about, please excuse me ladies I'll catch you up." The two old ladies smiled politely at Finn and walked off into the crowd.

She draped her arm around his shoulders and guided him away from the stage. "That was well timed my lad, those two old biddies could easily have bored me to death if you hadn't come to my rescue."

"Your welcome. Is the day going well then?"

"Oh, so far so good, are you ready for the contest? It's starting in about a half hour." Granny said nodding a quick hello as she passed one of the other elders.

"As ready as I'll ever be, I ate a slice of bread on the way down the hill."

She patted the boy encouragingly on the shoulder. "Good; good, it doesn't do to run on an empty stomach. Why don't you have a wander around and I'll see you at the start line. I suppose I'd better to return to my duties."

***

Linus Dane could hear the cheering village from up on the cliff top. He had taken over the watch from Will Dane at lunch time as arranged.

It hadn't been difficult to persuade Will to let him take over as watchman, he had nearly bitten Linus' hand off when he had offered.

Linus was in no mood for festivities in any case, he had seen the relief in his parents faces when he told them that he wasn't attending the solstice with them. He couldn't blame them really; even he could see that he was like a dark cloud hanging over the house since his mishap.

It would do his mother good to relax for the day. She had been walking on egg shells since he had recovered. He had always been bad tempered, but since his return his temper could flare without warning at the slightest thing.

He found it difficult to admit it, but he was actually beginning to enjoy the panic he caused his mother. Fear was a powerful thing.

His father was a different matter, he could barely bring himself to talk to Linus and had taken to coming home quite late. It was almost as if he waited each night until he knew that Linus and his mother had gone to bed.

When he had arrived at the watchman's cave Will Dane was waiting, already packed up and itching to go. Linus had had to endure a few pleasantries and yet more gratitude and promises to return the favour before Will had run up the steps to the cliff path.

Linus put his bag inside the cave and when he was sure that Will would be far off, along the cliff, he went over to the alarm bell hanging there on its' rusty old metal ring.

Linus tilted the bell carefully towards him away from the rock and slid his free hand inside the bell taking a firm grip of the heavy ringer. He tugged at the ringer, pulling, twisting, groaning with the effort; then with a sudden snap the ringer loosened.

He spun the ringer round between his fingers once, twice, three times and it was loose, slipping out of his grasp and landing on the rock with a thud.

He carefully returned the bell silently back to its previous position and then bent down picking up the heavy ringer by the rope tied to the end. He hefted the rope in his hand, feeling the ringer's weight before swinging it round in a wide ark.

He let it spin round three times to build momentum, released the rope and watched the ringer sail through the air towards the surf. Then it was gone under the water with a small splash.

That should do it, he thought sliding his back down the rock face to sit on the ground by the entrance to the cave.

He sat there, for the rest of the afternoon, staring out at a sea as empty as his heart.

***

The day went well, Finn actually enjoyed the contest; he ran well, wrestled strongly and finished first in the swim. It wasn't quite enough though, the problem was that he actually quite liked the other lads who were competing.

His efforts all lacked the venom he had always reserved for Linus. Linus had always bested him in everything but the run, but this year without Linus to run against Finn had come in third.

The overall victor had been Jamie Miller, who had competed out of his skin. It was probably something to do with his obvious infatuation with Elspeth the reigning Sun Maiden.

When Jamie had been crowned with white seashells, to much cheering, Finn was the first to congratulate him with a good hard clout on the shoulder. "Well done Jamie boy, if she's not impressed with that, I'll eat your britches!"

"Thanks Finn, do you really think she'll be impressed?"

"What Maiden wouldn't be impressed?" Finn replied with a smile.

Soon after, Jamie and Elspeth were the centre of attention in the marriage ceremony. Once they were wed and had been paraded through the crowd on a flower decked litter, they presided at the head of the large feast which had been laid out by the womenfolk.

There was steamed fish with aromatic herbs, all types of vegetables some that had been candied with honey, large round stone baked breads and at the centre of it all a large hog that had been spit roast to perfection, its sides golden, glistening with fat.

Finn joined the queue and soon had a large platter in his hand which was overflowing with delights. He found some space on the corner of one of the long tables and sat down to eat.

He had just filled his mouth when a large wooden cup was plonked down on the table in front of him. He looked up and saw Will Dane's smiling face. "Get that down your neck lad, you did well in the contest today. Pity you didn't win, especially since I had a little wager on you myself."

Finn smiled wiping the grease from his chin with the back of his hand "Sorry Will, I'll try to do better next year."

"Don't worry about it. Now go easy on that brew it's pretty potent, I've only had two and I feel like my head's stuffed with duck down." He took a large slurp from his cup letting a little of the brew trickle down his chin onto his already stained shirt.

"I'd best be off before the wife catches up with me. See you later." And he was off, staggering into the crowd of diners. Finn smiled at a few of the disapproving faces before returning to his own plate.

Chapter 15

By the time the feasting was finished the sun was already sinking low towards the horizon. Several large torches had been lit and set around the feast and a large fire burned to ward off the chill of nightfall.

Finn had managed to stash the best morsels from his meal into a cloth. It was only right that he share his feast with Merryn, she had probably never tasted some of the fine delicacies that had been served.

As the sun sank the older and more sensible villagers began to say their farewells, they would go back to their cottages and sit in front of their hearths for a spell before heading to bed.

Not that the festival had ended completely, the younger, more energetic villagers would continue the party well into the night, before exhaustion and booze overcame them and they slept where they fell.

It was time he was back on the cliff, he got up and was about to walk through the village to the cliff path when he saw Granny approaching. "Are you well fed then my boy?"

"Yes Granny, couldn't eat another thing" he said patting his full stomach. He wondered how he would stay awake all night. He was tired and stuffed, a good recipe for a sound nights sleep. It was a good job he hadn't finished that cup of beer Will had given him.

Granny held out a small bundle. "You should have accepted Norman's offer to watch for you tonight, you could have enjoyed yourself with the other youngsters. Here, I wrapped up one of Agnes' sweet chestnut pies; It'll make a good midnight snack for you up there on the cliff top."

Finn smiled, he would much rather spend the night down on the beach. "Thanks Granny, I'm sure I'll be glad of it later. I'd best be off now, Linus will only whinge if I'm late." He gave the old woman a hug and was off.

When he got up to the watchman's cave he found Linus sitting by the entrance, knees drawn up and wrapped in his folded arms. "Oh! it's you Finn, sorry I was miles away there" he said quickly clambering to his feet. "How did the festival go? I could hear the cheering from up here."

Finn smiled. "Oh it went well enough, young Jamie won the contest."

"That's good. I'd best be going, hopefully my parents will have saved me some food from the feast." He picked up his bag and was gone up the steps without saying another word.

Finn shook his head; that was the most pleasant conversation he had ever had with Linus. It just wasn't right; he really wasn't the same since he had come back.

***

When Linus got to the village he crept quietly down past the cottages to the far side of the beach, well out of reach of the light from the bonfire and torches of the feast.

Once there he walked back and forth for a moment or two eyes cast down to the sand searching, before he tripped and fell flat on his face over the stick he had stuck into the sand earlier that morning.

He stood up cursing and dusted the sand from the front of his clothing, picked up the disturbed stick and jabbed it hard, back into the sand. Then he bent and rummaged about in his bag, he took out one of the two lanterns he had stolen from home that morning.

It had had four sides fashioned from a mesh of woven wire, but he had blocked all but one side with pieces of heavy cloth. He hung the lantern on the hooked top of the stick, checking that the un-blocked side faced out towards the mouth of the bay.

He quickly opened the mesh panel and lit the wick in the small cup of rendered animal fat which was inside. He closed the door and took a few steps back towards the water to check that the light was visible.

Then he walked straight back from the beach up the small sand dune towards the village. After a few moments of searching he found the second stick he had jammed into the sand. He kneeled down and took a quick look around before dipping into his bag for the second lantern. This was exactly like the first with three of the four sides blocked off. Once he had hung and lit this lantern too, he walked quietly back towards the beach.

He walked across the beach to the waters edge and turned. The two lanterns burned brightly, one right above the other: He had lined up the sticks the day before, while everyone else was too busy with festival preparations to take much notice. The lanterns shone straight out of the bay and should be visible from the open sea. All you had to do was approach the bay entrance with the lanterns aligned one above the other and you could pass safely through the rocks into the bay. He smiled, it was all set.

A sudden scream made him start. He turned and threw himself down flat onto the sand. After a few seconds of silent panic, the scream turned to laughter as the maid who had been dancing on top of a table at the feast, was grabbed and subjected to a truly vicious tickling.

Linus got up and made one more quick check of the lanterns, then pulling his cloak tight around him he was gone, off into the shadows.

***

Finn waited as long as he could after Linus had gone before lowering down the rope. He couldn't put his finger on why, but his conversation with Linus had left him a little uneasy.

When he clambered down the cliff face he waited looking up, expecting to see Linus' gloating face looking down any moment. When several minutes had passed and there was still no sign of him, Finn sighed, relieved and walked across the beach to Merryn's rock.

He smiled when he saw the dark familiar silhouette sitting there waiting for him. "You took your time tonight, a few more minutes and I was off. I thought you must have found yourself some pretty little *landling* girl at the festival."

Finn sat himself on the rock by her side. "Well I did have a few offers but I told them that I was saving myself for this bad tempered selkie wench I'd met."

"Bad tempered! Well you obviously can't be referring to me, so who is this other selkie you've met?" She said folding her arms and pretending to sulk.

"Another selkie, I'm lucky to have survived one of you. I think if I met another it might just finish me off……………… unless of course she was prettier?"

She smiled, wrapping her arms around him. "You are silly, now give me a kiss before I change my mind." He gladly obliged and they kissed tumbling off the rock onto the sand.

After a few moments Finn rolled onto his side and propping his head up on his hand he gazed down at her face. It was softly moon-lit but as usual she seemed to glow with a light all of her own. "What are you thinking in that pretty head of yours?"

"Oh nothing really." She hesitated and then appeared suddenly sad. "I was just wondering how I'm going to be able to leave you to finish my wandering."

Finns heart sank; it suddenly felt like a cold stone within his chest. He felt the panic rising in his throat at the thought of not seeing her again. "Don't go." He said his voice cracking, as he fought to hide his desperation.

She turned to look at him, her eyes wet with tears. "But I must go Finn, I must return to my homeland. I'm needed there."

"Then I'm coming with you."

"I've already explained Finn; it's forbidden. You would be taken and executed, I couldn't bear that." The tears spilled from her eyes and ran glistening down her cheeks.

Finn pulled her close feeling her tears soaking through the thin shirt he wore. "Why don't we go away together? I could fix my fathers old boat. There must be somewhere close to your home where we could both live, a small island or something?"

Merryn looked up into his dark eyes. "You would leave Bruann? But it's your home, it's where you belong."

"You, are where I belong, I realise that now……… I love you."

"I love you too." she said throwing her arms around his neck, pulling him down to her waiting lips.

Time stood still as they lay there entwined on the sand, lost in each other.

***

The world was dark: the last revellers had fallen asleep, most in a drunken stupor that they would pay for in the morning.

Linus had sneaked in through the door and crept quietly into bed. He lay there, still eyes watching the roof as he struggled with what he had done. Sleep would be a blessed relief but it refused to come. The sleep of the righteous, his grandmother used to say. He hoped she was wrong.

Granny had stayed at the party as long as she dared. It just wasn't the done thing for one of the elders to spend the whole night supping ale and dancing…… pity. She had gone home and after one last cup of ale by the hearth she had gone to bed. She lay there now lost in slumber, as dreams of past days swum in her head.

The burning torches down at the festival had long since spluttered and died, smoke rising from the charred tips straight up into the windless night sky.

Out past the cliffs, Finn lay on the dark beach, the comforting weight of Merryns head resting on his chest as they both slept.

No one noticed as the long dark ship glided along the coast. The glistening oars dipping almost silently into the water, pushing the sleek craft forward through the slight swell.

The lookout leaned forward, toes gripping the gunwale, his arms wrapped round the carved dragon at the prow as his keen eyes scanned the cliffs. Suddenly he saw the narrow opening in the cliff wall and the two tiny lights beyond.

Without a sound he raised his arm and slowly swung it to port. The helmsman who had been waiting for the signal leaned on the heavy tiller and pushed the wide leaf-shaped rudder against the sea.

With a low whooshing sound the boat came around. The men at the oars kept the same steady rhythmic stroke as they pushed the craft relentlessly onward.

The helmsman watched the lookouts raised arm as he shifted it, right then left keeping the lights perfectly aligned and the long-ship passed through the entrance of the bay, oars almost brushing the walls of the cliff.

Once they were safely through the lookout ran to the stern of the ship and raised his arms. On the signal the men at the oars immediately pulled hard and the ship lurched forward as the prow rose out of the water. The stroke doubled as the men pulled with all of their might and their craft scudded across the bay.

Then with a loud grinding noise the bow slid onto the beach, the crew immediately raising their oars, straight up in the air, safely out of the water. Within seconds the oars were stowed and the first man was out, heavy feet hitting the sand with a thud, then a second, then a third.

When all forty one were on the sand, there was a bright ring, as swords were drawn, glinting in the bright moonlight. The large figure in the centre raised his hand and with the slightest flick of his wrist they ran like shadows into the village. The wolves had been unleashed.

Chapter 16

The first shrill scream dragged her back from the depths of sleep. She lay there, still, eyes shut listening as she heard a second scream, abruptly silenced.

Granny silently rolled out of her bed and barefoot, moved across the earth floor to the hearth where she picked up the long knife she used to prepare the food. She then hid, back to the wall on the hinge side of the doorway.

She stood there listening, blood pounding, deafening in her ears, forcing her body to be still, slowing her breathing, preparing for what was to come. There was another scream then the sounds of a scuffle, closer now, most likely the cottage next door.

Then they were there, the scuffing of heavy feet on the step outside. The door was eased slowly open and they entered. There were two of them, looming, dark; they smelled of damp wool and stale sweat. They stole quietly into the cottage and as they crossed the floor she saw a dull glint from the dark helmets they wore.

Once they were well clear of the door Granny silently leaped forward; knife in hand. Seeing the sudden movement, the closest intruder quickly turned, swinging his sword in a wide vicious arc. But she was not there to meet the blow as she ducked forward, rolled across the floor and under the sword as it sang through the air. As she passed his feet, she sliced deftly with the knife, feeling the edge bite into flesh as it severed the tendons behind the man's knee.

He grunted and fell heavily on the floor, dropping his sword with a clang as he reached down to stem the flow of blood from his wounded leg.

Granny regained her feet just in time to side step a sword thrust from the second would be assassin. As she pirouetted aside on the ball of her left foot she sliced forward once more with the knife, cutting through the skin of his sword hand at the wrist. The searing pain immediately loosened his grip on the heavy sword which clanged to the floor. As she passed she linked her left arm around the inside of his elbow. She continued her dance around the man, pulling the arm trapped in the crook of her elbow, round behind his back as she threw her right arm around his neck in a deadly embrace.

Any thought of struggle was immediately stalled as he felt the edge of the vegetable knife scrape against the dry stubble of his neck.

Leaning in like a lover she whispered. "Who sent you?" Pushing the blade a little tighter against the skin.

"Raghnall." He hissed through gritted teeth.

That was all she needed to hear, she swiftly slid the blade across his throat, shoving him forward, where he fell on top of his comrade who still lay there, blood oozing from his damaged leg, through useless fingers and onto the floor.

Picking up one of the discarded swords, she made for the door and stepped out into the night, sword hidden in the folds of her skirt. The air was now filled with the screams of villagers and the thick acrid smoke of homes already put to the torch.

As she picked her way silently from shadow to shadow towards the beach she saw the devastation which had been the raider's handiwork, few of the closely packed homes escaped as the fire quickly leaped from roof to roof. It was mid summer and the thick heather thatch was tinder dry. Several bodies lay where they had fallen, cut down as they had tried to flee, homes and families forgotten in blind panic.

She tried not to look at the faces of the dead, they were friends, neighbours. There would be a time for remembering, mourning, crying, but it was not now. Now was the time for hiding, surviving, clinging to life at all costs.

As she neared the beach she heard the scuffing of feet and quickly dived for cover behind a small cart. She watched from her hiding place as a small group of villagers who had survived the initial attack were herded, hands bound, towards the beach, their escort dishing out a blow here and there to encourage them on their way.

They were injured, terrified and huddled together for comfort, shivering in the warm summer night. As the group passed she saw Jack Spraggan towards the rear, mouth bloody, right eye black, swollen, almost closed. His grand-daughter limped along beside him leaning on him for support; her face matched his, bruised and battered her clothing dirty and torn.

Once the group had passed Granny slipped out from behind the cart and followed at a safe distance keeping to the shadows.

As they neared the beach she saw the bright ring of light cast by a large fire. The raiders had set light to one of the villagers precious boats; it served well as a bonfire. The prisoners were driven towards the light where a loud hoarse voice ordered them to kneel on the sand.

Granny darted silently along the low sand dunes, taking up a hiding place behind another of the boats, within earshot of the beach where she could clearly see the frightened villagers as they struggled to their knees, next to the bonfire. At the waters edge she could just make out the dark outline of the raider's ship looming menacingly over the beach.

Once the villagers were all on their knees, the only sound, quiet sobbing, a dark figure stepped into the light.

He was fatter than she remembered, older too but then it had been a long time. As the fire flickered on his face she could make out the familiar vulpine features, the long, thin nose with a small bump near the bridge, remnant of a fight long forgotten. The eyes were deep set under high arched brows, ice blue and just as cold. His lower face was hidden now, behind a thick grey beard the front of which was pleated and sported a collection of small dark beads. He had always been a striking man, tall with wide powerful shoulders. These remained but there was heaviness about his frame now that he had never had in his youth.

Raghnall approached the cluster of terrified people, casting his piercing gaze across them. "What kind of welcome is this for your new master?" He asked threateningly. There was no answer to his question only a low whimper from one of the children as he buried his head in his mother's breast.

Raghnall watched as his prisoners cowered in fear and a small smile began to form at the corner of his mouth.

"We have no master!"

Raghnall turned, surprised, to see Jack pushing himself to his feet. "The people of Bruann are masters of our own destiny." He said standing at his full height, staring defiantly back at Raghnall with his one remaining good eye.

Raghnall swallowed down his initial rage and forced himself to walk calmly towards the standing prisoner. "Who are you, who dare to speak out?"

"I am Jack Spraggan, chief of the council of elders. I would ask your name?"

"I am Raghnall Kin-Slayer, warlord of the northern sea, lord of Hofstadir and now master of this small fleapit village, or what's left of it." He replied glancing over Jack's shoulder towards the burning village. "Since your village is now mine, I will do what I like with it. I will take whatever supplies I wish, fresh water, valuables and perhaps even a hostage or two. Now get back on your knees, my patience is at an end!" He glowered at Jack as if daring him to refuse.

With a heavy sigh Jack lowered his head and bent his knee. He did not move quite fast enough for Raghnalls liking and a swift boot soon found Jack face down sprawled on the sand. "That's better" he growled, securing Jack in place with a heavy foot on his back. "Does anyone else have any objections?"

The villagers all fixed their eyes down to the sand none of them wishing to anger their captor further.

Raghnall called one of his men over. "When the men have finished with the village have the ship loaded with food, drink and whatever else has been found, we sail at first light." Then pointing at Jack.

"Take this fool to the nearest tree and hang him, it'll be a good lesson for the rest of them."

Jack was grabbed by rough hands and pulled to his feet. His grand-daughter ran to his side but her cries were quickly silenced by a powerful blow to the face and she lay slumped on the sand, the rest of the captives too terrified to help her.

The two men tasked with the execution dragged Jack back across the beach towards the village. The old man had little fight left in him and his feet dragged behind him across the beach, toes ploughing furrows in the sand.

Just as they had rounded the dunes the execution party found Granny standing there blocking the path before them. "Had a little too much ale has he?" She asked pointing at the condemned man and laughing.

"Move aside you old crone! Unless you want to join him?" Said one of the raiders drawing his sword and levelling at Granny as they tried to manoeuvre around her.

Granny blocked their way once again. "Now, now there's no need to be rude. Did your mother never teach you to respect your elders?" She asked showing her palms.

"If you won't move aside then I'll just have to move you." Said the raider, thrusting his sword into the sand and stepping forward to grab hold of the old woman.

As he grabbed her under her arm-pits Granny grasped the collar of his tunic with both hands and pulled him forwards. As she did so she fell onto her back, her foot swiftly thrust up into his stomach launching the heavy warrior over her head and through the air.

The second raider watched in shock as his comrade landed with a thump, flat on his back, knocking the air from his lungs with a loud gasp. Before he could react the old woman sprung to her feet and in one fluid movement the sword which had been thrust in the sand flew forward finding a home deep in his chest. He clutched uselessly at the sword before falling onto his back, dead before he hit the sand.

Granny quickly crossed to the first raider who was crouched on all fours coughing as he struggled for breath. She dispatched him swiftly with the sword she'd stolen earlier, still hidden in the folds of her skirt.

Jacks bonds were quickly cut and she helped him to his feet as he rubbed his chaffed wrists, trying to force the blood back into his numb hands. "What happened here?" He said indicating the two fallen raiders.

"Just a bit clumsy, that's all. Now run and hide Jack, Raghnall will be rather upset when he hears that you escaped." She leaned in and kissed his face, trying to pick an uninjured spot amongst the bruises.

Jack turned to run along the back of the dunes away from the raider's ship. He took two steps and stopped, turned round and asked. "What are you going to do Thora?"

"It's time I said hello to an old acquaintance Jack. Now what are you waiting for run, someone needs to help re-build once they've gone. They'll need you Jack." And she turned away from the old man and strode off towards the beach.

Jack watched her back for a few seconds; she somehow seemed taller than he remembered. Then he turned and ran as fast as an injured old man could, not stopping until he was hidden in the darkness of a small copse of birch trees a short distance from the edge of the village. Once there; he sat, exhausted and watched his beloved village burn, his old eyes clouded by tears that stung his damaged face.

Chapter 17

Raghnall stood at the waters edge, the keen eyed foreman watching his men's handiwork. Most of the village was alight now and the survivors were being gathered on the beach where his men could watch over them.

He had sailed this firth many times, most of the small towns and villages on its coast were under his protection. Strange how this little place had passed by un-noticed. Still he was here now; the ship would soon be loaded up with as much as it could hold. Probably just yet more fish, grain and whatever trinkets his men could find, these people had so very little to interest him.

He sighed; it was not like the old days when there were vast hoards of gold and precious stones to be taken. But then that was back in the days of the High Jarls, they were all gone now, rotting in their graves, most defeated at his hand. No one had the will to oppose him anymore, mores the pity. Still these little raids kept his men occupied, warriors were best kept busy it stopped them over indulging and getting soft or bored and he knew from bitter experience that bored was worse.

He shook his head and took a deep breath, clearing the nostalgia. With a little luck there would be a couple of reasonably pretty maidens in this village; that would provide a little light relief and lift his mood for a while. With that thought in mind he strode over towards the prisoners to inspect the goods.

As he crossed the sand he saw a lone figure walking down onto the beach from the dunes, he squinted through the gloom; just an old hag. He pointed at the nearest of his men. "You! Go and bring that straggler over here to join her friends!" He said, waggling his thumb in Granny's general direction.

The warrior nodded his head once "Yes my lord" and he trotted over towards the woman his sword clanking dully in its scabbard as it bounced at his thigh.

Raghnall turned back towards the gathered prisoners. There was a sudden muffled grunt and a dull thud, he turned and saw the old woman still making her way towards him across the sand. The warrior he had sent to fetch her lay where he had fallen, a lifeless shadow on the sand. "What manner of witchcraft is this?" He called as he planted his feet squarely in the sand, throwing his cloak over his shoulder clear of his sword arm.

The old woman stopped just out of sword reach. "What brings the great Raghnall to so humble a village?"

Since she had dispatched one of his men so effortlessly it seemed prudent to humour the old crone a little. "If you know of me, then you understand that I go where I wish, am I not master of the northern seas? This village has escaped my attention for too long it would seem, humble or not."

"It would appear that age has not diminished your arrogance. It would be better for every one that you and your men leave this place now. This business can bring no good."

There was something familiar about this woman, a memory long since forgotten, she was fearless, few dared to stand before him let alone criticise his actions. Now he came to think of it even her voice was familiar. But no, it couldn't be her, she had been dead for an age. "You seem familiar old woman, have our paths crossed before?"

"I'm surprised you remember my Lord, it was quite some time ago and you were always quite self absorbed. Still time has changed us both; there was a little less of you when we last met, it would appear that your appetite is for more than just mere violence these days." She said pointing towards his expanded middle.

"Be wary old crone or you will find that the passing years have done nothing to soften my temper. I am still at something of a loss, as I said you seem familiar. I would ask your name?" He said, freeing his sword from its scabbard with a rasp.

Moonlight glistened on the keen edge of the sword as it was levelled at Granny's throat.

"I'm surprised at your poor memory, time really can't have been kind to me at all, but I can remedy that." Granny drew back her shoulders and straightened up throwing the weight of the accumulated years from her frame like a heavy cloak.

She then reached back and untied her silver hair shaking it loose, as she did so the silver fell from her hair like a dusting of snow blown from a pine tree, leaving it raven black, shimmering darkly in the moonlight. She tossed her hair back once again away from her now taught and un-lined face and fixed Raghnall with a defiant stare.

His sword wavered in surprise.

"…………..Thordys? But how is this possible?"

She produced the sword from within her skirts, touching the edge to his, squaring her hips ready for battle, gripping the cold sand with her toes, this may after all be a very brief return from the dead. "It would be better that you leave now Raghnall if you remember you never once bested me with a sword."

"Perhaps so Thordys, but I'm guessing that many years have past since you last held a sword in anger. We have so much catching up to do, unfinished business if you will." He too squared his stance flexing his knees a little. He was almost looking forward to this, although he had to admit she always had been very good with a sword.

Some of the warriors began to edge closer to offer their lord assistance but he halted them with a wave of his hand. "Stay back! This is my fight!"

He began to circle Thordys in an anti-clockwise direction and she did likewise keeping him out of range, watching his gate, his posture, seeking out any sign of weakness.

He too watched, more in surprise than anything else, he had thought her dead, gone for years. She had gone into that cave alone; she insisted that it would be better that way, quieter. He had waited outside the cave with the others; he remembered the rocks around the cave entrance; black and cracked, baked by the dragons scorching breath.

He lunged forward at her chest, more of a probing jab than anything else, she parried the blow away and immediately countered, slicing in an arc towards his left shoulder, he sidestepped and they turned to face each other again.

He smiled "Not too shabby, you've clearly kept in practice."

"Well I'll admit I did warm up a little with one or two of your men earlier on. Not up to much are they?" She said smiling back. She had to admit she had missed this, just a little.

"Did you hear that men?" He bellowed, still circling, sword in hand. "Let me introduce your critic. This lads, is Thordys Gildenhelm, slayer of dragons, destroyer of trolls and at one time my very good friend."

It was her turn to attack, she feinted a slice under his sword and to his right side, but with a deft twist of her wrist this became a direct thrust at his now exposed belly. He saw the thrust just in time to throw his weight onto his back foot and pull back from the blow. The tip of her blade cut through his tunic and opened a small cut in the flesh.

He looked down at the wound. "Only a scratch. Now tell me Thordys how did you escape from that dragon? We waited for you to come back out of that cave, but no sign of you, just one very angry dragon who seemed a little upset at our intrusion. Still roasting fifteen of us must have cheered him a little."

She winced a little at the thought, she knew exactly why the dragon, or Haldor to name him; was quite so angry. "It's a long story and my memory isn't what it used to be."

Raghnall twisted the beads at the end of his beard. "I have a proposition, throw down your sword, become my guest and I will spare this village and what's left of its' inhabitants. We can discuss old times at our leisure during the voyage."

Thordys looked over at the nearby villagers cowering on the sand surrounded by Raghnall's men.

These were not good odds at all, even if she did win this fight, there were still at least ten others to deal with close at hand and they were bound to turn on the villagers the minute the duel swung in her favour. She just needed to get him away from the village. "How do I know I can trust you?"

"As you said yourself, it's only a humble village, beneath my attentions really. I give you my word."

She thought for a moment then threw her sword onto the sand at his feet. "On my knees I assume?"

Raghnall nodded his head. "If that's not too much trouble." He turned to his men. "Bind her tightly and have her taken on board!"

Two of his men ran over with a length of rope, she could smell the salt herring on their breath as they bound her arms together behind her back. Raghnall slid his sword back into his scabbard; now that she had been restrained he strutted over to her and stroked the smooth skin of her cheek with the back of his hand. "Such a striking woman, how could I have failed to recognise you? We'll speak properly later. No hard feelings now but that little scratch you gave me smarts a little."

And with that, he landed a vicious punch on her left cheekbone. Thordys felt sharp pain before the world went black; she was unconscious before her face hit the sand.

"You two, get her on board. Make sure she is tied firmly to the stern post, I don't want her getting loose." He turned back to what was left of the smouldering village. His men had had enough fun for one night, time to get them back on board and set sail with the tide.

He ordered the return to the ship and there were three loud blasts on the Drottinns' horn. As he passed near to the edge of the dunes a figure approached from the shadows. "Was the raid a success my lord?"

Raghnall smiled. "Yes Linus, very successful. You could say it has been a night full of surprises."

Linus looked round, worried that he may be seen. "And what of our deal my Lord? I have done as you asked, the village is yours. I can't remain here after all this, take me with you."

Raghnall considered the matter, the boy was ruthless, scheming; he had been all too quick to save his own skin and put his companions to the sword when they had stumbled upon them a month ago. The only thing that prevented his own execution was when he offered to guide Raghnall to this village. He reminded Raghnall of himself as a young man. A flattering thought yes, but was there room in the world for two?

"I am a man of my word Linus, get on board."

Chapter 18

It had taken most of the day to climb up from the shore where they had beached the ship. The path was rocky and the sun, now high in the sky, beat down on their backs warming the leather and iron-bound armour they wore.

Thordys stopped and lifted the water-skin she carried to her parched lips. Looking down from the mountain she could hardly make out the sea through the haze. They had emerged from the heavily wooded mountain side and now that they were above the tree-line the ground had become dry and rocky.

She was tired, tired to her very bones but that was not purely due to the long climb up the mountainside. It was this, all of it, the constant campaign, the war that was being waged month after month, and for what?

She looked back down the line of men, thirty handpicked warriors from the ranks of Raghnall's ever expanding army. This was a fool's errand in any case, fighting the High Jarls was one thing, they were rich and complacent, far too occupied in their lands and wealth to maintain a decent standing army. Their assaults, and there had been many in the past few months were continually met by a hastily conscripted host of poorly prepared farmers and peasants. It was all too easy really.

She would be the first to admit it, the men needed a sterner challenge but this, this was madness.

Raghnall had heard of the dragons hoard from a travelling soothsayer all too keen to read the entrails and pander to Raghnall's growing vanity. He had foreseen a great kingdom with Raghnall on a throne, all the world in the palm of his hand. Amazing what could be seen in the hastily spilled guts of a chicken she thought.

"Thordys!"

She quickly replaced the stopper in the water-skin and ran to the front of the line where Raghnall stood waiting. "There you are, thought you might be getting cold feet."

"Not likely my Lord. I was just checking on the men, it was a long hike up from the beach, wanted to make sure no one had been left behind."

Raghnall turned back towards the mountain top, impatient, already bored with the conversation. "The soothsayer said that the cave was on the west side of the mountain, facing the setting sun, we should be able to see it by now."

Thordys shielded her eyes with her hand and scanned the mountain side. "The most likely spot seems to be that small gully, it faces due west."

Raghnall could almost smell the gold, enough to at least double the size of his army. "Come on then!" He called as he trotted ahead, making a bee line for the corrie.

Thordys sighed. "Here we go again" and broke into a trot a few yards behind him.

She had been fighting by his side for several years now; at first it had been great, he was charismatic, dynamic, as he tried to outdo the legend of his father. She stood by his side as his domain had grown; they had fought battle after battle together until she had become one of his favourites her own tactical ability and skill at arms closely matching his own.

He was ambitious, driven even, but it was more than that, it was never enough he always wanted more. No sooner had they conquered one town or city than he was looking hungrily at the next, as his lands grew it just fed his appetite, there was always another place to wage war, another land to add to his collection, more people to be put to the sword.

The violence sickened her now; at first she had enjoyed combat, the combined rush of fear and adrenalin. Then slowly she had become numb to the thrill, it was simply a means to an end, a necessary evil if you will. Recently she had begun to realise that it was just plain evil.

But not Raghnall he revelled in the violence of war, most leaders would stay on the edge of the battle, directing their troops from a distance but not him; he was always at the heart of the battle, eyes wild, lost in the red mist.

Even after the fight his punishment for those who had opposed his will was cruel. This served well at first, as his reputation grew so did the shadow of fear that he cast. Many towns surrendered immediately in an attempt to escape his wrath only to find that no sooner had their new lord entered the gates than the executions began.

He reached the corrie first and threw down his pack as he waited for the rest of the host to catch up. Thordys, only a few seconds behind dropped her pack too.

She looked around, surveying the hollow, yes this was the place; she could see a wide cleft in the rockface, the opening of a cave which appeared to carry on deep into the mountainside. The rocks around the entrance were black, cracked and scarred by heat.

She turned around to find that the rest of the men had arrived and were gathering in a loose circle around Raghnall. He sat down on a rock waving his hand as he did so gesturing for them all to sit. "This is it lads, just as the soothsayer described, we have a few hours till sunset so the dragon should be asleep. We should strike while he slumbers." They all nodded and grunted their agreement to the plan.

Thordys spoke up. "Lord, why don't we wait until sunset? We could hide until the dragon departs then plunder his lair whilst he's gone."

"What's wrong Thordys? I thought you had faced dragons before, not scared are you?" Raghnall asked with a grin.

"Yes I have faced their kind before, and yes I am scared. You should be too. If we all troop into the cave like you say we won't have a sleeping dragon for long and if we do reach his lair I don't fancy our chances fighting him on his territory. That's if there's only one of them."

The oldest of the men spoke up. "She's right my Lord, it'd be folly going in there to face him. We should wait out here to ambush him as he leaves, we brought ropes, we could snare him as he leaves the cave. He won't be expecting that."

Raghnall nodded his head. "Not a bad idea, at least we would have room to fight out here and there will probably still be enough light to see. Someone should take a look inside the cave though; just to make sure he's there and that there's only one of them. I wouldn't like to tackle two of the buggers."

The men all shifted uncomfortably, staring at their feet trying not to make eye contact.

"I'll go in" said Thordys. "I'm smallest and a lot lighter on my feet than any of you lummoxes."

She stood and prepared for the task, leaving most of her armour and kit behind a rock at the edge of the corrie. She took her sword and helmet with her, the sword hanging over her shoulder; the helmet would protect her head whilst clambering about. There would be no room down there for a shield.

As she approached the cave entrance she saw that the men had already begun hanging ropes across the gap, ready to ensnare the emerging dragon. She turned, smiled at Raghnall and entered the gloomy cavern, holding a small torch before her.

The cave floor was easy to walk on, smooth, scoured out by the dragons scaly belly over an age. She continued steadily downhill, until looking back she could no longer see the light from the entrance.

She felt a small draught as the flame from her torch flickered, strange so deep down. As she followed the draught she found a wide crack in the wall of the cave. It was wide enough for her to squeeze into but much too small for a dragon to pass; she ignored the passage and continued downward.

Suddenly the cave opened out, she could sense that the space was bigger, less confined, the dim light from her torch did not reach far enough to light the walls any more and she couldn't see the roof of the cave. She thrust the torch before her and stepped warily ahead.

As she reached the centre of the cavern she saw it, only a glimmer at first but as she slowly crept forward it became clearer, gold, it could only be gold, shimmering in the torch-light. It was more gold than she had ever seen, coins, cups, statues, bracelets, crowns, all manner of trinkets lying heaped in a great pile. Some of the pieces were set with sparkling jewels which glittered and sparkled as she moved her torch.

She looked right and left taking in the sheer size of the hoard. Then looking up she saw him, lying coiled on top, using the great pile of treasure as his bed. She almost dropped the torch. He was truly magnificent, huge and ancient; she had never seen a dragon of such size.

His scales glistened in the light almost as brightly as his golden mattress. She followed the line of his back from his pointed tail, along the sharp scales of his spine to his majestic head which was resting on his fore-paws. His wings lay neatly folded along his back and she watched his huge chest slowly rising and falling, deep in slumber.

She stepped backwards slowly, on tip-toe, re-tracing her steps back to the passage; they may need more men.

Then something caught her eye, just to her right perched a-top a pedestal of stone. It was round; a little larger than a man's head and seemed to glow dimly with a light all its own. She approached, curious; it was like nothing she had ever seen. She peered at the ball. It was predominantly blue, a deep shimmering blue covered in odd intricate silver shapes with jagged haphazard edges cutting into to the blue.

It appeared to be perfectly spherical at first but as she ran her hand over the surface it felt rough, there were jagged ridges rising up here and there from the surface with glistening white tops. The areas of blue were smoothest; she reached out and touched the blue with her finger-tip and the surface gave a little, casting ripples over the still surface. She pulled her hand back and let out a small gasp, it wasn't solid it moved, like water.

She put down her torch and lifted the ball from its pedestal. When she brought it close to her face and looked closely she could see where the silver shapes met the blue, some of the edges were ragged and harsh the others smooth and white. Some of the shapes were familiar somehow, she looked even closer until her nose was almost touching the surface, the small dark dots she had noticed were actually small clusters of what looked like buildings; that was it, they were towns, villages.

No wonder some of the shapes looked familiar, they matched the charts that Raghnall's scribes had made, depicting the extent of his conquests. But that was only a tiny area of this sphere, most of it was completely un-known to her.

Then she suddenly realised, this was the world, the whole world.

"Quite something isn't it? Holding the world in your hand." the voice was little more than a whisper but reached out filling the dark unseen corners of the cave.

She turned around and saw the dragons deep green eyes piercing the gloom. "So it is the world, all of it. But how?" She said; too curious to remember to be terrified.

"Yes, my little thief, it's the whole world. I should know; I have seen it all. Now please put it back carefully, I'd hate for it to get damaged whilst I'm dealing with you." The deep silken voice dripped with menace.

"Yes, you're quite right, it would be such a shame if I were to drop it." And with that she stretched out her arm balancing the globe in the palm of one hand.

"Careful now little one, that is important. It is the only one of its like and it is very, very old." He stood up shifting his position on the golden bed and sending a small avalanche of gold coins down the slope onto the ground. "Put it down and you may fill your pockets with gold, as much as you can carry. Now that's what you really came for, is it not?"

"Please don't insult my intelligence master dragon, the moment I put this down will be my last on this earth and we both know it."

The dragon smiled. "Very good, very good, not anywhere near as greedy as the rest of your kind. Surprising, but still just as rude though. Yes, I am dragon, but if we are to converse, kindly use my given name, I am Haldor."

"As you wish Haldor." She said sitting herself up onto the pedestal in place of the missing globe which she still held outstretched in her hand. She had never spoken with a dragon before and to be honest she had perhaps exaggerated her previous dealings with the beasts a little.

Haldor considered the small human sitting before him. It had been some time since anyone dared to climb up to his lair; he had hoped that he had been forgotten really. He was old, very old, ancient even, he spent most of his time sleeping these days, it took an age to gather enough gold but he had decided that once he had enough it would be a shame not to make the most of it. It was quite the most comfortable thing in the world gold. He cast his eye over his beautiful bed with a sigh and was about to go back to sleep when he saw her. Oh yes! the woman; that's right, that's what he had been doing. "You have my name thief, but I do not know yours and despite your actions calling you thief seems more than a little rude."

She thought for a second, was it wise to give a dragon your name? She couldn't remember any advice against the practice. Well what harm could it do, she would most likely be dead by morning in any case. "My name is Thordys; Thordys Gildenhelm."

"A fine name for a thief, especially such a brave thief, did you think you could just tip-toe in here and help yourself? I may be old but you must know that we dragons are notoriously bad tempered." As if to drive home his point he flicked the tip of his tail, scattering a little more gold off his bed and across the floor of the cave.

She looked down again captivated by the globe she still held in her hand, it was amazing, she turned it over in her hands examining the far away lands she had never even dreamed existed. Then she realised, this ball was priceless, of more importance than all of the gold in this place, all of the gold in the world even. With this ball as a guide anyone could sail over the horizon in the sure and certain knowledge of what lay ahead; nothing would be unknown any longer. She did indeed hold the world in her hands.

She suddenly realised she could not allow this sphere, this knowledge to fall into Raghnall's hands. With this ball he would be unstoppable; land after land would fall under his heel. There would be no end to the bloodshed, the violence, the misery. She saw it all, the dark cloud stretching across the world.

She shook her head to clear it of the image. "I have a proposition for you master Haldor."

The beast's eyes narrowed as he moved his great head down towards her. "Very bold, trying to make a deal with a dragon. Go on then amuse me, I'm listening."

"You are wise great Haldor, you must realise that one such as I would not set out on such a quest alone. There are thirty warriors, armed to the teeth waiting outside your cave. They plan to surprise you as you leave tonight. I am their slave; a thrall, expendable. They sent me down here to spy on you and report back to them." She gave out a little sob, hoping that she had been convincing enough.

Haldor pulled back his great head and lifted himself slowly from his bed. "Only thirty men you say. Ha, they will rue the day they were born!"

"Be wary master Haldor, they have set ropes to ensnare you as you leave this cave. They are great warriors, well versed in the arts of war."

He spread his wings wide flapping once, flexing the muscles of his huge back. "I will be back presently little Thordys, you will be rewarded well for your assistance." And with that the great beast clambered down from the gilded bed scattering coins and trinkets onto the floor and was gone, up the dark passageway towards the surface.

As soon as she saw the tip of his tail disappear into the cave she whipped off the cloth she had tied round her torso to silence her armour and used it to wrap the globe, tying it tight to form a bag with the knot for a handle. Then she ran out into the passage, as she made her way up towards the entrance she saw bright flashes of yellow light and loud roaring as Haldor unleashed his fire upon the attackers.

She tried not to think about the men she had left there to face him, it was necessary and in any case they had come here expecting a fight.

She found the cleft in the rock-face that she had stumbled upon on her way down and squeezed in. She could smell fresh air on the breeze and trusted that if she followed her nose she would find a way out onto the mountain side.

Then all she had to do was get as far away as possible from a very angry dragon.

Chapter 19

Finn woke slowly; he could feel her, warm skin against his own, her head lying heavy on his chest. He lay there eyes shut scared to move a muscle in case he broke the spell. He could smell her hair; feel her warm breath tickle as it drifted across his bare chest.

Through closed eye lids he could sense that it was growing light, it was no use, he needed to wake up, and there were plans to be made. He opened his eyes and looked down at his sleeping beauty, her skin seemed to shimmer in the dim light of morning, he reached down and softly ran a finger over her silky cheek, she flinched a little then opened her eye just a chink and smiled. Her soft lashes gently brushed his skin.

That smile, it lit the morning brighter than the rising sun, he felt his heart swell a little in his chest and pulled her closer to him. Then they kissed softly and lost themselves once more.

Finn broke the silence. "It is getting late; I should be back at my post."

She frowned a little and then smiled at him, resigned to the fact. "I know, I just wish you could stay."

"I wish I could stay too, but we can't be found out, not now. I'll have a look at my father's old boat today, see what repairs it needs and we'll speak again tonight. We'll be able to sail away from all of this and be together, forever, just you and I." He kissed her again and then sat up and began to get dressed.

"I wish we could just go now, I hate these long lonely days." She said tossing his shoes over to him.

"I know Merryn, not much longer. Now run, quick, the watchman will be here soon."

They had one last brief kiss before she was running off into the waves and he sprinted back to where he had left the rope dangling from the cliff.

When he got to the top of the cliff he looked out into the surf and saw her dark head, bobbing just above the water, he blew a kiss and waved before he began to pull up the long rope.

He coiled the rope and quickly stowed it in the watchman's cave, then ran out, took up his usual seat on the rock with his back to the steps and waited. He scanned the empty sea, more out of habit than anything else, but it wasn't empty this morning.

There was a ship, quite far off but it was definitely a ship he could clearly see the large square sail.

He watched for a few moments, heart in his mouth, barely breathing, but it was fine, it was heading away, almost at the horizon now, heading almost due north. He let out a loud sigh of relief; that had been close; just wait till he told the day watchman.

Come to think of it where was the day watchman, he should be here by now, even allowing for a hangover. He looked east and saw that the sun was now well clear of the horizon. The watchman should definitely be here by now.

He climbed off the rock and made for the steps, eyes down watching his footing on the slippery stone. When he had safely reached the top he looked up, across the bay towards the village.

An ominous cloud of dark smoke hung over the village, thin wisps coiling, climbing up to meet the dark mass from what was left of the houses down below. Homes of the people he knew and loved. He looked up the hill towards his cottage and saw that even it had not escaped the blaze.

He felt faint as he stood there frozen, listening to the blood pound in his ears, how?…... What had happened?

Then he was off, down the path, blind panic, running on legs he could barely feel below him. His feet thumping on the rocks and stones, he didn't slow as he entered the village, running past the burnt out shells, house after house. He stumbled on blindly struggling to see, though tear filled eyes that stung with smoke. He ran on, on, only stopping when he reached home.

He stood there breathless, it was wrecked; the roof rent open by the fire, like a dark wide mouth screaming silently at the sky. He trod wearily on shaking legs up the garden path, reached out for the charred smouldering staves that were once the front door and stopped, frightened of what might await him inside. He took a deep breath, wiped the tears from his eyes with the back of a hand and stepped in.

It was gutted, the stone walls blackened with smoke and soot. There was a smouldering pile where the burning roof had collapsed under its own weight. He pulled a timber from the door frame and using it he prodded around the inside of the cottage. There was nothing left untouched by the flames, but she was not there, Granny was definitely not there, she must have escaped the fire.

He threw down the timber and ran out of the cottage, the street was deserted all of the houses had suffered the same fate as his own. He wandered downhill, towards the beach, the devastation was everywhere. He tried not to look at the dark shapes that had fallen, clothes stained, dark with blood, fearful that recognition may pitch him over the edge of despair. The smoke hung thick in the lanes, stinging his eyes as he passed.

The destruction reached all the way to the beach, he saw the remains of several boats, their ribs exposed like stripped carcasses on the sand. The survivors of the night were there, all huddled together for comfort around a small fire.

As he crossed the sand he was spotted, it was Billy; his face barely recognisable, blackened with soot, bruising and dried blood, the past nights events writ large on his features. "Look! Here comes the so called watchman!"

They all turned to look; their ravaged faces fixed masks of rage. The first was on him in seconds, fists lashing out wildly, knocking the wind from his lungs. Then a blow to his face snapped his head back and he fell to the ground, the metallic taste of blood filling his mouth.

He rolled himself into a ball on the sand as he felt the blows rain down on him, all of their grief, anger, pain, and sorrow poured from them in wave after wave of rage.

"Stop this! Stop it! Stop it!" Shouted Jack Spraggan as he threw himself into the melee, tearing the crowd apart, as he struggled to reach Finn. "Leave the boy alone, it's not his fault!" When he reached Finn he raised a stick lashing out with it to beat back the last of Finn's attackers.

Billy looked up from where he now lay sprawled in the sand. "Look what happened Jack, look! He was supposed to be keeping watch, supposed to warn us, raise the alarm but he didn't, and look, just look……..it's gone……..all of it, gone!"

Jack put down the stick and kneeled down, laying a fatherly hand on Billy's shoulder. "I know Billy, I know, but beating the lad won't change a thing. I'm sure there must be an explanation."

He looked over to where Finn was crouched on all fours, coughing and spitting blood into the sand. "Well Finn? Is there an explanation?"

Finn slumped back onto his knees; he held his aching head in his hands. Then in a weak voice, little more than a whisper he spoke. "I fell asleep." Not really a lie, he thought.

Jack shook his head, disappointed. "Well, it's not much of an excuse but listen. It's not all the lads fault, this raid was well planned, and they knew exactly how to negotiate the bay. Even if Finn had seen them coming and if he had managed to raise the alarm; we wouldn't have had nearly enough time to get everyone to safety."

"That may be so Jack, but we might have had the chance to put up more of a fight, get the women and children away up into the woods. I for one want him out of here, there's no place for him in this village. He is bad luck, always was and that's all there is to it. " Said Billy. His words were greeted with nods and grunts of agreement from the rest of the survivors.

Jack sighed and nodded his head, he was exhausted and it would do no good to oppose them. "Very well, if that's the view of the village he will be sent away.

Billy; see if any of the boats are serviceable enough to cast him to the sea."

Billy nodded and taking two of the men with him they went along the shore to examine the boats to see if any had survived the night undamaged.

This was the tradition of the village; the sea provided for them, it was their mother. Their dead were cast to the sea and as he had been outcast, Finn too would be sent out upon the sea, his fate rested now in the hands of the waves.

Jack turned and began to walk away along the beach. "Finn, come with me lad!" Finn did as he was told and followed the old man as he walked.

When they were out of earshot Jack spoke, eyes staring ahead as he walked. "Listen lad, there isn't much time. The village was destroyed by a man calling himself Raghnall, does that name mean anything to you?"

Finn thought for a moment, it was difficult; his head was still spinning from the shock of the morning, not to mention the beating. "No, no I don't remember ever hearing that name."

"Well I suppose that's no bad thing. The problem is that according to my grand-daughter this Raghnall seemed to know Thora, your granny."

Finn stopped. "What did he do to her? ……………..is she dead?"

Jack turned and looked at the boy's worried face. "It would probably have been better if she was, but no he didn't kill her. He took her with him, alive. Or at least she was alive when she was put onboard ship."

Finn's head ached, it was all too much. "But how could he have known her? I don't understand."

"Nor do I Finn, your Granny has been here in this village for thirty years or more. I don't know anything of her life before that; she wasn't one to talk about the past. Now it seems we know why." Jack put his hand on the lad's shoulder. "I'm sorry about the rest of them Finn, but you failed in your duty, it would be wrong of me to oppose their wishes. Come on now, Billy's finished checking the boats over."

Finn followed the old man back along the beach towards the villagers. What would he do, he had never known anywhere else, this was his home. Then he saw the angry faces waiting for him, hate filled every eye, it burned to look at them so he stared at the sand between his feet instead.

Jack stopped and looked questioningly at Billy. "Well?"

Billy stood up. "There's two that escaped the worst of it. One's a little scorched along the gunwales, but we'll need a serviceable boat to feed us. The other isnae too bad, the hull's sound but she'll need a new mast and sail. There's a mast we can salvage off one of the other boats and there's a sail that will patch."

Jack nodded. "Good, good, how long do you need to make her ready?"

Billy ran his fingers through his sooty hair. "We can have her ready by morning."

Jack turned towards what was left of the village. "Very well then, he will be cast out at dawn."

The villagers grumbled their agreement. Then a voice spoke up, "I won't have him down here with us, he's bad luck!" This was greeted with nods and grunts of agreement from all.

Jack held up his hand to silence them. "Alright then, he'll be sent to the watchman's cave until dawn.

He can spend the time there alone reflecting on his failure."

Finn turned and began to shuffle off along the sand. The first stone struck him with a dull thud on his back. He had no time to react before the second hit him on the back of the head and set his ears ringing. He broke into a run just as he was struck by a third, then a fourth, by then thankfully he was out of range.

He didn't stop running until he had left the beach and was on the rocky path back up to the cliffs. He put his hand up to the back of his head; his hair was sticky with blood. He gingerly felt down through the hair to the scalp, just a small cut thankfully but he could feel the growing lump beneath.

When he got to the watchman's cave he sat on his usual rock and tried to gather his thoughts, it was too much to take in. The village was destroyed, it would take years to re-build, friends, dead or injured, they all hated him now but he couldn't blame them for that. Granny was gone with this Raghnall, who she seemed to know somehow, how was that possible? How could she know the likes of him?

There were too many questions, it was all too much. Unsurprisingly his head began to ache. He shook it, big mistake, the pounding in his ears just got louder, he could feel his shirt sticking to his back with sweat and the panic begin to rise in his chest.

He stood up and ran into the cave for the rope, quickly making it fast and clambering down the cliff face to the beach. He didn't stop to undress and ran into the water. The first couple of waves slowed his legs suddenly and he fell, headlong into the icy waves.

He lay there, floating face down, letting the cold water numb his fevered body and wash the sticky blood from him. He held his breath for as long as he could. The urge to breathe was so strong, all it would take was one good breath, one deep cold breath and it would be all over. His chest began to burn, his head spinning once more and then he stood up; drawing in a huge lungful of air. He turned and trudged back towards the beach, his limbs heavy, weighed down by his sodden clothing and despair.

Chapter 20

Merryn slipped out of her seal-skin and emerged from the water, draping the smooth shimmering skin delicately over her arm. She shook the water from her hair and looked along the waters edge for him.

The sun was slipping away for the night and the jagged cliffs threw long shadows along the beach. The tips of the breaking waves foamed and glittered in the last light of day as they glided, whispering onto the sand.

He was there, a dark shape on the sand a short distance up the beach. She smiled and her heart lifted as it always did at the sight of him. She broke into a trot as she rushed to be with him, but as she drew close she slowed. She saw him more clearly now in the failing light, something was wrong , he sat there curled in a ball his knees pulled up to his chest, head slumped between his knees. She slowed to a walk and as she reached his side, she slowly stretched out a hand to gently touch his shoulder.

He jumped a little and his head snapped up, eyes wide in fear. She saw his face, bruised and battered, barely recognisable. There was dried blood at the corner of his mouth and his left eye was swollen and almost closed. His eyes flickered with recognition and the fear was gone, he sighed and let his heavy head fall back to his knees.

"What happened? Your face, your poor face!" She keeled beside him wrapping him in her arms. He flinched a little as she gently squeezed his battered body; she relaxed her grip and felt the tension leave him as he pressed himself against her seeking warmth and comfort. He buried his face in her lap and wept his body wracked by painful sobs.

When the wave of desperation had passed, he sat up and hurriedly wiped the tears from his eyes. He pulled away from her and fixed his gaze once more on the waves rolling onto the sand. "It's gone Merryn, it's all gone." His voice was flat, pathetic, little more than a whisper.

She reached out laying her hand on his. "What do you mean gone, what happened?"

He shrugged her hand away. "It's all gone, the village, destroyed, gone, they're all dead and it's all my fault. I should have been watching, up there on the cliff watching, not down here.........with you."

Merryn shook her head. "I don't understand, what happened to the village? You, your face?"

He pulled the back of his hand across his face once more wiping the tears from his eyes, oblivious to the pain. "Raiders came, they destroyed everything, they're all dead. The village is nothing but rubble and ash. I should have been watching, there to sound the alarm."

"That's terrible but it's not your fault, the raiders would have come in any case, you couldn't have prevented that, you weren't to know."

"But it was my job! All I had to do was sit on the cliff and watch, that's all, but I messed it up, simplest job in the world and I couldn't do it properly. If I had just been there to raise the alarm, they would have had time to get away, up onto the hill, time to run and hide. They're dead Merryn, and it's down to me!"

Merryn sat there silent, searching for the right thing, any thing, to say, some soothing words to make it alright, but there was nothing, so she sat there in silence.

After a few moments he spoke again his voice flat, emotionless. "I'm to be punished in the morning, cast to the sea, alone, it's better than I deserve really."

Merryn said nothing and reached out again to hold him.

He felt her touch and pulled away; shrugging her hands from his shoulders. "Leave me alone! Don't touch me!" He shot to his feet and began to walk away, back towards the cliffs.

Merryn jumped to her feet and followed "Finn!....... Finn!....... Don't go, just stay a little longer. I can join you in the morning; you don't have to be alone."

He spun round "Don't you understand! They were right, they were all right, I'm a jinx, cursed. Everything I touch, everyone I've ever loved is gone, I destroy everything!"

"But I love you, doesn't that count for anything?"

"But I can't love you, I won't allow it. Go away Merryn, go far, far away, go home, forget you ever knew me!" His eyes were cold, his injured features fixed.

Then he turned and walked slowly away across the sand, his heart slowly crumbling to dust in his chest.

Merryn just stood there, every fragment of her soul willing him to turn around and come back to her. She stood there, burning in her skin as the setting sun pushed the jagged shadows of the cliff closer and closer; until she was swallowed at last by the darkness.

***

Morning found him, sitting atop the cliff, watching the grey horizon. He slowly cast his eyes along the shoreline below, but the beach was empty, she was gone.

He had barely moved since he'd climbed back up the cliffs the previous evening, his body was cold and stiff, he felt like a part of the rock itself. He kind of wished he was.

He heard the scuffing of feet on the stone steps and a warm hand on his shoulder "It's time lad."

Finn slowly turned his head round to face the old man. Jack's face looked worse that it had the previous day, the bruising had developed fully and his right eye was completely closed. If it weren't for the grim look on his face he could almost have been winking. "Come with me now Finn, the rest of the village are waiting down on the beach."

Finn sighed, slowly uncurled his legs from under him and stood up stretching his stiff back. "We'd better not keep them waiting then. They'll be glad to see the back of me."

Jack nodded and smiled as much as his battered face would allow. "Something like that." He turned and gestured for Finn to follow him back up the steps.

When they reached the top of the path he could see the villagers huddled together down on the beach. Parts of the village itself still smouldered slightly, a bitter reminder of his failure. He cast his gaze quickly down to the rocky path below his feet.

As they trudged down the hill toward the beach Jack spoke, his voice little more than a whisper. "We don't have much time lad so I'll be brief, listen well. I've hidden a little food and water in the bow of the boat, it's not much but it's enough keep you alive if you are careful. There are a couple of lines and hooks there too, for when the food runs out. When you clear the headland turn due north, your need to get to a place called Holfstadir, that's where the raiders have taken Thora I think. I travelled up that way in my youth; it is far to the north near to the lands of ice and snow. I can't really tell you much more than that. She's a brave woman your granny but she can't hold out indefinitely. Do what you can to help her lad."

Finn looked up at the old man surprised.

"Don't look so shocked, I don't really agree with this punishment, it's too harsh, but they've all lost so much I can't go against their wishes. In any case you might be the only chance that Thora has. Hush now, we're almost at the beach."

As they neared the gathered villagers there was a low muttering, Finn kept his eyes fixed on the sand just in front of his toes.

Jack raised his voice. "Is the boat made ready?" Billy grunted and nodded his head, face fixed like stone.

Finn felt a hard shove on his back and he stumbled forward towards the boat, feet splashing in the water. He grabbed the gunwale and quickly threw his leg up over the rail and into the small craft. Strong hands pushed the boat away from the beach and out into the bay. He heard a lone voice shout. "Good riddance!" but other than that the only sound was the rhythmic slap of the small waves against the bow.

He quickly set the sail, letting out as much as he could to catch the light breeze. Then he leaned on the tiller and pointed the bow of the little boat towards the gap in the cliffs.

In a short time he was out on the open sea, his small craft bobbing like a cork on the waves close to shore. He brought the sail in a little, and watched it swell and crackle in the stronger wind out on the firth. Pulling hard on the tiller he struck his course due east, making for the headland, where he now knew his journey would take him north.

He turned and stared out towards the cliffs; he could just make out the small cleft of the watchman's cave in the hard granite. By habit his eyes drifted down to the beach below, it was empty of course. He let out a sigh, unaware that he had been holding his breath, and wrenched his eyes from the coast fixing them straight ahead towards the empty grey horizon.

Chapter 21

All of the world was darkness.

Her heavy head, swung left, then right, then left again. She heard the bones of her neck creak and grind one against the other with every sway and her aching brain seemed to rattle inside her head.

She could smell metal? No blood; that was it, never a good sign. She heard waves rushing, breaking and the piercing screech of a gull on the wing, caw-cawing for food, always hungry. Such stupid beasts, but quite pretty she was reluctant to admit.

My; her head hurt, must have been some night she thought. If she could only stop the swaying, that might help. She tried to move a hand up to steady her swinging head, but no, it was stuck fast, so was the other hand now that she tried it.

Then she felt the rope, tight about her chest, she was trussed up like a hog! Then slowly she remembered. The previous night's events came trickling back, the smoke, the bloodshed, the death and destruction, and there in the centre of it all, him, just as he always had been.

She tried to open her mouth to lick her dry lips but a sharp stab of pain from the left of her jaw was enough to force a rapid re-think.

Her head was slowly clearing, the dense fog of unconsciousness lifting a little. She could hear the creaking of rope and timber in time with the swaying of the ship she now realised that she was aboard.

There just beneath the sharp smell of blood which was still thick in her nose was the unmistakable heavy musk of stale sweat and men.

She heard footsteps drawing closer then stopping abruptly with a scuff. "Set course north by north-east, we've had enough fun for now it's time we were heading back."

"Yes my lord." Came the reply and her lead-heavy head swung right as the ship changed course.

The footsteps drew a little closer and she felt a rough hand on her left cheek. "Still out of it I see."

"Yes my lord; not moved a muscle since she was brought on board." Said the helmsman who sounded so close she could have reached out and touched him, if her hands weren't bound that is.

The feet scuffed as he turned and started to walk away. "Call me as soon as she wakes."

Decision made then, best stay just as she was, postpone the inevitable. Her head was far too sore for any type of interrogation in any case. She stopped fighting, gave in and allowed the dark fog to draw in and swallow her once more.

***

Morning found Finn huddled in a ball in the stern of the small boat. Sleep had been fitful and sparse at best, the soft swell had done it's best to lull him off to sleep but as exhausted as he was, his injured mind and body seemed to conspire against him. Every passing ripple shifted the weight of his bruised frame against the unforgiving timbers and he was immediately jolted back to consciousness once again.

He rubbed his gritty eyes and looked towards the heavens. The stars were fading now, snuffed out one by one by the grey dawn slowly approaching from the east. He had checked his course several times during the night ensuring that the bow of the boat was pointed in the general direction of the cluster of stars they called the axe. The heel of the axe pointed towards the only unmoving star in the night sky which remained, constant, hanging in the sky above the north of the world.

Not for the first time in his short life, he wondered at the stars, there were so many of them and what exactly were they. They had so many names, some he could remember some he couldn't, anyway the names seemed to change depending on who he asked.

Granny seemed to know them all and had a story to tell about each one it seemed. He wondered briefly if she was staring out at the same dawn as him.

He sat up and drew back his shoulders, flexing his stiff back as best he could. The night had been cold and long. He had lost sight of land just before nightfall; there was nothing out there but sea now, miles and miles of endless grey sea.

He checked his course one last time and tied the tiller firmly in place. The morning breeze was beginning to stiffen a little and he adjusted the ropes, pulling in and reefing a little sail, before clambering to the bow of the boat. Jack had done what he could but the provisions he had provided were meagre at best.

He broke off as much of the dense brown loaf as he dared and wrapped the remainder back up in the cloth. It would be just enough to stop his growling stomach for a little while. With a silent *thank you* to Jack he sat himself down and set his teeth to work on the course crust, while he stared blankly north at the slowly approaching horizon.

***

She came-to for a second time with a small groan and found her dry tongue stuck to the roof of her mouth. It took all her willpower to hoist open her crusted eyelids and let the bright morning light pour in. The light pierced her skull like a needle, as she blinked to let her eyes adjust.

There was a loud bellow. "She's awake my Lord!"

She looked up to see Raghnall striding towards her down the middle of the deck. The ship was long and thin, built for speed. The men on board were seated either side of a narrow walkway, oars pulled in and stacked along the length of the ship, as the favourable wind billowed out the striped sail and sent the craft ripping through the sea.

He sat himself heavily on the gunwale to her left. "I was beginning to think you would sleep all day Thordys."

She rolled her tongue around her dry mouth. "Couldn't spare a little water could you?"

Raghnall pointed at a man on the nearest bench. "You! Fetch some water."

Once she had slaked her thirst Raghnall dismissed the man with a small wave of his hand. "I am sorry about the lack of hospitality Thordys, but as you can see you've lightened my crew quite enough for one trip."

She looked along the length of the ship and noticed one or two empty spaces. "Your standards have slipped a little, they were almost too easy."

He gave a slight nod. "Yes, you're probably right you know. Warriors are not what they used to be. Not like the old days. You must miss it a little?"

"I turned my back on all of that long ago; I barely remember any of it now"

He reached out a hand and raised her head, examining her face. "You've barely aged a day since I last saw you, what's your secret? Magic?"

She stared into his cold blue eyes. "That's a very long story and one which I'll save for another time. Tell me, what brings an old man like you out raiding?"

He smiled and laughed, more of a low rumble in his chest really. "I do like to keep my hand in, you know. It wouldn't do to get soft and feeble like some old crone. Anyway once I'd heard about your little village, lying there, right under my nose for so long, I was curious. I just couldn't resist."

"While we're on the subject, how exactly did you find out about Bruaan?"

"I was wondering when you'd get round to that." He turned toward the bow of the ship. "You there lad! Come here!"

Linus stood up from a seat near the bow and reluctantly walked towards them. So, they had been betrayed, all of them betrayed by one of their own. She stared at the boy as he approached, the wild rage slowly fading, giving way to bitter disappointment. "Oh Linus, what have you done boy?"

Linus looked her in the eye for an instant, before looking away and refusing to meet her gaze. "Linus! Look at me boy! Have you any idea what you've done?"

"He just did what anyone else would have done Thordys, he saved his own skin." Raghnall said placing a fatherly hand on Linus' shoulder. "Yes

Linus here was very helpful. Anyway enough talk for now, there will be plenty time for talk when we get back to Holfstadir. It's been quite a while since you were there Thordys, you'll barely recognise the place." With that, he stood and he and Linus walked back towards the bow, leaving her there, alone.

Chapter 22

It had been three days now, three days since he had seen land, three days staring at the wide featureless grey sea. He had been fortunate though, the winds had been favourable, slowly pushing him further and further north.

The sea had grown wilder as he drew north, the waves were now taller than ever and the small boat was being thrown around wildly. Climbing the steep slope to the foamy crest where he caught a brief glimpse the horizon before the boat slid back down into the hollow. Salt spray filled the air as the prow cut into the water and his clothes were soaked and heavy.

The meagre provisions had run out at nightfall the previous day and today morning had arrived; cold, grey and hungry.

He cast the short length of line and hooks just after dawn. Lacking bait he had torn the scrap of cloth Jack had used to wrap the food into long thin lengths, tying a strip to each of the hooks in the hope that they would flap in the current and entice some foolhardy fish to take a snap.

He pulled in the fishing line for the third time that day, nothing yet. Still, fish mostly like to feed in the early morning or at dusk. So hopefully, he let the line back out again.

Finn sat down, bracing himself against the mast and stretched out his shoulders. The pain of the beating was easing a little; he still had the odd nagging ache here and there though.

He missed her.

He let his eyes shut and tried to picture her face; smiling at him in the silver moonlight. It was there, just barely. She was fading though, the more he wracked his memory to sharpen the image the quicker the edges seemed to fade and blur. A small fragment at the back of his mind worried that some day he may not be able to remember her face at all.

He had been such a fool.

No, worse than that, he had been cruel. He had lashed out at her, driven her away, blamed her for *his* mistakes. She was better off without him. He deserved this misery, this punishment, this lonely grey existence.

But he had hurt her; he had seen it in her eyes. She didn't deserve that.

The sail crackled a little as the breeze shifted, bringing him swiftly back to reality. He slackened the ropes a little, letting the sail fill with the growing wind. It was hard to check his course with any precision in the daylight but he reckoned he was still pretty much alright. It was past midday and the sun had already started its slow descent towards the west.

The west, Meryns homeland was to the west.

As he crested the next wave he snatched a glimpse of the western horizon and wondered where she was. She would have gone back home, he was sure of it, back to her family and friends, back where it was safe.

Far away from foolish boys like him.

***

Just after dawn the next day she saw the high mountains appear on the northern horizon. They were just as she remembered, jagged and wild, the tips capped with snow, even now, in midsummer. Thordys watched their slow approach in the early morning light; they would make port by late afternoon at this rate.

Her arms ached; they had untied her from the stern post that morning so at least she could sit down even if her wrists and ankles were still bound tightly. In a way she was quite flattered that he was still so wary of her after all this time.

She was no fool though, there would be a time for escape, for revenge, but this was not it, not yet anyway.

She cast her eye round the ship as the crew awoke to greet the dawn with groans and huge yawns. They had spent the night lying on the deck between the sea-chests which doubled as benches for rowing, their heavy woollen cloaks pulled over their heads as blankets against the chill sea air. She tried not to make eye contact; she had lightened the crew too much to be a welcome guest on board this ship.

The warship had been at sea for several weeks by now and the stench of unwashed bodies lay heavy on the deck where she sat. She tried to hide her disgust as the men took turn relieving their bladders and worse over the side.

Breakfast was served a short time later, and the short length of rope attaching her wrists to the gunwale was briefly untied to allow her to eat. She chewed the course grey rye bread, teeth working fast as she eyed the point of the spear which was levelled at her chest while she ate.

The bearded oaf holding the other end of the spear smiled coldly, he was holding himself back she could see it in his face. She wouldn't give him any excuse to strike.

When she had finished her sparse meal her hands were made fast, tied tight to the gunwale once more. She could see a flicker of disappointment in her captors face, and she struggled to suppress a smile. She had obviously relieved him of a friend or two.

Shortly after breakfast she saw Linus approaching down the middle of the ship. He crouched down on the deck and smiled at her. "Comfortable?"

She forced herself to smile back. "I'm fine. What do you want boy?"

"Oh, nothing much, I was just curious that's all. I always thought you were a bloody witch, nice to see I was right. So which is your true form, this, or the craggy old crone? Or are you really something much worse?"

Thordys shook her head wearily. "What does it matter to you either way, you clearly don't give a damn about much. What do you think the great and powerful Raghnall will do with you now? Now that you've served your purpose? I mean, you're of little or no use to him now."

"He has more use for me than for you witch! The only reason you're still here is by his say so. Every man on this ship is just itching to kill you, me included!" And with that he left.

Linus made his way back to the place he had been given near the bow of the ship and sat down. Why had she been taken aboard anyway? It made so little sense. This was his big chance, a fresh start. Raghnall was power and just being close to the man made him feel powerful too.

The bloody village deserved to burn, it had confined him, stifled him for too long, he was bigger than that, too big to live in his fathers shadow or behind his mothers skirts.

He was free now, well almost, she was the only reminder of that life now, sitting there at the back of the ship like some kind of harpy, niggling at him, pricking what little conscience he had left, better she had died with the rest of them.

***

Just as she predicted, the ship entered Holfstadir fjord in mid afternoon. The entrance was just as she remembered; a narrow cleft between the towering mountains, the sides of which thrust skyward straight out of the water. The mountain sides passed by so close, she felt she could just reach out and touch them.

Once inside the narrow fjord the wind dropped almost immediately and the huge square sail hung there lifeless for the first time in days. The men in the rearward places quickly lowered the sail on its long heavy ropes while the men a mid-ship pulled the sail round so that the long wooden beam, the yard, ran along the centre line of the ship.

Once the sail was safely lowered onto the deck and furled tidily, the men un-stacked and passed out the oars. Each man then took the leaf shaped end of his oar and passed it through the round oarlock just below the gunwale. The men outnumbered the oars two to one, meaning that while the first man rowed the second man could rest; they would then swap places and the ship would continue onward its pace unbroken.

When the oars were almost all in place Raghnall came striding to the rear of the boat. He passed her an almost imperceptible nod of the head before sitting down between her and the helmsman. He then picked up a large cudgel and brought it down on the centre beam of the ship with a loud hollow thud. At this signal the men pulled hard on the oars and the ship heaved forward, cutting through the water. Raghnall kept up a slow steady beat and the ship made its way inland.

When they had travelled almost a league the fjord took a sharp turn to the south, and there lying before them on the shore to starboard lay the town of Holfstadir.

He had been right Thordys could see that much had changed since she had last been here; she guessed that the settlement had at least doubled in size since she'd last seen it.

Holfstadir had been founded on the largest flat piece of land along the fjord and consisted of a wide triangular piece of ground at the base of a large mountain the locals called Midtfjel. There were several narrow paths which climbed up and around the mountain but almost everything came into or out of Holfstadir by sea.

Thordys could see that barely any of the land lay unused, there were long-houses, shacks, workshops, warehouses occupying every viable scrap of land, some even jutted out over the water propped up on stilts. Smoke belched from forges down by the waters edge and the lazy breeze wafted the un-mistakable stench of a tannery out to meet them. The whole town was soot-stained, dirty and loud.

Raghnall turned and seeing the shock in Thordys' face he laughed. "See, I told you it had changed a little. I control everything now, all goods and wealth must come here, by law. My law. The merchants must trade here and all must pay me for the privilege of doing so. In return I protect their interests; it's a very profitable arrangement for them and for me. Well mostly me, and in any case they have very little choice in the matter."

She kept her face on the town, seeing a small group of children fighting in the mud by the waters edge.

"You must be so proud, it's a town of rats and you are the king rat, master of all you survey. Squalor. There is nothing noble here."

She saw a flash of anger in his eyes, then it was gone, he snorted and turned away from her to give directions to the helmsman.

There was a long pier which jutted out into the sound, several trading ships were moored there and were being hurriedly unloaded. Large bales of wool, goods and barrels were being lifted onto the pier using block, tackle and wooden cranes fixed to the uprights of the pier. The dockworkers barely looked up at them as they passed.

There standing on the pier, nearer the shore, Thordys saw the most shocking sight of all. A group of around ten people were huddled together, an assortment of men women and children, all bound in chains and wearing iron collars. They were obviously the latest cargo to have been unloaded, and were clearly the most valuable commodity traded at Holfstadir, *thralls*!

The helmsman brought the ship to bear on another slightly smaller pier, which was lower in the water. Thordys could see that this pier had another use all together, moored on both sides of this pier were warships like the one in which she sat. She counted eight, tied up and ready to put to sea, although there were several empty spaces at the pier.

As they drew alongside, someone on the pier threw a rope, which was quickly made fast to the bow. The men quickly drew in the oars and the ship was pulled in to the dockside.

Chapter 23

The sun came up in the morning just like it had the day before. The sea's mood was calmer now, the wind had dropped during the night and he had been able to let the sail out fully to take advantage of the steady south westerly wind.

At least he wasn't as hungry as he had been the day before, he had pulled the fishing line in just at sunset to find a rather small pouting that been stupid enough to take a snap at the flapping piece of rag. It was the kind of fish the men of the village would have thrown back; too small even to be worth the effort of gutting, but to Finn it was a very welcome meal, even cold.

He had unhooked it carefully and swiftly knocked its head against the thwart, stunning and killing the little fish swiftly. Then he'd used his teeth and fingernails to pull back the skin exposing the delicate white flesh. He had nibbled most of the meat from the bones before he'd realised it, with some difficulty he restrained himself and set a little of the remaining fish aside. It would make a better breakfast than he had eaten for days and what he couldn't eat would make good bait.

That morning breakfast was all too brief, but once he had eaten the remainder of the little fish he threaded the remaining guts, bones and skin onto the hooks and leaving the damp strips of rag attached he gently let the line out over the stern.

He tied the end of the line firmly to the tiller and then stood up checking that all of the line and hooks had played out true, satisfied; his eyes drifted up toward the southern horizon and he saw them.

He counted quickly, seven square sails were spread out across the horizon. They were making much better progress than his small tub; these were sleek, narrow warships, made for speed, battle and the open sea. They would be upon him by the end of the day; there was nothing he could do about that. He could never dream of outrunning them and going around them wasn't really an option; with so many eyes to each boat they would surely have seen his small sail by now.

There was nothing to be done about it, he turned away from his fate and sat down at the tiller to await the inevitable.

***

Thordy's trip up through the streets of Holfstadir had provided little to surprise her. The storm clouds had crowded in and the muddy gutters were soon overflowing with rain water, urine and other human waste, the stench was so strong she could almost taste it.

The townsfolk bustled along the sides of the rainy streets, business as usual, heads down, quickly stepping out of the way of her heavily armed guard. The town buildings appeared to be huddled together, as if trying to shield each other from the deluge. Every spare foot of space was occupied by some form of structure, all of them spewing smoke and noise and stench out into the air around them.

The torrential rain had started as soon as they had stepped onto the dockside; it tumbled off the heavily thatched roofs, down the sides of buildings, forming rivulets in the mud and sweeping the accumulated human effluent downstream towards the fjord.

Thordys looked up between the clustered roofs; the sky was lead grey and felt every bit as crushingly heavy. It will take more than rain to wash this place clean, she thought.

They continued their uphill trudge; until the buildings began to thin out and they emerged from the town to approach a high stockade, the walls of which had been formed from the trunks of pine trees taken from the surrounding hills, they were firmly bound together and their ends buried deep in the thick loamy soil. As they continued around the circular structure they came to a narrow recess which housed the large heavy gate.

The party stepped into the recess and halted, they stood in a short tunnel fashioned of wood. In the gloom she could see bright arrow slits running along either side of the passage and rainwater streamed down upon them from the round murder-holes above their heads.

After a short pause she heard the bolt being drawn back with a heavy thud and the iron studded gate swung slowly open to admit them. They emerged from the gloom of the entrance tunnel back into the lashing rain and onto a large open square. She walked onward as she was led across the rain splattered muster ground and into the largest of the long-houses facing the gate.

The roof of the long house was pitched in a high "v" with an extended eve which provided a sheltered passageway around the outsides of the building. The entrance took the form of a large double door which was guarded by two thugs, the thickness of their moustaches only exceeded by the thickness of their necks.

They both bowed their heads as their lord and master entered. Thordys resisted the urge to bait the sentries as she was lead in by her escort; it was cruel to mock the hard of thinking after all.

The long-house was the largest she had been in for many years, there had been one larger once, but that was so long ago, another lifetime. The high rafters crossed at the apex of the roof, at the height of four men, or there about. There were eating benches set out on either side of the fire that burnt in a long hearth which ran down the centre of the large open room.

The heat from the fire was a welcome friend; she had almost forgotten what warmth was after the long voyage and the march up through the squall.

Raghnall threw off his sodden cloak, letting it fall carelessly to the floor; he rubbed his hands together and held his palms out in the general direction of the warming hearth. There was an all too brief flicker of calm as he gazed around his hall, and she was reminded of the man he had been all those years ago.

He turned towards her and the spell was broken. "Welcome to my humble home Thordys. It's been a long day old friend and I thirst for ale and the warmth of a maid. We'll discuss your fate after a good nights sleep."

"Chain her to the post there." He said pointing to one of the large timber pillars supporting the roof trusses. "But keep a close eye on her."

With that he walked off toward the rear of the hall where he parted the heavy dark drapes as he entered his private chamber followed by a large scruffy hunting hound.

***

The warships were upon Finn just before evening, as he had predicted. As they drew close he stood and lowered his sail, reefing it neatly as he swung the yard around to stow it lengthwise.

Then he stood there arms folded legs braced against the soft swell, watching as two of the ships drew alongside, dwarfing his little boat between them. He glanced between the round shields braced against the gunwales of the ships and tried not to wither under the glare of the broad hairy faces staring back at him.

As he drew level with the mast of the ship to his left he saw that two of the warriors had risen up from their positions and had ropes in their hands. Then as Finn passed they swung the ropes, sending iron grappling hooks sailing in two high arcs towards his little boat. He ducked down fearful of being struck by the grapples and heard them land almost simultaneously on the bottom of the boat with a dull thud, they rattled as they scuttled across the boards, and their sharp prongs found purchase in the clinker-built slats of the little boat.

There was a sudden lurch as the men heaved on the ropes drawing the boat in alongside their long-ship. The gunwales of the crafts clattered together and when Finn got himself back up onto his feet he found himself face to face with the business end of a long spear.

The helmed figure wielding the spear turned to his men and laughed. "It's just a sprat lads! We should chuck this little fish back."

There was a chorus of grunts of agreement coupled with raucous laughter from up and down the ship. One of the men holding the end of a rope turned and spoke up. "He's seen us now my lord. He knows our number and course; it would be folly to set him free. If we are to throw him back as you say, best kill him first."

The leader took a moment to think. "You there, sprat, what is your business being so far out at sea in such a pathetic little craft?"

Finn warily looked up. "I am a little lost I fear. I intended to travel to Holfstadir, but I have only a vague notion of how to get there."

The spearman nodded. "Hmm, and what, pray tell, is your intention should you arrive there safely?"

Finn hesitated, unsure as to how much he should tell the man. Well he had little to loose, his voyage if not his life was most probably over now in any case, the truth would have to suffice. "I am trying to find my Grandmother, our village was attacked by warriors from Holfstadir and she was taken prisoner."

The leader turned to his men and laughed again. "Quite a rescue, eh lads?" Then he withdrew the spear and turned away. "You two, don't just stand there, help him aboard!"

Four thick arms reached down and hauled Finn up onto the deck of the warship. The men were packed in tight, sitting in two rows down either side of the craft. There was little room to stand in the narrow passage which had been left down the centre. Before he knew it he was quickly padded down and the small knife he'd been left by Jack was removed from his belt, after a cursory examination it was tossed overboard.

The leader handed his spear to one of the men and lifted his dark helmet from his head. "I am Harald, Jarl of Torsund, leader of this small outing. Who are you sprat?"

He didn't like being called a sprat but he held his tongue. "My name is Finn Marwick of the village of Bruann."

Harald scratched his beard and shrugged. "Never heard of the place, still never mind. I suppose you'll be wanting to keep your boat. You there! Fix a line to his boat, we'll tow it for the time being. Are you hungry? You look hungry."

Finn nodded. "Yes, I am hungry. I've been fishing for the past couple of days but I've not had much success, only one small pouting and that was yesterday."

Harald gave a small chuckle. "I'm surprised you've caught anything at all way out here, especially with that seal hanging around the stern of your boat. Odd though, I've never seen one this far out from shore. Come on there's some broth left I think."

He led Finn to the stern of the ship where he sat down by the helmsman and gestured for Finn to sit beside him. Harald nodded to one of the men sitting nearby, who produced a long twisted horn, he blew two short sharp notes and then the notes were repeated from the other ships in the convoy.

"So Finn Marwick what was your plan? What were you going to do when you got to Holfstadir?" Harald said filling a small horn cup from the pail of steaming broth that had been brought up from the bow.

Finn looked up blankly, his mind still trying to make sense of what Harald had said, he hadn't noticed a seal, was it her? No probably not, he was an idiot to hope.

Finn reached out with both hands took the cup and quickly brought it to his mouth, the hot steam carried the scent of mutton and his stomach lurched, reminding him just how hungry he was.

"Careful now, it's hot." Said Harald; steadying Finns wrist.

Finn sipped at the warm liquid and felt it flow down his gullet into his hollow belly. Once he had drained the small cup, he sat back and wiped his mouth with the back of a hand, and quickly glanced out past the stern post. "My plan? In all honesty I don't really have one. My only thought was just to get there. I suppose I will just try to find Granny once I get there." He said with a small shrug of his shoulders.

Harald took the cup and re-filled it from the pail. "It's not much of a plan really, is it? Well the first part is in hand for we too are journeying to Holfstadir. As for finding your grand mother, well the

259

bad news is that if she was taken there as prisoner she is most likely destined for the Thrall market."

Finn took the cup. "What's the Thrall market?"

Harald smiled. "You really are a strange one; you must be a long way from home if you've never heard of a thrall. Who does the menial work in this village of yours, who mucks out the animals, who tans the leather, who tills the soil?"

Finn drained the cup once more and looked up. "We all do our share; we pull together. If there is a market for these thralls as you call them, do you mean to say that people buy and sell other people?"

Harald gave a small laugh. "Of course people buy them, Holfstadir has one of the busiest thrall markets there is."

Finn shook his head. "That's just not right; no one should be able to own another person. People are not property to be bought and sold, surely you must see that?"

"I see a lot of things; but mostly I see that you've much to learn about the world." Harald laid a friendly hand on his shoulder. "The Lord of Holfstadir, Raghnall, controls the sale of everything in these parts, thralls included. He grows richer and more

No Such Thing as Home

Ciaron Fox

A tale of love and
loss inspired by
traditional
Celtic and Norse
Folktales.

Available at

amazon kindle

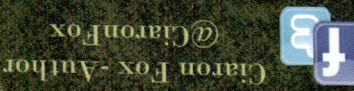

amazon.co.uk

Ciaron Fox - Author
@CiaronFox

powerful every day. He strips all the lands about him bare, taking from all of us and leaving us with a mere pittance. This small fleet you see is made up of several of us Jarls, we're all agreed that it's time for a change. We are bringing war to Holfstadir and with a little luck, an end to Raghnall."

Finn nodded and waited for a few moments as Harald stared off angrily at the horizon. He handed back the small cup. "Thank you for your kindness Harald, I can't remember when I was more in need of a warm meal."

Harald smiled, "You're very welcome lad; nothing makes friends like a common enemy. Night's drawing in, grab a blanket and get some rest we should make landfall tomorrow."

Finn took the heavy blanket that was offered and finding a space up in the nook of the bow; he draped the blanket over his shoulders and curled up. He took one last look down the length of the ship and out past the stern, where he saw his little boat being tugged along at the end of a long rope.

Was she there? There was no reason for her to be, but deep in his heart he hoped she was. He sent a silent thought out to her over the waves. Then warmed with food and wrapped in the blanket; he quickly fell fast asleep.

Chapter 24

A loud clatter woke Thordys immediately, her eyes flew open and she sprung up to her feet, well almost.

The chain connecting her to the post had been threaded through a set of ankle irons and it would only allow her to stand upright as far as a low crouch. She winced as the manacles cut into her wrists and ankles and fell backwards onto her backside with a thump.

She looked around and found the source of her rude awakening, one of the young housemaids had dropped the pail of water she had been carrying. She was hurriedly mopping the spill up with a large cloth, clearly worried about the potential punishment that might follow her clumsiness.

The longhouse quickly began to bustle with activity, she sat there, ignored, a spectator to the scene. The fire was quickly set by a young boy, who brought in several armfuls of timber and laid it neatly in the long hearth. He set quite a small fire, it was only morning and the fire would be built up during the day to fill the whole hearth by the time evening arrived.

The two guards who had been tasked with her supervision during the night sat there bored, either side of the post; they were bleary eyed despite having taken turns in sleeping during the night. The oldest of them sat there leaning forward on a bench, his head sitting heavy on his forearms, hands gripping the long spear which acted as a prop to the whole unsightly heap of a man.

She nodded in his direction; then raised a hand as best she could in the manacles, to get his attention. "Oi! Fatso! I need to go."

He looked at her blankly as if it were the first time he'd seen her.

She sighed and shook her head. "I need to pee, you dullard!"

He nodded his head and grunted as the penny finally dropped. "Yes, yes, just wait there!"

Thordys shook her manacled hands at him, making the whole chain rattle and waking up his drowsy companion. "Not much choice in the matter, have I?"

The guard walked over to the far corner of the longhouse, to the left of the large entrance door and then returned a few minutes later with a bucket draped with a scrap of leather. He plonked the bucket down on the earth floor next to Thordys and smiled. "There you go."

"Just delightful!" She said as she pulled black the leather cover and released the stench, the bucket was at least half full. "At least have the decency to look away!" She said as she lifted her skirt and squatted over the pot.

When she had done, she replaced the cover and sat back down against the post. The guard grunted at the boy who had previously set the fire and he quickly ran over and carried the heavy bucket out of the door. She noticed that the boy wore a dull iron collar around his neck, as did all of the other housemaids and cooks. The collars confirmed their status as thralls, property of their master the "mighty" Raghnall.

What new disappointment will this day bring? She thought as she gazed out of the open door at the brightening world.

***

When dawn arrived it illuminated the mountains which had crept up overnight to obliterate the northern horizon. They were huge, much larger than Finn had ever seen before and their tops were frosted white with snow. They glistened slightly pink in the warm light cast by the rising sun.

He got up and stretched rubbing the sleep from his eyes as he looked around the waking ship. There was already a pot steaming over a small fire which had been set in a stone bottomed firebox just to the stern of the mast, the prevailing breeze blew the delightful scent of warm porridge along the length of the boat.

After a short stop to relieve himself over the side he made his way down the length of the ship in the hope of scrounging a small bowl of breakfast. When he reached the cooking pot a man sporting the most unruly red hair and whiskers looked up and smiled exposing a row of stained teeth. "Morning sprat! You'll want some breakfast then?"

He dipped a ladle in the steaming grey gruel and filling a couple of small bowls he handed them both to Finn. "Do me a favour and take one of those bowls back to Harald. He asked me to send you along to see him when you'd woken up."

"Thanks, I'm sorry I don't know your name Sir." Finn said smiling awkwardly.

"The name's Leif, and there's no need to be sorry about it. Shouldn't go through life apologising youngster, makes you seem weak. Now hurry along before that porridge gets cold, it'll taste bad enough hot!"

Finn did as he was told and reaching the stern he found Harald sitting next to the helmsman. "I brought you some breakfast sir." He said, offering the small bowl.

Harald took the bowl and grunted for Finn to sit. Once he was seated he pointed out past the bow. "See those high mountains there?" Finn nodded.

"Well Holfstadir lies in amongst them. I've been there twice, Raghnall likes to gather together all of the Jarls once in a while to remind them who's really in charge. He likes to lord it over us all, showing off, you know? He puts on games pitting his best warriors against ours in various events, archery, wrestling and the like?"

Finn nodded still eating his porridge; Harald needed no prompting and continued almost as if Finn weren't there.

"Well he has the place a little too well defended you see. He sits there in his lair at the top of the town, back to the mountain, looking out over the whole fjord. He has watchtowers along the shore looking out toward the sea. He knows that's where the threat will come from." Harald paused for a moment to take a small spoonful.

Finn looked up and felt obliged to fill the silence. "Then a sea-borne attack like this seems a little pointless."

Harald laughed. "Exactly, exactly! I was right; you're really quite a sharp lad." Harald focused his attention back to the porridge bowl. He shovelled a large spoonful into his mouth, leaving a smear along the fringe of moustache on his top lip. "Well you've two choices youngster, you can either join our little party or I'll have to leave you behind, if you get my meaning. Can't let you go spoiling the fun."

Finn weighed up his options, which had just rapidly diminished. The thinly veiled threat was not wasted on him. In any case by the sound of it he had no chance of getting anywhere near Holfstadir on his own, but as part of Haralds war party he would at least have some chance of success slim as it might be.

The decision really made itself. "Yes, I'm with you. I've never handled a sword in my life but I have chopped wood once or twice. If you'd be good enough to loan me an axe I'll do my best."

Harald smiled broadly. "Great that's settled then. We should make landfall by noon."

***

Linus tentatively opened his eyes; the lids seemed to creak like poorly oiled hinges. He slowly pulled his head up from the low bed he lay in; peeling his lips away from the dried pool of saliva he had created during the brief few hours of sleep. He pushed himself up onto his elbows and slowly looked round the longhouse.

The place was strewn with men, lying where they fell, as if some great battle had taken place. Well he supposed it had really, thirty men against two barrels of ale, good odds, but the ale had quite obviously won!

The young wench lying next to him groaned and rolled over taking most of the blanket with her and exposing his bare behind. He struggled for a moment trying to remember her name; he never had been much for names. It was no good he couldn't remember and what did it matter in any case, there were plenty more like her. The ache in his bladder forced the issue, no going back to sleep then.

He got up and tugged the blanket away from the girl, much to her obvious disgust. Then with the blanket draped over his shoulders he shuffled across the floor and out of the door. A quick walk around the longhouse brought him to the earth bank which was built up against the stockade wall. The bank was formed both to support the wooden wall and to provide the thin walkway from which the top of the stockade could be patrolled. He relieved himself with a sigh onto the ground letting the puddle run downhill between his bare feet.

He turned back to the longhouse, which would be his new home, for a while anyway. He had been granted an *oar* on board the Sea-Stallion, a fine ship which was due to go back to sea soon. The crewmen of each ship were allocated their oar and also a bed in the ship's longhouse. Last night's debauchery had been by way of welcome from his new crew, although in truth they seemed to require little excuse for a party.

He stumbled back towards the longhouse, stepping gingerly around the wet patch in the dirt. He had better get himself dressed, they were to spend the morning at the dock, preparing the ship and taking aboard supplies, they were heading north soon apparently. He could hardly wait.

Chapter 25

Once they had reached land the flotilla of ships formed a single file as they made their way up the narrow fjord. The sails were quickly furled, stowed and Finn watched as the experienced crew quickly deployed the long oars. They swiftly fell into a steady rhythm as they pulled the ship through the water deeper and deeper inland.

They wound their way round the snaking path of the narrow inlet until looking back; he could no longer see the entrance to the sea. Then, rounding the next bend he saw several ships lined up on a narrow strip of muddy beach, he quickly counted the masts, fifteen in all.

Surprised, he turned to Harald, who just laughed. "You didn't think this was it, did you? It will take more than just seven ships to take Holfstadir."

Harald's crew pulled hard on their oars as the helmsman picked his spot and aimed the prow of the ship at a clear patch of the beach. The ship softly slid to a halt in the sticky mud. The oars were neatly stowed alongside the furled sail and the crew hopped over the side.

Harald turned to Finn. "You coming?" He said as he swung his leg over the gunwale.

Finn quickly followed suit, his feet landing with a squelch in the slimy mud. Haralds crew quickly merged with those of the other ships as hearty handshakes and welcomes were exchanged. Finn felt very out of place, perhaps it was his lack of arms or armour, his hairless cheeks or just his size? He suddenly felt quite small; perhaps *sprat* wasn't so far from the mark after all.

"Harald! Late as usual I see!" Finn turned towards the booming voice. If he'd felt small before then now he felt positively tiny at the hulk of a man who parted the crowd as he approached.

Harald turned, smiling. "Magnus! I heard you were dead!" The two men grabbed hold of each others forearms before trying to squeeze the life out of each other in bear-hug.

Magnus squeezed hard lifting Harald off his feet. "Enough, enough, I give up, you big lummox!"

Magnus released his captive with a hearty laugh and then caught sight of Finn. "Brought one of your serving boys with you?"

"This is a passenger we picked up on the way. He was heading off to Holfstadir alone, on some kind of fools errand, a suicide mission really. I like him, he's a bright lad, I'll vouch for him." Harald said placing a hand on Finn's shoulder.

Magnus shrugged. "Good enough for me. Come on there is much to discuss."

He led them through the throng, to the edge of a small woodland, where a large sailcloth had been hoisted up into the tree line to form a covered shelter. Magnus stepped into the shade and sat down by a small fire which had been lit, Finn kept his distance standing just outside the shade of the large canopy.

Four older men were already sitting around the fire in a rough circle, bright eyes shining through hairy hardened faces; Harald made a half-bow in recognition. "Greetings, fellow Jarls."

There were a few muttered responses before Magnus spoke. "It is good to see so many old friends gathered to the call. We are all of one mind, here for one purpose. Raghnall has grown too powerful by far, his greed and demands on our people and our lands has become too much to bear."

One of the older men spoke. "Yes Magnus, what you say is indeed the truth and I like my fellow Jarls have answered your call. I would however council caution. Are we sure that this endeavour will be successful? I for one would not like to bear the brunt of Raghnalls vengeance if we fail in this."

"Then quite simply, we must not fail." Said Harald his eyes fixed. "My people will have barely enough grain to last the winter if we meet Raghnalls demands. I will fight my way out from under this yoke, or I'll die trying."

Magnus raised his hand. "Well spoke Harald. But I will not force any to follow me into battle against their will. Gunnar you may council caution but in truth the time for caution is long past. If you are not willing to join us then you may take your men and go without recrimination."

Gunnar held up his hand. "I'll make my decision when I have all the facts."

"Very well." Magnus began to draw a map with a stick in the bare earth. "We are well aware of Holfstadir's position. It is too well protected to allow a successful sea-borne assault. The fjord is too narrow, our ships will have to proceed two abreast for several miles before attempting to land on the beach. This will mean a staggered landing, forcing us to fight on too narrow a front; the first two boats in will be met with the full might of Raghnall's men and have the impossible task of trying to hold the beach whilst the other ships land their men."

The other Jarls nodded, grunting their assent. Gunnar spoke up. "Raghnall has ships enough to fill the fjord and harry our ships as they land. This is indeed folly?"

Harald took the stick from Magnus. "Then we must force Raghnall to fight us on two fronts. Magnus will lead the seaborne assault, ensuring that the ships are packed together as tightly as we dare, so that they can make landfall in quick succession, or better still all together as one force. The quicker our warriors are on dry land the better. You must draw the ships together and land like a fist."

He waited; enjoying the tension. "I will, in turn, take one third of our host over the mountains to the slopes of Midjfel." He said pointing at the mountain behind Holfstadir with the stick. "We will descend upon Holfstadir from the mountain side like a hawk swoops upon its prey. Raghnall will have already set his men to the defence of the beach, all of his defences have been fixed upon a sea-borne attack; they have been for years. By the time he diverts his men to the defence of his stronghold it will be too late." Harald pierced the map of Holfstadir with his stick, sat back and folded his arms, satisfied.

Gunnar stared at the map on the floor for a long moment. "It's a fine plan. You have me and my men." The rest of the gathered Jarls nodded and grunted their assent to the plan.

Magnus stood ending the meeting. "Good, it's decided then. Go and make your ships ready. Harald you will need a good days head start to get over the mountain, you must be away by midday. We will mount our attack on Holfstadir at noon tomorrow. I will signal you when the bulk of our host makes landfall and Raghnall is fully engaged on the beach."

They all stood and made their way back towards their ships, there was much to do.

***

The hound nuzzled in close as he rubbed the small hollow behind its left ear, the fur felt course under his hand. The dog was getting old, slow in the chase, more fond of a bed by the fire now, but he was the closest friend he had had in many a year. He sat there brooding, his breakfast, long cold, lay on the low bench before him.

Why was she back? He had thought her dead for years, as dead as the others who had been stupid enough to follow him to the dragon's lair. But she had returned, and now so had the dream.

He had woken in the small grey hours of morning, thrashing, blankets twisted around his limbs, the skin down the left side of his body screaming in pain as if newly burnt only yesterday.

His shield had proved little protection from the dragon's breath as it turned to ash and crumbled in his hand. He had passed out from the pain and fallen slumped behind a rock, forgotten, while the beast incinerated the rest of them, well the ones too slow or foolhardy to flee.

When he had come-to and made his painful way back down to the ship he found the remnants of his broken host gathered on the beach. Thirty men had climbed that mountain, only nine remained. The price was too great; the beast could keep his bloody hoard.

He stood with a groan and crossed the floor towards the hall. He could see her through the gap in the drapes, still chained to the post as he'd ordered. She was young still, while he had grown old and tired. So very tired. He had always known she was some kind of witch.

Yes, but she had been *his* witch. She had saved him from the battlefield, tended his wounds, wounds that by right should have killed a youth like him. She had brought him back from the very jaws of death. It was wrong, or at least that's what they whispered in dark corners when they thought he wasn't listening.

She had become even less popular when he had taken her into his bed. He had heard the whispers; she had possessed him, brought him back from the dead and now owned his soul. Nonsense, she had taken his heart that was all. That heart had died when she had, burned to dry ash, just like his shield.

His arm brushed against the rough spun wool of the drape sending sharp needles of pain down his side and to the tips of his burned fingers. He winced and shrunk back from the entrance, no one must see this pain. Weakness would not do, it was strength that had kept him on top for so long, strength of arm and when that failed strength of will.

He slowly lowered his aching carcass into the chair and once he was settled he called for his healer. The salve smelled fowl, but it would ease the pain, for a while at least.

After a short while the old man entered the room, he immediately busied himself dropping herbs into a bowl and pounding them to mix with whatever stinking waxy substance he used as the bulk of the salve.

Now, what should he do with the witch?

Chapter 26

The long march up the mountain started easily enough; they followed the narrow paths carved through the dark pine wood, by the beasts of the forest. Finn had been given a heavy sheepskin cloak to wear around his shoulders; which would also serve as a blanket to ward off the night time chill on the mountain tops.

As per his wish he had been given axe and helm. They had had no armour to spare but he didn't mind, the climb would be difficult enough without lugging a heavy mail shirt.

The forest was dark and the heavy scent of pine hung in the air as the warriors brushed against the lower branches, scattering needles as they passed. There was no sign of game, but that was little wonder given the noise that over two hundred men made as they crashed their way uphill along the narrow path.

All too quickly they emerged from the forest onto the lower slopes of the mountain; they clambered across thick tiring brush and sedge for a time, the thick cloying mud threatening to remove their boots with every step, until they found another path leading up the hill. This one was a little wider than the path through the forest; the soil had been worn down over the years, exposing the rock and loose shale underneath which was compacted as if by the passage of feet over an age.

Finn was surprised to see such a path up there in the mountains, he turned to Leif who had been trudging along silently at his side for the past few miles. "I didn't expect to find a path up so high. It's so wide, it's almost a road."

Leif kept his eyes to the ground mindful of where he placed his feet on the rough track. "It's a Troll path. Should be safe enough while it's daylight though."

Finn did his best to hide his shock and continued to walk alongside the older man, although he couldn't help lift his eyes every now and again, searching the dark nooks and clefts in the rock face.

By the time the sun began to fall towards its watery bed in the western sea they had almost reached the mountain top. The wind was strong up in the heights but that was pleasantly cool after the long hike. The sea to the west stretched flat and bright in sharp contrast to the jagged peaks which surrounded them on the other three sides.

The falling sun threw sharp shadows across the cliffs and gullies and Finn wondered how many trolls lived there, there could be whole clans of them, he thought, all of them hungry and beginning to wake, now that night was approaching.

They continued uphill for another league or so until they came across a wide saddle of land where the downward slope of two peaks met. The ground was dry and springy underfoot from the thick growth of moss over the years. At the head of the column Harald raised his hand, signalling the stop and the men quickly busied themselves setting camp for the night.

Finn followed the lead of the others and set down his cloak, helm and axe in what looked like a favourable spot for the night. He was exhausted from the climb but he wandered through the makeshift camp as Harald organised the first watch of the night.

He had just given his men their orders when he saw Finn approaching and waved, beckoning him to come over. "How are you young Finn, tired from the climb?"

Finn nodded. "Yes, it was quite a climb, but it's almost worth it for the view."

Harald cast his eyes around for a second. "Yes it's quite something isn't it?" He pointed towards the next valley to the north. "See there, where the mountain side drops back down into the mist. Holfstadir lies down there in the dip. The peak just to the east there is the summit of Midtfjel."

Finn looked up to where the mountain vanished into the clouds. "We're nearly there then?"

"Yes, if we break camp at first light we can carefully make our way down the mountain and be in position for the attack at mid-day. With so many men it will be more treacherous to descend the mountain; one slip could ruin us all."

Finn didn't know what frightened him more, the impending attack on Holfstadir, the climb back down or the thought of a long dark night up there on the mountain.

Harald smiled and put a reassuring arm around the boy. "Don't look so worried my young friend, what's the worst that can happen? Die well, you'll meet a beautiful Valkyrie and you're assured a place in Valhalla. In any case I'll see you safe through this."

After a moment or so he pulled away and landed a playful punch on Finn's shoulder. "Now go and get some food before it's all gone, these gannets will leave precious little."

Finn smiled and walked off to get some food, cold mutton and rye bread, Harald had forbidden the lighting of any fires, worried that the light or smoke may be seen in the fjord down below.

***

As the light faded and the tide drew back exposing the mud and rock at the edges of the fjord, the seal hauled herself out of the water and up onto the rocks. She found a nice flat stone to lie on and lifted her tail up off the mud pulling her body into a shallow crescent.

The ships were still pulled up on the opposite shore, their masts leaning like a row of pine trees in a gale. She'd watched them all afternoon from the safe deep water in the middle of the channel. It had been so tiring keeping the ships in sight overnight; as she followed them toward the land. Once she'd reached the fjord she had been quite exhausted. There had been too many eyes ashore however to rest up, seal meat would be as good as any other and she'd no intention of letting that happen.

Now it was dark enough, the men had lit their camp fires and the smell of smoke drifted across the water. She could hear them laughing, someone started singing, some raucous ale-house dirge no doubt.

Was he over there? Sitting by one of the fires, sharing a joke maybe?

The anger flickered briefly in her chest, the thought of him laughing, joking by the fire while she lay there, tired and miserable. No, no he wouldn't be joking with the others, she felt sure of it. He shared her pain; he still loved her, in spite of what he'd said.

She had longed to speak to him, floating there in that miserable little boat, she almost had, but no, what if he rejected her again?

He couldn't really have meant what he had said, there on the beach, he was angry, upset, he was just lashing out; it wasn't really even her fault, or his. Someone would have found the village eventually. So she had kept her distance, keeping pace with the little boat as it drifted slowly with the wind and tides.

She couldn't bring herself to sever the tie, their last words would not, could not, be the words they'd shared on the beach, she simply would not allow it. She would wait, follow, and when the time was right they would be together again, even if it was only to say farewell.

She took one last look back towards the resting fleet, the fires still burned bright against the encroaching dark, holding back the shadows for a time. The seal closed her dark eyes against the night.

***

He slept, or tried to, wrapped as best as he could in the sheepskin. He was clearly much bigger than a sheep and its meagre skin did little to shield his legs from the icy winds on the mountain top, even when he curled up as tightly as he could.

It was almost a relief when he was roused to take his watch. About ten of them were arranged in a rough circle on the outer edges of the camp, he'd been given a small horn to blow to raise the alarm. He had no idea how to actually blow a horn, it wasn't a skill he'd ever acquired, but really how hard could it be?

Now this on the other hand, this was familiar, wide awake, in the middle of the night, pitch dark, keeping watch. It seemed that fate would allow him no escape. He was doomed to be forever the night watchman.

He could hear faint snoring over his left shoulder, then there was a grunt as someone obviously kicked out, this silenced the snorer, but only briefly.

The wind whipped across from right to left and he could see the heather bowing to the pressure of the passing wind. In the dim light of the stars the movement could almost pass for waves on the sea.

He put up his hand to stifle a yawn and saw something move; it was close by, over where the prevailing wind had harried a bare rock-face over hundreds of years causing the rock to slowly shed its surface in small nuggets. This had left a scar of loose rock and scree that was slowly, ever so slowly working its way downhill to the foot of the mountain.

It was nothing, he was sure of it, just a trick of the light, the wind or something. He fixed his gaze on the rocks, then remembered that he always saw better in the dark if he didn't look directly at an object, he shifted his gaze slightly and then noticed that he had been holding his breath. He let out his breath with a soft sigh and felt the tension leave his shoulders.

He watched and waited, there it was again, the large round boulder at the foot of the cliff moved a little. Then it moved a little more and uphill!

He reached for the horn around his neck, but then thought better of blowing it, what if he was mistaken?

He shuffled forward sliding downhill a little on his bottom. Then crept slowly towards the cliff-face on all fours, feeling sure what little noise he was making would be hidden by the wind. He crept around the side of a stunted juniper bush keeping low to the ground and poked his head out for a look.

The boulder was still moving, shuffling almost; then he saw the surface of the boulder ripple in the breeze. It was covered in fur!

Dread raised the hair along the back of his neck. Oh great, he had found a bear and now he'd crept so close that there was no way he would be able to get away. The best thing he could do now was to lie as still as possible and hope the bear lumbered off soon.

He wiggled his hips pushing himself down as low as he could in the dense heather and waited, watching the bear.

There was a sudden gust of wind, it ruffled the juniper branches and blew his fringe forward over his eyes. He quickly flicked the hair out of his face and froze. The bear had suddenly stopped moving, that was definitely a bad sign.

He could hear a loud sniffing sound and watched in horror as the bear began to slowly turn around raising itself up onto its hind legs. There was a glint of metal and a dull thud as the bear put down the large sack it had been holding in its right hand. Finn's mind was racing, why would a bear have a sack?

But this was no bear, it was clearly a troll.

A pair of tiny eyes glinted from either side of the largest fleshiest nose Finn had ever seen, no wonder it had smelled him. Long thick curled hair tumbled down the sides of its head, but even this thatch barely hid the huge bright metal ring the troll wore in its left ear.

Before Finn could even move the troll had taken two huge steps forward and was bending over him menacingly. A great hand reached out with a light jingle as the heavy metal bracelets around its wrist clattered; then it stopped, fingertips just inches from his head.

The troll sighed and sat down, resting it's almost non existent chin in one huge hand. Its heavy brow furrowed deeply as it cocked its head to one side contemplating the tiny human.

Finn sat there silent and more than a little confused at the fact he was still alive. The troll's eyes were not quite so little this close up; they were just dwarfed by that huge nose. It just sat there, staring at him and he was sure he could hear it humming a low tune to itself, this was becoming awkward; what was the proper way to address a troll, sir, madam? In all honesty it was very hard to tell which one was sitting here in front of him.

Just when he had decided to break the tension and speak up, the troll nodded, quickly, stood, swung its heavy sack over one shoulder and strode off downhill, into the night.

Chapter 27

The mist floated on the surface of the fjord as the sun struggled to crest the mountain top. Unnoticed she slid silently beneath the surface leaving small eddies twisting in her wake, she could afford to get a little closer this morning, the men were already hard at work making the ships ready.

Their purpose was clear, most of the shelters, barrels and chests of food remained where they had been set the previous night. The ships were being loaded lightly; their only cargo appeared to be weapons and men.

There was no laughter, not like the night before, no jokes, no singing, all of the men were clearly fixed on the job ahead, their faces grim masks showing little or no emotion.

She watched them tighten ropes, fixing their round shields to the gunwales and then one by one each ship was pushed out off the beach and into the channel. The oars slid out like the spines of some huge poisonous fish and then rippled sinuously as they gently dipped into the water, pushing each ship forward through the mist.

One by one they slid from the beach and struck out for the open sea. She watched each one closely, searching the men at the oars hoping for at least a glimpse of his face.

When the last ship had left the shore she swiftly fell in line at the stern, wherever they were going; she was going too. What was the alternative? The decision made itself; she had never been one to leave a task unfinished.

***

Finn had sat his watch till the dawn, eyes fixed on the spot where he'd lost sight of the troll, if indeed that's what it had been. For the first hour or so he'd waited, horn at the ready, he felt sure that it would be back, and probably with several of its friends in tow.

He wasn't sure how to defend himself from a troll attack; come to think of it he wasn't sure how to defend himself from much of anything. The one thing he could do and do right this time was raise the alarm.

He wouldn't be found wanting in that regard again. So he sat there waiting, twisting the horn in his fist.

When the first tense hour or so had passed and there was still no sign of, well anything at all really, he began to relax a little. He still kept hold of the horn, just in case. Had it really been a troll? He couldn't be sure, it certainly seemed big enough and ugly enough if the tales were to be believed.

But it hadn't attacked, that was confusing. All the stories involving trolls he had heard as a child usually ended in doom for the people involved. There was generally a lot of bone grinding, to make jelly. Trolls appeared to like jelly, a lot.

When the sun began to rise over the mountains and there was still no sign of the troll's return, he could finally relax. Trolls didn't like the sun, everyone knew that, the sun meant safety and warmth, but for trolls it invariably meant death, well death in the form of being turned into a large boulder for all eternity. No, any troll worthy of calling itself a troll would be safely underground by now.

The breaking dawn brought a fresh wave of cold as droplets of dew started to form on the tips of the heather. Finn stood, stretching his cold stiff muscles, his watch over, he drew the sheepskin cloak tight about his shoulders as he made for the middle of the waking camp and a cold breakfast. It was going to be a very long day.

***

Raghnall had avoided entering the hall all day, much against his better judgement. No doubt the men would be gossiping already, he sometimes wondered if he had mistakenly hired fish-wives instead of warriors. It seemed almost cowardly hiding like this but he felt safer brooding in his chamber, seeing her only made him remember. No good would come from wallowing in the past.

He remembered her skin, so warm under his hand, her touch raising gooseflesh on his skin……

But no, madness, weakness, they were akin. He would harden his heart once more, she had been dead to him for more years than he cared to count, she would be dead again before the day was out, there would be no return for her this time.

He untangled the fur from his legs and slipped out of his bed. What brief sleep he had managed had been spoiled once more by the dragon, the burns were not the only wounds which refused to heal it seemed.

Memory was a curse, since her return he had replayed it all, from the first moment he had met her. He had surprised himself at how much he could recall; every conversation, every look, every moment, no matter how brief; played back in intricate detail in his minds eye. She had bewitched him again, possessed him once more, perhaps they had been right all along.

He found himself standing at the entrance to the hall. She was there, just on the other side of the heavy drape hanging over the doorway. All he need do was walk in. She was there, in his hall, chained to his post, his prisoner, guarded by his men. Why was it then that he felt trapped?

He was chained indeed, chained to this life: the man he had created was so much bigger than he was. He was known, revered, but mainly feared, everywhere. He had understood quite quickly that the people would never love him. That had been his liberation; if they could not love him then they must fear him, truly fear him.

True fear was absolute and true fear was what he had nurtured. Not the common type of fear, like that of a child who has angered its parents, or a dog who has stolen its master's dinner, that fear is always tempered by love.

True fear, the kind that made grown men weigh and measure every word uttered lest it proved to be their last; that was what he had harnessed. True fear depended on strength, swift action and anger. There could be no mercy, no hesitation, a glimpse of the slightest chink in this armour and the illusion was lost.

He had already hesitated too long; he should have spilled her blood there on the beach that night, in front of her friends. Time appeared to have had little effect on her but he was damn sure that cold steel would end her.

He felt the anger rising in his belly like an old friend. He must remove this weakness; he must destroy the witch, completely.

The serving girl almost dropped his breakfast as she pulled back the drape and found her master standing there glaring. She quickly ducked her head and navigated a wide course around him as if his rage itself were a physical barrier.

As quietly as she could she laid the food on the low bench and collected the supper which had lain untouched since her last visit the previous evening. She was hastily leaving the room when he broke the silence. "Summon Olaf to my chamber!"

"Yes my lord."

He turned away from the serving girl, she was forgotten already and walked over towards his breakfast, decision made, he could feel his appetite returning. He selected an apple and began to turn it over in his hands examining the skin for blemish.

He needed to send a message to the world; he had already hesitated too long over this matter he must remind them who he was. The fear must be renewed.

Burning was the usual disposal for a witch. It was quite entertaining, the crowd always cheered, it was as if they were all joining in the witches terrified shrieks and wails. The pitiless flames heard nothing as they licked and caressed, devouring first hair, then clothing then matter itself, rendering their guest charred twisted and unrecognisable.

He felt the inferno surge, slipping under the skin of his left arm, his tortured fist snapped closed on the perfect apple. Fingertips driving in like a claw, breaking the skin and bruising the soft flesh below.

The pulse of agony shimmered across his face like the flicker of the flame in his minds eye and it was gone.

His sinews relaxed and he released the spoiled apple to roll onto the floor. No, there would be no fire for this witch. He must be there to bear witness to her destruction and the risk of shaming himself in the face of the flames was too great.

As they said there were many ways to skin a cat and indeed there were just as many ways to rid himself of this woman.

Chapter 28

Thordys' shoulders strained against the ropes as the wheels of the little cart sought their own route through the deep ruts in the muddy lane. The rough hemp wound tightly around her shoulders chafed against her already bruised skin.

His thugs were efficient she had to grant them that, a quick inventory revealed that there was very little of her body that had remained unscathed. She flexed her fingers, or tried to, the damage was extensive, she was pretty sure that all but two of the fingers of her left hand were broken. Surprisingly there appeared to be three unbroken digits on her right hand, she logged that in the plus column.

Her face had, typically born the brunt of the assault, her jaw ached and her nose felt as though it was only held in place by congealed blood. She could open one eye just a little; the other had puffed up and closed in on itself.

The cart jolted as the rough-hewn wheel struck a rock which lay submerged in the thick mud. She coughed and felt shattered ribs grate on one another in what remained of her rib cage. The blood trickled down her chin onto the already soaked and torn tunic which hung like a rag from her shoulders.

She could hear the slow steady plod of the horses hooves, that and the fact that she had been pitched forward since they had left the stronghold suggested that they were making their way downhill towards the shore. She had been told nothing of what was going on; she had not spoken with Raghnall since they had arrived at Holfstadir and was not sure quite what to make of his absence. She had tried talking to her captors but they were either too scared or too stupid to converse with her.

She thought she'd caught a glimpse of him, just briefly in the main hall, in the seconds before she had passed out. He had been watching from a seat in the shadows silent, his men knew their business and needed no direction from him.

She heard a course "kraa!" as a lone raven circled high above.

The cart straightened up as the roadway flattened out. She raised her head a few inches and peered out of her remaining good eye. They were nearing the centre of the town; the grimy townsfolk were gathered together in wary huddles, watching the passing procession. She took some reassurance in the fact that they didn't seem to be enjoying the spectacle and let her too-heavy head drop once more.

She heard the tone of the hooves become hollow as the pony pulled the cart onto the jetty and the wooden wheels crossed the planks with a steady thunk, thunk, thunk.

The cart stopped abruptly and the wheels rolled back a little as they rocked to a halt in the hollow between two boards. She felt rough hands tugging and untying the ropes from about her and then she was lifted bodily from the cart and propped upright on unsteady legs.

The thug behind her took a handful of hair in his fist and tugged her head upright. Peering from her eye she saw that she was on the edge of the jetty. The townsfolk had been gathered along the shore to bear witness to this. She was just working out what *this* would be when she noticed the long boom hovering above.

One of the hoists normally used to unload the ships had been swung directly overhead; she saw that a sizeable stone had been fastened to the rope by an iron ring. The stone waited ominously on the jetty just a step or two away.

Raghnall sat, mounted, where the jetty joined the shore. His horse pawed the wooden boards, unsure of the man-made surface beneath its hooves. He settled the beast and raised his hand; a horn was raised and sounded. Once the echo had returned from across the fjord there was silence.

"People of Holfstadir! I Raghnall, your Lord and protector have long brought you peace and prosperity. You ply your trades in safety and your works are the envy of all the world. I have brought you here today to bear witness to the destruction of one who would disturb that peace. Behold……. a witch!" He paused for a moment and watched the reaction of the townsfolk.

"This witch has lain hidden from me for many years, hidden from the law we all live by. She threatens the safety and very existence of you all, and for that she must now die!"

Thordys was shoved forward towards the stone; her hands which had been bound behind her back were unfastened. She saw that a loop had been tied in the rope about seven feet up. Her hands were yanked upwards and her wrists made fast to the loop.

Her body hung there, a dead weight dragging at her already aching joints, pulling her tortured ribs apart. She scrabbled forward with her toes and was able to climb inch by inch onto the rock. Once there, she found that by standing on the tips of her toes she could bear a little of her weight and ease the pressure on her arms.

There was a creak as the rope pulled taught and raised the stone with its passenger slowly off the deck. She swung to and fro as the boom was swung out over the fjord, and then inch by inch the rope was lowered until she felt the cold water gently washing the blood from her toes.

There was just time for a glimpse of the silent crowd before the rope was suddenly released and she dropped, breath driven from her lungs with a gasp once more, just as it had with the punches that had arrived with today's dawn.

She hung there, weightless in the depths by the dockside, the chill entered her body, bringing numbing relief to aching bones and bruised flesh. Her hair loosened the bonds of blood and grime and floated around her head like a veil in the breeze.

She braced her body, fighting the urge to open her lungs, to breathe in the cold fluid. The spasms began in her chest, racking her body, like spears plunged through her damaged ribs. Just as the moment arrived that she felt she could bear no more, there was a tug on her wrists as the rope was pulled taught, hoisting her inch by inch out of the water.

Her wet hair hung down, shielding her face from the watching crowd. She peered through and saw him sitting there, arm raised, impassive in his saddle.

A short way along the jetty stood Linus, he caught her eye and just had time to smile and nod in recognition before Raghnall lowered his hand once more and she was plunged back down.

She knew the routine; she had seen witches tortured before, it was always cruel and un-necessary. She would be lifted and dunked several times until she either dropped from exhaustion or drowned. She braced once more, ready to fight her own body, to deny her lungs from betraying her; she would not allow him or that bloody traitor Linus the satisfaction.

Whoever was operating the winch was clearly well practiced, he had done this before, just as she felt she could hold on no longer there came the welcomed tug on her wrists and she was dragged upwards into the light once more.

The dockside was silent, as she hung there waves lapping at her ankles. All was, as it had been moments before, his arm was raised, her life lay in his fingers, she dangled there, hanging on the rope and his whim. She felt the moments passing marked by the throb of the blood pulsing in her ears and braced once more for the plunge.

She heard a faint "Baruuuuuuuuuu!" as a horn sounded in the distance. The single note was immediately joined by the sound of other horns, this time louder and closer.

The townsfolk stirred in spite of their armed escort, and she saw the assembled masses turn to look down the fjord toward the sea. Raghnall tugged at the rains and his horse turned neatly on the spot. His arm fell and she quickly followed, dropped below the waves, forgotten.

She heard the muffled thump of running panicked feet on the jetty. There would be no rescuing tug on her wrists this time, as the rope above her fell slack and the rock, her fellow passenger, dragged her to the bottom. She suppressed the rising panic, opened her mouth and let the water rush in to fill her aching lungs.

Chapter 29

Linus had never been to an execution before. Well there had been Ian and Jon but that had been a private affair, more intimate, being that it had been staged for him and him alone. This was something else altogether.

He looked over at the wretched woman, dangling there by her wrists; he had spent most of his childhood staying well out of her way. She had always frightened him a little. Somehow she seemed to see right through him, to the dark little thoughts he had hidden from all the others.

She didn't look so frightening now. Come to it she was barely recognisable at all. She had had such a beating, he had never seen anyone's face so swollen and bruised. Still she probably deserved it, she was a witch after all and he'd seen all the proof he needed of that. The way she had transformed herself, revealed her true form, it was not natural.

This dunking goes on for far too, long he thought, as she was dropped into the sea once more. Better she was killed quickly, gruesomely, but quickly, that would have been much better. That would have been a real spectacle.

He looked around the gathered crowd; there was no enjoyment here, no entertainment. The townspeople were only here because they had been ordered to be. They clearly had no love for their lord, sitting there, high in his saddle looking down on them all.

They did fear him though, and that was better, infinitely better. Someday, thought Linus, someday people will fear me as they fear him. That was true power.

Thora was hoisted out once more; she hung there dripping, like a wet rag. Linus shook his head, not again.... just kill the woman and be done with it.

Suddenly there was a loud "Baruuuuuuuuuu!"

Linus turned toward the sound as did all the others there on the pier. He looked down the fjord and saw a ship in the distance. No, not just one, there were many, all rowing single file and making good speed towards them.

He turned to Raghnall, he had turned his horse, arm still raised for Thora's next drop. For just a moment Linus saw surprise in the warlords face, then it was quickly replaced by anger. Raghnall dropped his arm and Thora was dropped for the final time, a plaything now forgotten.

With a shout of. "To arms! To arms!" Raghnall kicked his horse into action and made for the beach.

There was panic on the shoreline as the townsfolk scattered, back into the warren of narrow lanes where they lived. Linus followed the rest of his crew as they ran down onto the beach; there was no time to take ship and head off the attack. As the captain of the Sea-Stallion barked orders he took his place with the others along the narrow muddy beach. They stood there shoulder to shoulder shields overlapping. Linus pulled the long axe from the strap securing it over his shoulder and hefted it in his right hand.

The ships were almost abreast of them now; he counted at least fifteen. They turned towards the beach, their oars flapping like the wings of great birds as they bore down on the host gathered to meet them.

Linus' mouth was dry; he licked his lips and tried to ignore the warm wet sensation that was spreading from his crotch.

***

Finn looked along the line; the men were strung out along the edge of the forest hidden from sight in the shadow of the dense pines. He had taken up a spot lying behind a thick trunk that had fallen long ago and was beginning to rot down into the soil. Each man lay there silent within arms reach of his neighbour, awaiting the signal. The thick carpet of needles had muffled what little sound they had made when they had come, creeping stealthily down the steep slope.

He poked his head up over the log and looked down towards the town. There was a wide expanse of steep grassy slope between the edge of the forest and the fringes of the town. The space was clearly used as pasture and there was a small herd of goats clustered close to the rear wall of the fort below. There would be no hiding their descent; they would have to be quick and deadly.

The fort was their target, Harald had said as much as they broke camp that morning. They were to wait until Magnus' men had made landfall in the town below and Raghnall had committed his forces fully to defending the town. Then they would swoop down the mountainside, destroying Raghnall's stronghold before attacking the bulk of his men from the rear.

It had been about a half hour since they had watched Magnus' flotilla of ships enter the fjord. They had followed one another single file along the channel, sails stowed making way by oar, until as one, he saw them tack to starboard and break for shore.

He had been unable to see the landing from up here; the view was obscured by the steep slope and the roofs of the dark houses below. There was however no mistaking the dark smoke rising from the shoreline and the distant roar of battle.

He ducked back down and lay there, nervously grasping the shaft of his axe. The axe-head was smaller and much lighter than the heavy wood axe he used back home but then its purpose was entirely different after all.

Even laying there his legs felt weak, he wasn't sure if he trusted them to carry him down the hillside. He had visions of his already weak knees buckling underneath him sending him tumbling down the hill until he bounced into the side of the rampart with a thud.

He looked to the man on his left; his name was Snorri wasn't it? He was older much more experienced. Finn tried to work out of he was scared too, it was hard to tell, most of his face was obscured by helmet and beard. Snorri's eyes flicked up and caught his gaze. "Don't look so worried sprat. If all goes well we dine tonight in Raghnall's hall, if it doesn't then I'll pour you a drink in Valhalla. Either way we'll spend tonight drunk."

Finn gave Snorri the most convincing smile he could muster and looked away pretending to adjust his belt. There was a firm tap on his shoulder accompanied by a loudly whispered. "Make ready!"

He turned and passed the message to Snorri and word made its way from man to man along the edge of the wood. Finn turned and looked over the log again, the top of the wooden stockade was deserted and the fort was still, it would have appeared deserted were it not for the thin lines of smoke rising from the hearths within the walls. They waited, and waited, and then they waited a little more.

Suddenly, a lone burning arrow soared up from the waters edge, spluttering high in the sky above the town. That was it, the signal.

The long line of men rose from their hiding place and burst forth from the wood. Finn followed, his other options being rather limited and before he realised it he was rushing headlong down the grassy slope with the others.

His legs flailed wildly, struggling to keep his speeding body upright, he held the axe out at arms length in an effort to counterbalance and stay upright. Others in the line did the same as they surged down the hill.

Worst off during the descent were the men who bore the long trees which had been felled just that morning, the stubs of their branches left protruding for use as steps for scaling the rampart. They were carried by four men at a time, the men at the rear struggling to arrest the falling logs while the ones at the front leaned back as far as they dared, heels scrabbling for purchase.

There was no war-cry to accompany the headlong charge; they could not afford to be caught out there in the open. There was every chance that the best of their archers had been left behind to defend the ramparts.

As they reached the bottom of the pasture the slope lessened but the momentum they had built up carried them almost hard up against the walls of the fort.

The heavy ends of the scaling ladders were dropped, ploughing thick divots into the earth, as the men at the rear, clearly well practiced, heaved their end, which had earlier been the much thinner tree top, high into the air.

The logs rose, slowing at the zenith of their arc then speeding up, they fell with a series of satisfying thuds on the top of the wooden balustrade. In a matter of moments there were four routes up to the top of the wall.

They quickly rushed up the logs, the first men reaching the top just as the defenders appeared on the ramparts. Then fighting broke out on the wall itself as the invaders pushed out along the rampart, increasing their foothold on the narrow strip of earth that had been piled behind the wall.

Finn stood in line, waiting with the rest as they pushed forward towards the nearest ladder. The frustration was clear, they needed to be up there on the wall and quickly.

One of the others had clearly had enough; he broke from the line and ran headlong at the wall, as he neared the side he jumped, thrusting his foot at the wood as he swung his axe one handed above his head. The axe head cleared the top of the rampart and lodged there. The man then walked his feet up the wall, gripping the axe-handle like a rope. He had almost reached the top when, just as his head cleared the rampart his ascent was swiftly halted by the arrow that pierced his throat.

As he watched the man fall Finn saw that he had reached the foot of the ladder. He quickly took his place and clambered upward as close as he dared to the man in front. The branch-stump rungs of the makeshift ladder were now smooth and muddy, the rough bark having been stripped by the first eager feet to ascend. He felt the wood bow and bounce beneath him as they passed up its length. Several arrows whizzed past and another lodged in the ladder underneath him. He used the arrow as a makeshift foothold and continued upwards towards the fray.

Dead men littered the narrow path along the wall. Finn stepped from the ladder and felt his feet squelch in sticky bloody mud. He saw that they had pushed out from the ladders and now occupied much of the rampart, there were a group of defenders putting up strong resistance at the western corner and there was already heavy fighting down in the ward in front of the longhouses.

He moved along the wall clearing the exit from the ladder for the man behind and stepped gingerly over a fallen warrior. As he did so a hand reached out grabbing his ankle, he looked down and had time to see hate in the man's eyes, before an axe was swiftly lodged in the rear of the injured mans head. Finn freed his foot from the now limp hand and nodded thanks to his rescuer who was busy freeing his axe from the man's skull.

They had all but taken complete control of the rampart so Finn joined the others as they charged down the steep banking towards the battle in front of the longhouses. The group he was with picked up momentum as they rushed down the embankment and as they reached the small cluster of defenders they smashed into them like a wedge.

Finns shoulder smashed into the edge of a shield flipping it sideways and opening its owner's side to the sword of the man on his left.

Out of the corner of his eye he saw the flash of a sword swinging in a deadly arc as its owner tried to bring it down on his head. He used his forward momentum, ducked his head and threw himself forward, striking the swordsman just below the knees and sending him sprawling flat onto the mud.

Finn pulled himself up from the sticky mud and turned towards the fallen swordsman who was now on all fours. There was no time for thought, as he swung the light axe and brought it swiftly down on the middle of the swordsman's back. There was a dull thud; like chopping wood, only wetter.

He pulled to free the axe and found that it was firmly lodged in place. He pulled again, bracing himself with a foot on the dead mans shoulder but the axe wouldn't budge an inch. He let go the axe and bent down to retrieve the dead mans sword, he wouldn't be needing it now after all.

Finn turned, readying himself for the next foe and rushed forward with the others, lungs bellowing a roar, headlong into the melee.

Chapter 30

Merryn had followed the flotilla as it wound its way around the coast and into the next fjord. She heard the horns sounding as they made progress and at first thought that the fleet was announcing itself. Then she saw the narrow watchtowers on the shoreline and the beacons being hastily lit along the coast and knew that the alarm was being raised.

She could smell the grubby town before she could see it, spreading up the hillside from the shore like a dark mould. Smoke rose from hearths too numerous to count collecting in one ominously dark cloud hanging over the settlement.

She watched from the middle of the channel as the collected ships all turned right and the oars pulled hard for shore. The shallow hulls built speed as their sharp prows cut through the water and closed on the muddy beach.

The tide was high leaving only a narrow strip of mud before the town proper began. Armed men began to emerge, from the edges of the town onto the muddy strip and she saw a mounted warrior ride out along the length of the beach, hooves pounding, thrashing the shallow water into foam.

She ducked under and swam towards one of the piers that jutted out into the fjord. As she passed safely between the large wooden piles she surfaced and watched as the ships, almost simultaneously, run up onto the muddy shore. The crewmen immediately abandoned oars, there was no time to stow them now, and grabbing their shields from the gunwales they leaped over the side, into the shallows.

There was a short volley of arrows, some burning, from somewhere deep within the town, they rose in a shallow arc before dropping down on the beached fleet. Several men fell as the arrows missed poorly raised shields and bit instead into soft flesh.

She watched flames creep out along the boom of a ship, then pour down the ropes to reach the hull itself. Within moments the empty deck of the ship was belching thick smoke up into the leaden sky.

Merryn swam towards the shore staying under the shadow of the jetty; from between the wooden piles she watched the battle raging on the shoreline. There were no arrows now; both sides were locked in close bloody combat. Shields clashed, swords rang out, interspersed with the cries of the wounded and dying.

The water had grown shallow and she could feel the muddy bottom on her belly. She waited there unnoticed and struggled to remove her gaze from the carnage before her. Her dark eyes remained fixed on the horror, looking, searching, always searching for him. She watched as the attackers gained ground and moved up from the mud, over the narrow margin of grass and sedge pushing the defenders back into the narrow streets and lanes from whence they had come.

The fight moved onward, into the town and as quickly as that the beach was empty, the ships abandoned for the time being. Tiny waves rippled along the shore, no longer white crested but frothy pink with blood, lifting and dropping lifeless bodies onto the greasy mud. Smoke still rose from the burning ships slowly reducing them to hollow ribbed carcasses which would soon litter the shore.

She quickly slipped from her skin and folding it neatly she tucked the bundle up underneath the topmost horizontal pier support. Safely out of reach of the tide and out of the sight of prying eyes. Then she crept up along the side of the pier as it formed a ramp towards the town, braced at any moment to turn back to the safety of the fjord.

The waterfront was deserted; the townsfolk had obviously hidden themselves inside their houses or fled to safer high ground. She ran across the narrow gap and into a narrow vennel running between two storehouses. She hunkered down in the shadows and caught her breath; she should go back to the beach and check the fallen men, what if he was one of them? Finn was not experienced he was no warrior, he would be easy pickings. She closed her eyes; she had come so far and for what?

No, he was alive she felt sure of it, she would know if he were dead, she would feel it. She must press on she must see him; rescue him from this carnage before it was too late.

She wiped the desperate tears from her eyes with the back of a hand and slipped up the narrow passage. Merryn stopped at the end where it opened out into a wider alleyway which ran at right angles to the first. Washed clothes hung across the alleyway from slack drooping lines. She checked both ways and quickly ran across the alley, tearing a freshly washed tunic from the line as she went. She pulled the tunic over her head as she ran uphill towards the sound of battle.

***

The fortress had been taken and the last of the defenders dispatched. No mercy had been given and none had been asked, the defenders had fought to the last man. A group of women and children had been rounded up from their hiding places in the longhouses and made to sit down in the courtyard. The only thing saving them from the sword was the iron collar clasped around their necks. Thralls were too valuable a commodity to be squandered.

Finn tucked the stolen sword into his belt and limped across to the huddled women. He saw the fear in their eyes as he approached and he raised his grubby hands to reassure the prisoners.

One of the men who had rounded them up saw his approach and barred his way. "Hey! What do you think you're playing at!"

"Nothing, I mean no harm. I just want to talk to them, that's all. I've checked everywhere and there is no sign of my grandmother here, they might know where she's being held."

The warrior laughed. "What a cock and bull story! You just want first pick of them don't you? They'll be divvied up later, fare and square, now get lost!" He pushed Finn in the chest.

Finn tried to move around, past him, but was again intercepted and pushed away. "You're beginning to test my patience now boy!"

A small crowd had gathered just in time to see the two of them come to blows, Finn ducked a wild haymaker and threw his shoulder forward into the man's gut, sending them both tumbling onto the ground in a writhing heap.

The fracas had not gone unnoticed, Harald broke into the crowd. "What's the meaning of this?" He bellowed, as he kicked out at an exposed rump on the ground careless as to who its owner might be.

He reached down and grabbed Finn by the belt lifting him from the ground. "Oh! It's the mighty sprat. Get up the pair of you and explain yourselves!"

The older man picked himself up from the ground and quickly dusted himself off. "He was trying to get first pick of them thralls, that's all. I tried to explain that they'd be shared out later but he wouldn't have it."

Harald turned to Finn. "Is that so?"

"No. I was just trying to find my grandmother, you promised I could. I've checked everywhere and there's no sign of her. I thought they might know where she was." He said, pointing at the huddled slaves.

Harald surveyed the miserable cluster. "Ask them what you will, but be quick about it. We strike out from here in five minutes and since you two clearly have plenty of fight left in you, you'll both be joining me."

Finn ignored his erstwhile foe's angry glare and quickly approached the frightened captives; the first few he spoke to either didn't understand him or had been rendered mute. A young lad then grunted and nodded his head at him. "I seen a prisoner, brought back from the last raid, she spent the last week or so bound up in the big house."

Finn scrabbled over to the lad. "That must be her; she'd have been brought back here about then."

The boy shook his head. "Can't have been, she was no one's grandmother that one, she was far too young. Went by the name of flora or something like that."

Finn took the boys hands. "That must have been her. Where is she now? Where are they holding her?"

"She's probably dead by now, she got a hell of a beating this morning. The master said she was a witch and then they trooped her off down to the harbour to sort her out."

Finn sat there staring out past the boy, he was too late. She had been the one last fragment of his old life, of normality he could cling to, the one thing he hadn't completely messed up.

He'd destroyed the village; he may as well have burned the place down himself. He had lost Merryn too, driven her away when he needed her most, stupid, stupid, selfish fool that he was. He heard the villager's taunts of long ago, they had been right all along, he was dammed, cursed; everything spoiled and became rotten at his very touch.

He thanked the lad, got to his feet and then strode towards the gatehouse picking up an abandoned shield on the way. The men were gathering, readying themselves for the final assault down into the town. The best he could wish for now was a good death.

Chapter 31

The fighting had been fierce and if truth be told Raghnall's fears about the abilities of his men had been well founded. They were lacking somewhat in the grit of the previous generation, but then they were far more accustomed to alehouse brawling these days.

The shoreline had been far too easily lost; he had run down the first few fleeing cowards himself as a lesson to the others. It had not however had the desired effect and even in the full flight of his rage; he had been powerless to halt the rout. Raghnall and the select men of his guard had had little alternative than to follow the retreat up the winding narrow streets of the town.

They had reached the market square and this was where he intended to permanently halt the enemy advance. He trotted out to the middle of the square and swung down from the saddle, the battle would turn here, he must lead them himself from the front.

Raghnall quickly ordered his men to block the entrances onto the square with whatever they could to slow the enemy attack and he watched as carts and barrows were pulled into place and upturned. Then he strode to the centre of the square holding his sword aloft. "Form up, on me!" He bellowed.

His men gathered into three loosely formed lines in the middle of the square, the front line overlapped their shields and stood braced for the onslaught. Raghnall stood near the centre of the second line of men and cast his eye along the line, yes this would serve; his foes would break themselves upon the wall of shields as they trickled out from the streets and alleyways. They would pay for their insolence.

The first few attackers emerged from the narrow gaps that had been left. Their blood boiling with the heat of battle; they rushed headlong at the wall of shields, eyes and mouths wide as they screamed their war-cries.

His men held fast and this first small wave was repelled with ease. The attackers continued to arrive in the square, but with less haste. There was a loud shout and the attackers formed into a loose line to match his own. Their leader strode to the middle of the line, matching his position to that of Raghnall, he wore a masked helmet and carried a shield like the others but there was no mistaking him, a mountain of a man he towered a good head taller than anyone else in the square. Rage welled up inside him; it was Magnus, his supposed friend and ally.

Magnus' men continued to file into the square taking up position until their numbers almost matched that of his own. Raghnall could contain his anger no longer. "Enough of this! Charge!" He bellowed waving his sword in the air.

The two sides closed the gap and immediately merged into one seething mass, sword, axe and man.

***

As Merryn drew closer the sound of raging battle began to echo down the narrow passages. She seemed to be swimming against the tide of people fleeing their homes, not caring which way they ran; so long as it was away.

They barely looked where they were going as they ran carrying as much of their households as they could manage, pots, pans, blankets, children all gathered into bundles in their arms. Some, probably traders or merchants, pushed heavily laden barrows, the wheels rattling and clattering on the rocky lanes as Merryn jumped aside to let them pass. Their wives and children following in their wake, like families of ducks put to flight by marauding hounds.

Up ahead she could see that the buildings either side of the lane abruptly ran out as the narrow lane opened out onto some kind of open space. She moved in against the wall to her right and crouched down, approaching as carefully as she could. She jammed herself in behind a stack of baskets and poked her head around the corner.

The sight before her was grim. She had heard tales of war and battle since she was a child, told at the hearth of an evening by her father and uncles, tales of bold daring and glory. Nothing she had heard prepared her for this.

She watched in horror as swords cleaved limbs, sending bright droplets of blood glistening into the air. Axes dropped splitting shields and heads alike. Men clambered over friend and foe not caring that their way was paved with death and above it all the air hung fetid with the heat of exertion.

The din was terrifying, clanging metal on metal, metal on wood and the grunt and groan of humanity as it tried to both stay alive and mete out death in the same instant.

There in the middle of the tumult stood a giant of a man, his helmed head jutting up, like a solitary rock emerging from the waves. Warriors fell upon him time and again to be swept aside as he continued to carve his bloody way through the throng.

It was impossible to tell which side was winning, and she wondered how any man could claim victory from this.

As she watched a fresh hoard of warriors emerged from a street on the uphill side of the market square. They held back at first allowing the men at their rear to join and swell the throng before with a collective roar, they came running across the square, eager to join the fray.

Her eyes followed the charge. She had never seen men look more terrifying, their faces contorted in rage as they fell upon their foes, and there at the edge of the line, running, sword in hand, with all the rest, unmistakable as her own right hand, was the boy she loved.

***

The plan had worked perfectly, as they charged across the square Finn saw that Raghnall's men were completely lost in the frenzy of battle. Fully occupied with Magnus' attack, they were oblivious to their doom and did not even turn to face them as they slammed into their ranks from the rear.

The men in the back line were easily cut down with sword and axe blows from behind, most would die having no idea of the means. The surprise was however short lived and within moments Raghnalls' force had reorganised and gathered into a loose ring of men completely surrounded on all sides.

Finn found himself locked in a desperate duel on the periphery. The first blows had been exchanged in haste, both him and his opponent eager for a speedy triumph as they neared exhaustion. Finn had landed a blow to the man's shoulder but found that his foes axe had returned the favour by biting into his thigh just above the knee.

Both crouched, sucking in huge lungfulls of air, eyes peeping above battered shields as they gathered what little strength remained for another exchange. The man's face was obscured by his long grey tresses that hung dripping in sweat and blood. Finn searched out his eyes trying to anticipate where the next blows would be aimed and struggled to ignore the dull throbbing ache from his left leg.

Time seemed frozen, seconds like hours, all sound was lost, drowned by the rushing of blood in his ears. He felt every fibre of his being vibrating, charged, so alive now, with death all around him.

He sensed more than saw a slight change in his foe's posture as his weight shifted preparing to swing. His left arm raised the shield, catching the swinging axe's blade on the edge. As it lodged in the wood of the shield Finn kicked out hard with his right foot finding and buckling his enemy's knee. As he did so his sword arm drove forward sending the point of the hardened steel into blood and bone and bringing battles-end one man closer.

With leaden legs he stepped over the man's lifeless body searching out his next foe. All around him men were locked in grim exchanges, the dead and dying littered the ground like autumn's fallen leaves.

He felt a thump on his back, like a kick in the ribs, expelling the air from his body with a loud grunt, body thrust forward; his head snapped backwards making his ears ring. High above, he saw that the heavy grey cloud had opened to reveal a sliver of perfectly blue sky.

His knees hit the ground as exhausted legs folded under him. He looked down and saw the spear-head and a length of wooden shaft erupting from his belly. There was no pain, not yet.

He felt the blood rushing from his veins. He heard the wind whispering through the feathers of the ravens circling high above. He could feel the gentle waters of the fjord kissing the rocky shore below, at that moment he was everything; returning as he was to the dust from which he had been forged. Slowly his world became smaller as he felt the edges crumble.

The patch of blue sky was gone now, its appearance fleeting as the grey clouds re-established their tenure high above. Then the ravens began to arrive, uninvited guests eager for the feast.

Chapter 32

Merryn burst out of the alleyway, blindly scattering the baskets that had provided her with a hiding place. She ran headlong across the muddy square, heedless of the battle still raging in the centre.

Finn's executioner retrieved his long spear from the lad's back and moved on seeking out another foe, leaving the boy discarded in the mud with the others. The fighting swirled in ever decreasing circles, a tempest leaving the fallen scattered on its fringes, as Raghnalls force was whittled smaller and smaller. Battle's end was drawing near, the outcome inevitable.

She stumbled onward, eyes blinded by the tears which ran freely down her cheeks. Slipping in the gory mire she stumbled and fell clumsily onto her hands and knees but still she clambered forward toward him.

She pulled Finn onto her lap and cradled his warm limp body in her arms. Delicately she stroked her fingertips across his forehead, brushing the matted hair from his beautiful face. His soft kind eyes stared sightless up at her. She never had been able to describe their colour, it was somewhere between hazel and green, scattered with glistening shards of brown. Laughing eyes she'd always thought, but the light behind these eyes was gone.

She felt her body shudder as a wave of desperation flooded her; she fell forward over him clutching his still warm body to her own and buried her face in the nape of his neck. Her tears fell as deep in her chest, her young fragile heart crumbled.

They lay there, lovers locked in one last embrace oblivious to the cruel dark world around them.

***

They arrived with the wind, their horse's hooves soundless as the nine rode onto the square. Cloaks whipped and swirled about their shoulders in the growing storm as they swung down as one from their saddles and approached.

All nine wore masked golden helmets and were fully armoured and armed as men, but their garb did little to hide their femininity.

The horses nervously pawed the earth, unaccustomed as they were to the firm soil of Midgard below their hooves.

They strode silently into the wreckage of humanity which had been strewn by the battle and began the selection. The nine fanned out across the square as they progressed, stopping occasionally to reach out a hand to a fallen warrior.

As they did so the chosen warrior arose, leaving his broken body behind, an empty shell discarded on the ground. Without a word the chosen then slipped like wraiths back past fallen comrade and foe to wait by the nervous horses, while the Valkyrie continued their task.

Their passing went un-noticed; the only mortal eyes witness to their presence were the poor souls close to death; nearing the thin veil between this world and the next.

The first of the nine stopped once more and looked down at the two mortals lying in the mud at her feet. The poor girl was holding the fallen boy tight in her arms, rocking back and forth on her knees, keening as if soothing a babe in arms to sleep. Her tears fell freely; running from her face and spattering his tunic, as she stared down at the expressionless mask of the dead boy's face.

She stopped to ponder the scene before her, staying her hand for a moment. The emotions of the mortal world were not lost on her. To her eyes mortal love seemed fragile; all the more beautiful because of its briefness. These mortals lived and loved with death an ever-present spectre at their shoulder. They filled their short lives with friends, families and children, knowing that at any moment they must leave them all behind.

Was there ever a more pitiful sight than these two children of men lying before her? She sighed, the weight of her task heavy on her shoulders and held out a hand to welcome the fallen boy to Valhalla.

"Stop sister! Please!"

She looked up, shocked that anyone would dare interrupt her task. The woman stood before her barefoot and bloodied, her wet hair and clothing plastered to her pale shivering body. "Who are you, who dares address me so?"

The woman took a step towards her holding her hands out in front of her palms uppermost. "It's me dear sister, Thordys. Has it been so long that you have forgotten me?"

The valkyrie peered through the mask of her helm, her memory struggling to see through the years and the bruises decorating the woman's face.

Yes it was her indeed. "It has been an age sister. Rest assured you may be gone but you are quite surely not forgotten. Your folly is held up as an example to our younger sisters. Here once again we find you meddling in matters which are none of your concern." She turned away from Thordys, dismissing her to return to her task.

"Agata, this boy is very much my concern; I brought him kicking and screaming into this world and have stayed by his side ever since. He is dear to me sister, he is as near as it is possible to be my own son. I ask again for the love you once bore me, leave this boy behind?"

The valkyrie turned away from the dying boy once more. "So once again you place the needs of a mortal, above our duty to the All-father. Has your exile taught you nothing? Would you have me throw down my duty and join you living with these mortals, aimlessly wandering the lands of Midgard for eternity?"

Thordys sighed. "No sweet sister I would not share my fate with you, my path has been long and often lonely. The lives of men are all too short and what few friends I have made have been taken away from me all too soon. This boy is good sister, his life has been far too brief, allow him a little longer before you take him to the halls. Many have fallen this day, take another in his place. I will bear the blame, tell father I forced you; tell him what you like, what more can he do to me now?"

Agata removed her helmet and cradled it under her arm, the briefest of smiles flickered across her beautiful face. "I have missed you dear sister. Tell me was he worth it, the mortal you spared? Did his love make up for all that you lost?"

"If you're asking would I do it again? The answer is yes, my heart would not be denied, the years I spent with him were my best and my worst." She laid a hand on the valkyrie's shoulder. "Let me take this poor boy?"

"Very well, but be quick, do not let the others see!"

The valkyrie bent down and laid her hand on the boys injured abdomen, there was the briefest glow as the warmth of her fingertips spread into his body. His eyes flickered, blinking in the soft rain which had started to fall; there was a slight wheeze as his lungs lurched back into life. The girl holding him was so lost in her grief that she barely noticed the change.

Thordys turned to her sister. "Thank you Agata. I am forever in your debt."

"I know. Now hurry, get him away from this place before you are seen!" And with that the valkyrie replaced her helmet and returned to her duty.

Thordys tapped the young girl on the shoulder and she raised her head looking blankly up at the old woman. "We'd better get him somewhere warm and dry before he catches his death!"

"Leave me alone old woman, can't you see he's gone?"

"No, look girl, he breathes still. Help me get him up and we'll get him inside out of this rain." Thordys knelt down and pulled Finn's arm over her shoulder, urging Merryn to do the same. He hung limp like a rag-doll as they dragged him across the square his feet trailing behind him in the mud.

Thordys turned back as they reached the edge of the square; her sisters had completed their task and were mounting their horses. She fought the urge to wave one last time, how she longed to see Valhalla once more. "Farewell dear sisters." She whispered to the wind.

Chapter 33

Linus huddled in the corner of the small chicken coop, listening to the raindrops drumming on the loose planked roof. The chickens were gathered in the opposite corner of the small structure, clucking and eyeing their unwelcomed guest warily.

He had no idea how long he had been hiding there, but he was sure it hadn't been raining when he had lifted the narrow hatch and clambered in.

He had jammed himself into the far corner of the rickety structure and tried to calm his breathing, the angry chickens had just begun to calm down a little when he heard heavy booted feet running up the narrow lane.

Linus had held his breath and waited, sure that the footsteps would halt and that his hiding place would be easily discovered. But the footsteps passed by, clearly paying no heed to the back yard of the grimy hovel. All was quiet, apart from the low burbling of the indignant chickens.

The sunlight easily penetrated the poorly built coop, sending shafts of light across the dusty confines and illuminating the walls with bright narrow stripes. He had marked the stripes slow progress as the sun passed overhead. Or he had until the clouds had arrived destroying sharp relief and filling the coop with a diffused milky light. The rain had followed close behind the dark storm-clouds and now he could not be sure whether the storm was the cause of the gloom or if evening was drawing in.

The sharp smell of urine wafted up from his damp britches cutting through the heavy smell of chicken manure, but still he hid, motionless awaiting nightfall.

He had reasoned it out, it didn't matter which side had prevailed, either way he was dammed. If Raghnall had won the battle, he'd be sure to make an example of a coward like him. He'd watched him chase the first deserters, running them down from horseback. At that moment he'd have run too, but his quivering legs promised the venture little success.

If Raghnall had lost the battle his fate was just as bad, he'd been one of his men, coward or no, his fate was sealed. So he waited.

Come nightfall he'd be gone, out of this town and away, there must be paths out of the fjord, up into the high mountains. He'd put as much distance between himself and this hole of a town as possible, by dawn the next morning this place would be nothing but a distant memory.

His mind turned back once more to the battle, he had done nothing, absolutely nothing. His axe had hung limp and impotent in his hand as he just stood there watching them advance onto the beach; he had held up his shield to block the first deadly blow and then crumbled. His attacker had been dispatched by another of his fellow defenders as he cowered on his knees hiding in the shadow of his shield.

When he'd seen the rout begin he had been all too quick to join it. He had clambered up from the ground, axe and shield forgotten, abandoned on the ground. He tumbled into the town with the others, desperate to loose himself in its cluttered streets. How he had found his way to this foul sanctuary was anyone's guess.

He opened his eyes and saw with great relief that it was definitely getting darker; it would soon be time to leave.

What was that? He heard something; through the drumming rain. There it was again, drawing closer, soft slopping footsteps in the sticky mud. He tensed and held his breath, quite sure that his pounding heart would give the game away.

The footsteps stopped and the chickens began to fuss, how he longed to kick out at the stupid birds, but he didn't dare. The trapdoor to the coop opened suddenly and an arm reached in. He braced himself as the small fingers began fumbling blindly through the straw, clearly in search of an egg or two.

Finding nothing he heard the owner of the hand sigh and the door was yanked open a little wider. A small grubby head pushed into the coop and the hand continued to rummage further across the floor, a probing finger found his leather clad toe and stopped.

The little girls head snapped up and one pair of panicked eyes met another. Linus slowly lifted his index finger to his lips "Shuuuuush?"

***

The raucous din from the long-house went on far into the night. He saw them spilling out from the doors, slopping horns of his best ale and mead in hand. The local wenches had been all too quick to rush to the celebration, but he couldn't blame them for that, he had not been the most welcoming host of late and their only aim was survival, especially now that the balance of power had changed.

He tried to stretch his back a little which was nigh on impossible, trussed up as he was. They had tied his hands to his feet; which had made it easier to carry him by pole back to the fortress, like the carcass of some deer being brought home to butcher.

His ankles had then been secured to the bottom of a fence post within the pen he now shared with his pigs. No, he supposed that the pigs along with everything else he had owned were someone else's now.

Gods his back ached! The damp mud had soaked through his clothing hours ago and now the cold night air stole into his old bones. Whatever warmth he may have taken from the pigs was also denied him as they warily kept their distance from the human who still had the thick stench of death upon him.

The battle, if it was indeed worthy of the name, had been a farce. His men had been woefully outclassed; even his strongest warriors had struggled when they had been outflanked in the square. They had drawn into a smaller and smaller cluster as they were beset on all sides. He had known then that it was over and was almost relieved. He had fought on though; his death would not be bought cheaply.

His best men had fallen around him; they had dealt out more than their fair share of death that day, but they had fallen all the same, until at last he stood alone.

He lashed out at them over and over, with sword and boot alike but they held back refusing to engage him, refusing to strike him down. This was his fate, his destiny; he would die fighting bravely. Bards would sing of this day for years to come. He would not be denied his fate.

He began to shout insults at them, questioning their parentage, their manhood anything to goad them into action, he saw the anger flicker in their eyes but still they would not strike. They stood fast, an impassive circular wall confining him and his rage.

At last Magnus stepped forward. Yes this would serve; a worthy opponent at last. He was soiled with mud and gore and his long axe hung heavy in his hand. Raghnall raised his sword and hefted his shield to his shoulder, crouching in preparation for the duel.

But Magnus just stood there, his chest heaving. After a few moments he threw a small nod over Raghnall's shoulder and before he could turn he felt a dull thud as the cudgel cracked the back of his skull, then nothing.

He had come-to just as he was being carried in under his gates. By then the hard rain had already soaked him to the skin, he was unceremoniously dumped onto his back and the pole was withdrawn from between his ankles and wrists. His captors were enjoying their moment and rained down their laughter as well as a few well aimed boots and fists.

His imprisonment in the pig pen was not the last of the indignities thrust upon him, the stench of the pig-muck was added to by the addition of several buckets of night-soil tossed in his general direction. They had quickly become bored with hurling abuse, especially once the first barrel of mead had been tapped, so they left him there trussed up in the filth.

His ankles and wrists ached; the bonds were fastened so tightly he had lost feeling in his hands and feet hours ago. He had tried pulling at the ropes but that had just opened fresh cuts. His hands and feet were so closely tied that there was no possibility of using his teeth on the ropes. He had abandoned all hope of escape several hours ago.

That young whelp Harald had wandered over just before sundown. He had watched him approaching with the swagger of youth or was it just a little too much ale? He braced himself for another helping of abuse, but there had been none. Harald just stood there, silently contemplating the man in the mud. He fought the urge to hurl a little abuse of his own, but he was dammed if he would break the silence first.

After a few moments Harald raised his drinking horn in salute and with a rye shake of his head, he turned on his heel and sauntered back towards the celebration, without a word.

Raghnall's neck was aching with the effort of watching them celebrate. He was weary, so weary; he let his head drop forward onto his chest, closed his eyes and wished for death. Just like everyone else, death it seemed no longer heeded his command and refused the invitation, sending its inferior cousin sleep to visit him instead.

Chapter 34

Thordys had just finished kindling a small fire in the heavy field-stone hearth, when she returned to Finn's side. The girl with the tear streaked face just sat there staring down at the unconscious lad.

She looked around the room; it was obviously the home of some kind of trader, there were light crates and sacks stacked around the walls and fresh reeds strewn across the earthen floor. Their stay could not be a long one, the trader would most likely return in the morning when he was sure the battle had ended. He would be prepared for some disturbance and probably expecting a little of his stock to have vanished so there was no great harm in their being there overnight.

She found a small stone lamp and lit the wick from the fire, there wasn't much tallow left in the bowl but it would serve for the time being. The wick spluttered a little as she set the lamp down on the floor next to the boy.

Thordys flexed her aching fingers, the bones had healed swiftly as they always did, it did nothing to dull the pain though, she grabbed a burlap sack filled with some kind of grain and dragged it across the floor. "You Girl!" The girl looked up blankly. "Yes you! Raise his shoulders and we'll get this in underneath to support his head."

Merryn scrabbled across to the boy and did as requested. Once he had been lowered gently back onto the sack Thordys started to strip him of his clothing. "Go see if you can find some clean cloth, we'll need to dress his wounds."

Merryn returned a few moments later with what looked like one of the trader's shirts and handed it to the old woman. She looked down at Finn's naked torso, his pale body was battered, bruised and cut in various places, but worst of all was the blood oozing from the deep gash that had been left in his belly by the spear.

Thordys took the shirt, bit at the edge with her teeth and began tearing it into long strips. She handed the remainder of the shirt to Merryn. "I need strips like this, see? As many as you can manage."

Then she took a small bowl of water and began to wash the dried blood away, starting with the spear wound. Once it was clean she pushed the sides of the skin together with her fingers and sucked air through her teeth. "It'll mend, won't be pretty mind, but it'll mend."

She balled up a handful of the shirt material and pressed it onto the gash. With her free hand she reached over and took Merryn by the wrist. She pulled the girl's hand towards her and pushed it down to replace her own on top of the dressing. "Push down on the wound like this. I need to find needle and thread." Then she bustled off lamp in hand.

Merryn held the bandage firmly in place, she could feel Finn's chest rising and falling under her hands with each breath. The light from the hearth flickered across his soft face and for a moment she thought she saw a tiny smile pull at the corners of his mouth. His eyes were closed, deep in sleep now, not the cold dead eyes that had stared up at her in the rain but his eyes, he had returned. Her Finn. He was back. She fought the sudden urge to hold him, kiss him, feel his warm lips on hers again. She shook her head and dragged her thoughts back to the matter at hand.

She stared down at the bandage in her fists; the blood was seeping around the sides, not very much but enough to worry her just a little. She pushed a little harder and that seemed to stem the flow a little.

Thordys passed her the little lamp and knelt down on the earth floor. "Here, hold this close by. I'll need as much light as I can get." She carefully removed the dressing, gave the wound a thorough wipe and began to sew.

She pinched the sides of the cut together with the index finger and thumb of her left hand and used her right hand to wield the needle. "I found a whole reel of yarn tucked out the back, it's a bit thicker than I'd like but needs must. I never was much of a seamstress but I don't suppose he'll complain."

Once the wound was neatly closed with a line of eight knotted stitches, Thordys pulled Finn onto his back across her knee. The entry wound in his back was a little smaller than the gash to his front but the small pool of blood it had left on the floor was enough to make Merryn let out a small gasp.

"Don't worry girl, it looks worse than it is. He's plenty blood left inside him, that's what matters. Now come a bit closer with that lamp."

Once Thordys had stitched the wound, they spread Finn's wrecked tunic onto the ground and laid him down gently on top. "That should keep him up off the cold floor. Now go see if you can find a blanket, I think I saw a small bedroom out the back."

Merryn found a small low ceilinged room at the back of the building, there was a thick hay-stuffed mattress in the corner, a bit too bulky to drag to the hearth though. She grabbed the two rough woollen blankets from the bed and made her way back to the hearth.

When she got there she found Thordys gently stroking Finn's cheek and softly humming a low tune. The tender moment caught Merryn by surprise and she found herself standing motionless staring. The old woman looked up with a start. "Don't just stand there girl, bring those blankets here."

They laid one of the blankets over the sleeping boy, tucking the edges under to keep out any draughts. Thordys turned to the hearth and threw a fresh log onto the fire. "That's about as much as we can do. We'll see how he fares in the morning."

She picked up the second blanket and gently draped it across Merryn's shoulders. "It's cold and dark outside girl; you'd better go fetch your skin before someone else finds it."

Thordys saw the shocked expression on the girls face; raised an eyebrow and smiled. "I know a selkie when I see one. You're not the first of your kind I've had the pleasure of meeting." She nodded down to her sleeping patient. "You love him, don't you?"

The words caught in Merryn's throat, leaving her open mouthed like a fish drowning on air. She clutched the blanket tighter around her shoulders, suddenly quite cold and nodded.

Thordys sighed. "That's what I was afraid of." She knelt down by her patient and made a small adjustment to the blanket, gently smoothing it around his chin. "I suppose he's all grown up now, has the scars to prove it. Fat lot of good I did protecting him anyway."

With sudden realisation Merryn knelt down by the old woman "You're Thora, aren't you?"

Thordys didn't raise her eyes from the sleeping boy, she smiled a little at the familiarity of the girls strange accent. "Yes, there's those that call me by that name. He called me Granny."

The girl lifted her blanket-draped arm like a wing and shared the shelter of the woollen blanket with the old woman. "He talks a lot about you, you know? He loves you very much."

"Much good that did him! I was supposed to watch over him, keep him safe, not too much to ask was it? Yet here he lies, only just back from deaths door." She fumbled around in what remained of the tunic Finn lay upon and removed a small round stone from the hem of the collar. "And as for this pointless token, it was supposed to protect him."

Merryn plucked the small red stone from her palm and watched the fire flicker on its polished surface. "What was it intended to protect him from?"

The old woman smiled at the girl. "You mostly." She said with a laugh.

She stood up from under the blanket to put another log onto the fire. "I meant what I said about that skin of yours, you'd best go collect it sharpish. If I saw you scuttling out from under that jetty there's a good chance someone else did too."

Merryn bent over and planted a small kiss on Finn's sleeping forehead and he stirred a little. Thordys placed a gentle hand on her shoulder. "No time for that now child, hurry. Stick to the shadows and come back quickly. I'll see what food I can find in this hovel."

Thordys watched her run over to the door and lift the latch, tugging the blanket close around her shoulders with her free hand. "Your name child? Before you go."

The girl turned, bright eyes glinting through her dark tresses "It's Merryn." And with that she slipped out into the night pulling the heavy door shut behind her.

Chapter 35

Dawn finally broke over the mountains, and Raghnall watched the grim shadows slowly retreating from the courtyard. He had shivered most of the night in the thick oozing mud, his head mired in half remembered whispers, longing for the sun's warming rays on his back. He was determined he would savour this dawn; it would most likely be his last after all.

His back had ceased its incessant ache sometime in the small hours of the morning; it had finally given up all protest against this contorted posture and allowed him to get a little rest. He had stopped worrying about his hands and feet some hours before that, figuring that the numbness was actually proving to be a blessing. For the first time in years he was no longer plagued by the pain from his burns, how ironic that at this late stage he had discovered his apothecarie's secret ingredient, pig muck!

The old faces had visited themselves upon him one by one in the night. His father's cheerless stare, wordlessly informing him yet again of the disappointment he felt. The soft smile of his little sister, trying to soothe him as once again he wept himself to sleep despite the stinging pain left in his buttocks by fathers lash.

No matter how he tried he never could remember his mother's face, he could smell her skin though, lavender and honey. He had often been told how fair she had been but his only real memory of her now was of soft skin and flaxen hair.

Then the other faces came to visit, the cold grey faces, contorted in pain, pain that he had doled out time and again. Their names were lost to him, too numerous for anyone to remember really but they blamed him for that aswell. He should remember them. He had taken all they possessed, all that they had and all that they would ever be, the odd one had left their mark upon him too, writ indelibly upon his body in cold steel but he would join them soon enough and they delighted in that.

Then last of all was the inferno, bright, searing, scourging fire, the heat touching his being down to the very bones and beyond. Always the dragon-fire; it had encroached on his sleeping moments for years and would not be forgotten, not even now, so close to the end.

Across the yard they began to awake, several hundred of them with headaches to match his own, theirs however far more pleasurably gained. They emerged from the smoky longhouses, in various states of undress and disarray stretching in the morning sun. They could afford to be languid today, their work was done and everything he had wrought for himself over the years was theirs now.

Down at the gatehouse he watched as a small group of men were brought in under guard from the town. Their hands were bound and he could see that their faces were bruised and blackened even from so far off. His men he supposed, hunted down after the rout, well the fact that they were still breathing was testament to their cowardice. Damn them all, they'd have been better off had they died in battle, they'd have had a warm welcome in Valhalla at least.

He watched as the men, probably about twenty in all were herded into a small pen; like sheep and instructed to sit. They did as they were asked and he dragged his eyes away, ashamed to have once regarded these curs as his.

***

Finn awoke to the smell of wood-smoke and oatmeal. He slowly opened his sticky eyes and struggled to pick out the detail of the dimly lit room. After a few moments his eyes managed to focus on the smoke-blackened roof beams and thatch high above and he could feel rough-spun wool scratching against his chin.

He cast his eyes about the space but struggling to see anything else in the gloom; he turned his head a little to the left, a movement he immediately regretted as a sharp spear of pain shot down his neck towards his lower back. He gritted his teeth, fearful of crying out as he was still unsure exactly where he was.

He righted his head and decided against moving it to any position other than straight ahead. Then he tried to sit up from the half lying position he found himself in. He slid his elbows up a little, which to his great surprise didn't hurt too badly, then he tensed his stomach muscles in preparation for sitting up. That turned out to be a worse mistake than turning his head had been. There was a sudden ripping ache through the centre of his body and he let fly a dull moan as his body slumped limply back into its previous position on the floor. He passed out once more, slipping into a deep foggy slumber.

Thordys had heard his groan and shuffled over to him from the hearth; Merryn too rushed to his side and cast the old woman a questioning look. Thordys ignored the girl and felt Finn's forehead with the back of her hand, satisfied she lifted the blanket and checked the dressing of the spear wound. There was a little seepage of blood but that was to be expected, she bent low to sniff the dressing and finding all in order she gently lowered the blanket back down.

Merryn still wore a worried frown. "Well?" she said directing the question at Thordys.

The old woman nodded her head slightly. "He'll be fine, I think he just came round a little, probably tried to move or something stupid like that. He always was a pig headed lad."

Merryn looked down at the sleeping boy. "We shouldn't move him, it's too dangerous. We should keep him here until he's recovered."

The old lady continued stirring the small pot of oatmeal "And what do you suggest we do when the owner of this fine establishment returns? He'll expect full payment for board and lodgings. Unless that skin of yours has pockets I'm unaware of, you're worth just about as little as I am."

Merryn let out a deep sigh, there was no faulting the logic of the old woman's argument. "What's the big plan then?" She asked trying to keep any trace of sarcasm from her question.

Thordys handed her a small wooden bowl filled with a rather disturbing looking grey sludge. She took the bowl and cast a suspicious eye over the contents. "Don't look too closely, just eat it! It's the best I could come up with given the circumstances and limited ingredients."

She took her own bowl and perched herself on the end of a low crate. "The way I see it is this, our only real option for getting out of here is by boat. I've been here before and trying to walk ourselves out over the mountains would be difficult at best."

She took a mouthful of the grey slop and nodded in Finn's general direction. "Given the lad's injuries it's not an option. Even if we could avoid any dealings with the mountain trolls, he'd be too weak for the steeper sections of the climb."

Merryn was just going to ask for a little more information about these trolls when Thordys cut into her train of thought. "So like I said, the sea's the best option. Don't suppose you could shed any light on how the boy got way over here in the first place? I'm pretty sure I was the only prisoner taken from the village."

Merryn took in a large mouthful of the gruel. Her intention was to gain a little thinking time but she immediately regretted having put the substance into her mouth as the tasteless sticky gloop gummed up her tongue. She worked the porridge around her mouth, tried to ignore Thordys' expectant stare and decide just how much of the story to tell the old woman. When she'd managed to swallow and rid her mouth of the disgusting mouthful she began the tale.

She may have abridged the story a little, she left out a lot of what had happened between them on the beach in order to protect her own modesty and shield Finn from any further anger, but the important facts were all there.

Thordys sat there impassive, listening to the girl's tale. She struggled to keep her face a calm mask, fighting to hold back the emotion she felt. How could the village have cast him out like that? They obviously had no idea of Linus' part in the raid. They probably thought that Linus had perished that night, caught inside one of the houses and burned with the others. Did they really think that anything Finn could have done would have prevented what had happened? At most he would have gained them five minutes head start on the raiders, not enough time, not when you were dealing with Raghnall.

She let the girl finish her tale and then sat quietly for a moment or two digesting the facts. "So if I'm right we at least have Finns boat. With a bit of luck it's still tethered to the back of that long-ship."

Thordys placed her empty bowl on the floor and crossed to the door, she opened it just a crack and peered out. "It's getting bright; you have a look around and grab what you can from in here, anything that you think would be useful. I'll go and see if I can liberate a wheelbarrow or something."

With that she stepped out through the door, closing it silently behind her.

Chapter 36

Linus squatted in the mud with the others, he looked around at the dejected, bruised and battered faces but seeing none he recognised he let his eyes fall back down to the ground.

That little brat had screamed her bloody lungs out last night, sending the nervous chickens flapping all around the inside of the coop. By the time he had squirmed his way out of the hatch her entire family had rushed to her aid, having hastily armed themselves with whatever they had found close at hand.

They had lashed out at him with besom and boot, screaming voices accusing him of chicken theft among other heinous crimes. He had curled tight into a ball until the blows eventually came to an end, after a few assault free moments he risked raising his head and found that someone had gone to fetch *help* in the form of what looked like a group of warriors.

He had nervously raised himself into a sitting position under the watchful eyes of about ten of the townsfolk who surrounded him just itching for the slightest excuse to restart his thrashing.

He could see the girl who'd found him standing just outside the gate; she spent a few minutes speaking to the group of heavily armed men, before pointing at him.

The crowd had parted to allow the patrol access to the prisoner; it was during the next few long moments of his life that Linus realised that the "beating" he had received from the townsfolk on being found by the child was actually nothing of the sort. That had been just a delightful first course to wet his appetite, compared to the generous helping of pain that was served up by the patrol. Mercifully he had passed out just a few seconds after he'd heard the sickening crack of his jaw braking.

He still had the tinny taste of blood in his mouth this morning as he sat there in the muddy courtyard. He gingerly ran his tongue around his mouth, he had lost at least three teeth and the very idea of opening his mouth sent shards of pain rushing up the left side of his face.

Across the courtyard he could see a smith stoking the fire in his forge, the coals were beginning to glow white-hot as his apprentice hauled at the long handle of the bellows. The battle was over and he had found himself on the loosing side. Still as he'd already reasoned out there really couldn't have been a winning side for him.

The smith raked the coals sending showers of bright sparks curling into the morning air. He stared intently at the forge before turning and nodding to the guards. The guard in question was a hulking brute of a man, with sharp flinty eyes peering out from just above a huge set of whiskers. He stomped over to where Linus sat and swiftly yanked him to his feet by the scruff of the neck.

Linus staggered forward a few steps before he caught his balance and stood as upright as he could manage considering the manner in which his hands were firmly bound behind his back. The sudden change in posture sent sharp needles of pain coursing through his body, he would have cried out if he had been able to open his mouth to do so. As it was he tried desperately not to bear down on his teeth for fear of loosening what precious few he had left.

The guard pulled him the short distance across the courtyard to the smithy. He could only imagine what new horror awaited him there, apart from the obvious red hot metal. His mind raced with thoughts of what heated implement may soon be used upon his poor battered body, tongs, spikes or even a branding iron, all were a distinct possibility. He felt a cold sweat break out across his body and the world around him started to become a little blurred.

Before he had the chance to pass out they had reached the smithy, where he was forced into a sitting position on the floor with his back to the Smith's anvil. He felt the cold hard metal of the anvil against the nape of his neck and shivered despite himself. He closed his eyes and waited for the inevitable blow, as executions went he found himself woefully poorly informed.

As he sat there awaiting the heavy impact of, he knew not what, he heard a metallic rattle and felt cold steel being clamped around his skinny neck. He opened his eyes and desperately craned his neck to look down to try to identify the implement of torture.

"Oi!, keep still." The guard shouted as he took up a standing position in front of Linus and grabbed a firm hold of his face with both hands. This did nothing to soothe his injured jaw and he felt hot tears well in his eyes as he screwed them tight shut and tried to block out the pain and panic rising in his chest.

He heard the Smith slide the heated rivet into the clasp in the rear of his iron collar and smelled the burning hair from contact with the white hot metal. Three sharp strikes from the Smith's hammer were all it took to form the rivet, locking the collar in place and sealing his fate as a Thrall.

He was roughly yanked back to his feet, knocking the heavy collar forward and scorching the back of his neck with the hot iron. The iron felt rough and heavy about his neck, rattling on his bruised collarbone as he was marched out of the smithy to clear the way for the next prisoner.

A vast wave of relief flooded over him, he was alive, sore, broken and smelling of piss, but alive, and that was all that mattered in the end. He was escorted across the courtyard, past the long-house he had so briefly called home; to a small pen which if he remembered rightly had recently been home to a large herd of goats. The pen was already packed full of other bruised and freshly "collared" men. They shuffled apart, grudgingly making room for him to sit in the mud.

A thousand questions rattled through his aching head, although looking around at his companion's faces he quickly thought better of attempting conversation. He would just have to take each moment as it came.

***

Thordys surprised herself with the relief that she felt on seeing the little boat; bobbing there, safely tied up at the end of the jetty.

Its low squat shape betrayed its origin, it could only be from Bruaan, in all her travels she had never seen boats made so obviously for one purpose. They were broad in the beam, squat and drew little water; they bobbed like empty nut-shells on the surface of the sea. They were almost impossible to capsize and easy to drag across the shingle up onto the beach. Most importantly they could safely cope with the weight and drag of the huge sun-fish that returned to bask in the warm water close to the shore each summer.

She ducked her head back behind the corner and strolled as carelessly as she could manage back to where Merryn stood waiting with the long handbarrow she had borrowed.

The girl stopped fussing with the blanket they had used to cover Finn and raised her head questioningly. "Well?"

Thordys gave the girl her most reassuring smile. "All's well, they've tied the wee boat up at the end of the jetty. From what I could see it seems to be in good order. There's a bit of hustle and bustle along the shore, looks like they've had a busy morning." She lowered her gaze down toward the barrow. "How is the patient?"

There was no hiding the worry, writ plain across the girls face. "He's still sleeping. I thought he'd have woken by now!"

Thordys reached out and gently lifted her chin. "It's probably best he stays asleep for now. Come on lets shake a leg, I'll be happier when we're well away from here."

With that she took a firm grip on the handles of the barrow and pushed it out onto the dockside. She turned to coach Merryn as she walked. "Keep your head down and try to look miserable. It shouldn't be too much of a problem."

The two women slowly trundled the barrow across the track and onto the wooden jetty. The men working at the dockside barely spared them a second glance as they busied themselves landing and unloading the numerous long-ships which were now moored either side of the long wooden jetty.

All of the ships used in the assault on the beach had been brought safely to the dockside, the other ships which had been left behind in the neighbouring fjord had also now made landfall in Holfstadir. The ships were packed in so tightly that Thordys reckoned that she could probably run an entire lap of the harbour on their decks without getting her feet wet.

Her musings were brought to an abrupt halt by a rough voice. "Oi, you two, what you got there?" Thordys looked up to see a rather small man in his fifties, squinting at them from the prow of the nearest ship.

Before she could answer the man hopped effortlessly onto the jetty and strutted towards them. "Miserable, remember?" She whispered to the girl.

Thordys slowly raised her head a little, the man was a might shorter that she was, he sported a rather wispy red beard which was gathered into two braids either side of what seemed to be a rather pointy chin.

She presented the man with the most wretched expression she could muster and sighed. "Ours is a most upsetting burden my lord, my only grandson; more dead than alive, he may not last the day."

Merryn let out a small sob at the last comment and Thordys smiled inwardly, the girl was playing her part well.

The little man bent over the barrow and pulled back the blanket a little; he squinted down at Finn's sleeping face and nodded his head. "He was telling the truth then?"

Thordys did nothing to hide her surprise. "You knew him?"

The man straightened up and nodded. "Yep, we came across him on the way here. The fool was miles out at sea in that little tub." The man pointed a stubby thumb over his shoulder. "Said he was on the way to rescue his Grand-mother. I just thought his words were empty wind!"

Thordys let the smallest of smiles creep onto her face. "He did his best and all but died for his troubles. Either way I'd like to try and get him home; his mother'd never forgive me if I left him here."

He scratched his head a little and shrugged. "You can be proud of the lad; he fought well, kept his nerve even in the middle of it all. You planning taking him back home in that little boat?"

Thordys gave the man a small nod and said nothing in an attempt to hide the desperation she felt rising in her chest. She could of course just thump the little red-headed pest and make a break for the boat, but she knew that before they'd reached the end of the jetty both of their backs would be well feathered with arrows.

The small man suddenly about-turned towards Finn's boat and set off at a trot. "Come on then I'll help you get him safely aboard, if we're quick about it you'll catch the tide."

Chapter 37

Linus and the others had been herded out through the gatehouse and down into the town. He had spent the past hour working in group of ten; all iron-collared alike. They had been tasked with clearing the dead. It was heavy work hefting the fallen men up from the muddy ground and onto the large cart; he now understood the meaning of the old term dead weight.

Once the cart was well laden they followed as it slowly wound its way back uphill to the meadow behind the fortress. As they rounded the side of the stockade they found that another group of thralls had been put to work digging a large hole in the ground. They spent the next half hour un-loading the cart and filling the large grave with their gruesome cargo. His fingers clawed for purchase against the cold hard flesh as each of the corpses, frozen by death, tumbled into the deep pit. By the time they had emptied the cart his hands and clothes were greasy with blood and grime and his nose was filled with the fetid stench of decay.

Once the cart was empty they were loaded onto the back and allowed to sit for a few minutes rest as the cart was driven back down to the market square where the worst of the fighting had taken place. He was so tired that it took several minutes for him to realise why the bottom of the cart felt damp.

As they trundled down the hill he saw that most of the townsfolk had returned to their homes. The occasional face stared out at them as they passed, he was unsure whether it was anger or revulsion he saw in their eyes.

It took four trips up and down through the streets to clear the square. When the cart rolled back onto the square after the last trip up the hill he saw that a large bonfire was taking shape. Before he had time to search out a drink of water; he and his companions had been pressed to the new task of stacking the bonfire.

All manner of timber was passed from hand to hand along the line towards the top of the growing pile. Some of the wood was cut and squared and had clearly been foraged from broken buildings or ships, the odd piece was already blackened like charcoal and stained his already grimy fingers and clothes black.

By midday the bonfire stood so tall that a set of ladders had been fetched to help pile the last of the remaining wood on top. Once the job was finished he found himself being herded with the others to the side of the square where he was dolled out a helping of thin broth and a chunk of black rye bread. He scuttled over to the others, planted his bony backside on the ground and began to eat.

He quickly found that if he soaked the stodgy bread in the broth for long enough he was able to let it slip down his throat without having to trouble his broken jaw with chewing. Once the bread was done he lifted the bowl to his mouth and felt the warm broth trickle down his throat into his hollow stomach. He gently dabbed at the corners of his mouth with his grubby sleeve, put down the bowl and with weary eyes looked up to survey the mornings work. It would be quite a blaze, visible for miles; they were clearly planning quite a celebration.

***

Once they had laid Finn gently in the bow of the boat and covered him with a blanket, the wee man helped Thordys and Merryn lift the bits and pieces they had pilfered from the trader's stores on board.

He handed the blankets down from the jetty along with the small selection of dried fish and grain.

Thordys stowed their meagre provisions as best she could under the narrow bench at the tiller, figuring that it should provide some shelter from sea spray and stop the grain getting too damp.

As she reached up to take the last bundle, the man caught her eye and nodded his head towards the bow where Merryn knelt next to the boy. "Are you sure she's fit for the journey? Looks like she could use a few days rest and some fattening up before you set out."

Thordys turned her head a little. "Would that we could stay a little longer, she will have to be strong, we both will. The boy must be laid to rest at home, it is our way."

He gave a tiny nod and sucked a little air in through his teeth "Aye………aye. Well you're clearly set, pity though, you'll miss all the fun this afternoon."

Ignoring the implicit invite as best she could, Thordys safely stowed the last bundle, containing among other things the girl's precious seal-skin under the bench. "Thank you for all of you help sir, it would have been a devil of a job getting him on board ourselves. May I ask your name, so I can pass it on to the boy if he wakes?"

The man smiled. "They call me Leiff, he'll remember my piss-poor cooking if nothing else. Sure I can't persuade you to stay a while longer?" He asked hopefully.

When he saw he was wasting his time he bent to unwind the mooring rope before passing it to Thordys and pushing the boat away from the jetty with a stiff shove of his boot. "Fair winds and calm seas missus!"

Thordys dropped the stubby oars into their oarlocks and pulled hard, away from the jetty and out into the fjord. She saw Leiff raise a hand and wave before he turned and strolled back towards the shore.

Once she had rowed the little tub out into the middle of the channel and had tugged it around to face the right direction she stowed the oars and pulled the rope to raise the small sail. There was a usable breeze, she thought. What with that and the outgoing tide they should make reasonable headway.

She turned to Merryn. "Don't just sit there mooning like some fool, get over here and take the tiller. The boy will be fine he just needs to rest."

The girl clambered across the deck on all fours nervously bracing herself against the roll of the little boat as the breeze caught the sail.

Thordys let out a little laugh. "Ha! You've never been on a boat before have you? I should have known, sorry. Here, sit there and brace your back against the gunwale. Now keep your eyes out there on the horizon, I'll take the tiller for a while, you'll get to like the movement once you get used to it."

Merryn did as instructed and sat grey faced, staring at the passing shoreline. "The sea feels much different up here on top."

Thordys smiled at the girl, she looked so very young and fragile sitting there in her stolen rags. "Yes I suppose it must feel quite odd. I've never given it much thought. But then I've never really spent too much time down below, not if I could help it anyway."

***

By the time they came for him the sun was low in the sky, it had been the best of days, a good day, bright and dry. He had enjoyed feeling the sun on his back; even with his arse in the mud. Still all good things must end, who knew what tomorrow would bring and indeed who cared, there would be no tomorrow for him. There was only now, the present.

He felt each moment. Every fibre of his being felt alive; he had not felt so alive in years. In recent years, even in the heat of battle he had felt so little, no rush of emotion, no nervous energy, no fear, it had all faded over time. So slowly, he had barely noticed as each emotion slipped quietly away from the party, leaving him alone and numb.

It was the certainty of it all, he knew that now, he had known that he could not be defeated; his will was strong, too strong. He hadn't feared death because it had not even featured in his mind as a remote possibility, whereas it was a certainty now.

He would continue the charade though; act out the part of the glorious chief, all-powerful, spirit undefeated, even now at the end.

Heavy hands pulled him to his feet clearing his bound wrists from the post and the cords binding his feet were cut. His legs fell, heavy and lifeless below his body as he was propped up on the shoulders of his jailers. His leaden feet ached; starved of blood for so long he felt them pound as the life-giving liquid trickled back downhill.

He was spared the indignity of staggering like a toddler thankfully as he was dragged roughly out of the pig-pen and across the courtyard towards the gatehouse. By the time they reached the gate enough of his strength had returned that he was able to bear his own weight and as long as he leaned on his escort a little he was able to maintain what little dignity he had left, despite the stench of pig muck.

Harald, Magnus and the other Jarls were waiting for him at the gate. They were armed and helmed as if for battle and he quickly realised that his death was clearly to be a public event.

Harald removed his helmet. "I trust that your accommodation is to your liking? I must say that you have been a most gracious host, I have never seen a larder quite so well stocked."

He flashed Harald his most sarcastic smile "I'm glad you've all been enjoying your stay. Is there a little mead to spare? I'd like to wet my whistle before the show."

"We'll have our fill of your mead when this day is over. Now; enough of the pleasantries, lets not keep the good people waiting." Harald quickly tied a length of cord to the ropes binding his wrists and handed the loose end to Magnus.

The gates swung open and he was sure he saw a glimmer of a smile through the thick beard on Magnus' face as he gave a sharp tug on the cord and dragged him out into the road. They really had made an effort, he was surrounded on all sides by armed men and the whole party was lead by a drummer banging out a solemn rhythm.

He was glad of the protection if truth be told; it wouldn't do for some angry idiot with a knife to spoil the show and by the look of the crowd there were more angry idiots present than usual. The street was lined with people, some stared blankly almost confused at the scene before them and others yelled rather unimaginative obscenities as he passed.

As they rounded the first corner and turned downhill towards the market square Magnus edged close and bent down to whisper in his ear. "We've arranged a special surprise for you."

He looked up at the big man questioningly, but all he received in reply was a low chuckle which could barely be heard over the angry shouts of the mob.

The crowd grew in numbers as they approached the middle of the town, buoyed by the ones who had fallen into line behind. The noise was deafening now, he kept his eyes down carefully watching the rutted road, wouldn't do to stumble now, not in front of them all.

As they turned the last corner into the market square he glanced up and immediately wished he hadn't. There, out past the guards, out past the angry faces baying for his blood, in the middle of the square was his end.

There could be no mistaking the huge stack of timber, it was executioner and funeral pyre combined. He felt the familiar surge of heat engulf the left side of his body as the dragon-scarred tissue and damaged nerves called out; as if in recognition of an old friend waiting in the crowd. The sudden jolt made him stumble for the first time; he bit down hard on his lip fighting the urge to scream out in pain as he tumbled forward onto the cool earth.

He lay there curled like a baby, the calm façade lost as panic overwhelmed him completely. He could barely hear the roar of the crowd now, drowned out as it was by the surge of the blood pounding in his ears.

It was too late he was lost; there was no dignity to be salvaged here.

He was pulled to his feet once more, wriggling and squirming like a worm as hard fingers pressed into the tortured skin of his left arm. He heard screaming, shrill and primal like a snared rabbit struggling, pulling desperately to break free from the ever tightening cord. A small fragment of his mind recognised the scream as his own, but went unheeded, ignored completely, as the remainder of his consciousness tried to flee his doomed carcass.

Kicking and thrashing, he was more dragged than led to the pyre in the centre of the square. The crowd fell silent, their jeering chants redundant, shamed as they were by the disintegrating man before them.

Once on top of the structure he felt his knees kicked out from beneath him and he crumpled. His hands were hastily bound behind his back and then made fast to his ankles. His head slumped forward onto his chest as he knelt there like a supplicant before the temple, borne upward on a mountain of half burned wreckage.

His body was calm now; at the end, drained and exhausted by panic. He raised his head and stared out at the gathered townsfolk, blinking away salt tears as he fought to slow his breathing. Was that pity he saw out there in their eyes? Well, what was one more insult now?

The crowd were quickly blotted out by the rising smoke, swirled into crests and waves by the breeze as it rose like a blanket around him. The acrid fumes clawed at the back of his throat, scalding his lungs and bringing yet more tears to his stinging eyes. He jerked forward wracked by coughing as his body fought to clear the invading smoke from his chest.

He felt a single brief flicker of heat slap his face like a scorned lover. The smell of singed beard flickered briefly in his nose and he found that his eyelids had been fused closed by the flame.

His last few breaths were ragged and pitiful things, as the smoke crept into every nook and cranny, poisoning what little air remained within him. How stupid he had been all this time; so terrified of the scourging flames and yet dead, long before he felt their warm caress.

The crowd stood by, watching silently as the tall plume of smoke rose curling high into the evening sky.

Chapter 38

Their progress had been too slow for her liking, as they coasted along the fjord and out to sea pushed along by tide and the lazy breeze.

The watch posts dotted along the shore which had been so well manned only days ago were now deserted, smoke still rising lazily from one or two of the small huts on the shore where the watchmen had obviously been caught napping. She gave silent thanks that they were too far out in the channel to clearly see the fate that had befallen the occupants; the girl had seen quite enough bloodshed lately.

Little by little, Meryn began to relax as she grew accustomed to the gentle motion of the boat on the water. The strain of the past few weeks seemed to catch up with her all at once and she was quickly rocked to sleep, safe now, head tucked into her chest. Thordys shuffled along the narrow bench and gently pulled a blanket up around the girl's shoulders as best she could with one hand on the tiller.

She checked the sail once more and then stared back down the narrow fjord towards Holfstadir. At first she had expected to see at least one of the longships chasing them down, but the further away they got; the more she relaxed.

She had spotted the plume of thick smoke rising from the town about an hour or two ago. It brought her a little relief; they were obviously far too preoccupied to worry about their little boat.

She couldn't be entirely sure of the purpose of the fire and at first she feared that they had put the whole town to flame. After a short time though, when she noticed that the column of smoke hadn't grown any thicker, she guessed that it had to be a bonfire, that or a funeral pyre.

Either way the sun would soon set and the mead and ale would soon be flowing. Thankfully they would be in no fit state for very much until morning and by then she hoped to be well out to sea and forgotten, about as safe as they were likely to get.

The boy lay there, in the bow of the ship, face just visible poking out of the blankets, he hadn't stirred since they'd set out. That was good, the longer he stayed asleep the better, it would give his wounds a good start along the healing process. He was sure to have a lot of questions for them when he woke.

***

When the sun slowly breached the horizon the next morning they were almost out of sight of land. Thordys still sat at the tiller, she was cold, even under her blanket the night air had been chill. The last couple of hours, just as the sky had begun to lighten and day approached had been coldest as the damp sea air seeped into her bones.

She looked over her left shoulder at the retreating mountains and checked their heading before the stars were completely blotted out by day. It had been many years since she had been at the helm but the stars above were like old friends to her. No matter where she wandered during her long exile they had always been there; high above watching over her.

The two youngsters hadn't moved all night, she was envious at first but deep down she knew that even if she were able to leave the helm there was very little chance of sleep for her tonight. Her mind was still racing, replaying the events of the past few days over and over.

Things had changed completely; there was no going back. She would have to be honest with the boy, tell him the truth and hope that he was understanding and just a little forgiving. She had most likely lost him completely now in any case.

The girl began to stir from slumber with a low grumble as the dawn light reached her face. She opened her eyes slowly and stared warily over at the old woman for a moment, her eyes softened just a little and she sat up letting the blanket fall from her shoulders. She reached underneath the bench and her slim fingers touched on the small bundle containing her skin. Her fingers gently stroked the package for an instant before she sat back reassured and let out a small sigh.

Thordys set aside her misgivings and smiled over at the girl. "Good morning, sleep well?"

The girl rubbed her eyes with the back of her knuckles. "Better than I thought I would. How long have I been asleep?"

"Just overnight, you were clearly in need of a good rest." Thordys said reassuringly.

Merryn sat up and nodded over towards the bow where Finn lay sleeping. "Has he woken yet?"

The old woman frowned a little despite herself. "No; not yet, can you take the tiller for a little while? I'll go check on him and see what I can fix for breakfast."

The girl shuffled onto the bench and took hold of the tiller trying her best to copy the posture she'd seen adopted by the old woman.

Thordys gently helped her position her arm and fingers correctly around the tiller. "There, just like that. Keep the rising sun over your left shoulder and keep one eye on the sail, if it starts to sag then give me a shout."

Thordys clambered up towards the bow bracing herself against the roll of the boat and ducking her head underneath the crackling sail as she went. She knelt down by the boy, he was sleeping soundly and his colour seemed good. She gently drew back the blanket and seeing that there was no fresh blood on the dressing she tucked him back in gently.

Once she'd made her way back to the stern, she and the girl shared a sparse meal of stale bread and water, barely a word passing between them as they chewed on the tough crusts.

The next two days passed just the same, they took turns on the tiller while the other rested or slept, Finn didn't stir at all. At first conversation was sparse and stilted between them but as, time passed things grew easier. They became familiar with each others habits and much to her surprise Thordys found that Merryn was actually quite a likeable girl with a quick wit and a truly lovely singing voice.

The sea miles slowly passed as little by little they made their way steadily southward. On the second day the wind shifted a little to the west, much to Thordys' disgust, which meant a long day spent tacking a wide zig-zagging course in order to continue their southerly progress. Merryn soon got used to the procedure and after one or two sloppy turns; they were quickly able to work together to get the sail re-set and continue their course without too much difficulty.

About midday on the third day at sea Finn woke.

Thordys had been staring absentmindedly at the horizon when he mumbled loudly in his sleep. It seemed to wake the whole boat with a start.

Both Merryn and the old woman's eyes darted quickly to the boy, then to each other. Thordys signalled with a look and Merryn immediately took over the tiller while the old woman scuttled forward to tend to the lad.

His eyes were open but strangely glazed. He looked questioningly at her and opened his mouth like a fish gasping for air. He worked his tongue around the inside of his dry mouth and tried again, his voice croaky and little more than a whisper. "Where am I?"

She leaned in close, cradling his head and squeezed a damp cloth over his mouth letting droplets of water seep down onto his lips and tongue. "Easy now, easy, just relax everything is going to be fine."

He slowly worked the moisture around his parched mouth and tried again. "Is that you Granny? Where?…….. How?……."

She smiled at the lad. "You just ease up there; we're a long way out at sea, we're safe now, just you, me and young Merryn."

She saw the startled look in his eye and went on as reassuringly as she could. "Yes, I know all about her now, don't fret. Believe it or not I actually like the girl. Now you just take a minute or two to get your head straight, we've a few days sailing ahead of us yet, there'll be plenty of time to talk through this whole mess."

She leaned forward and slid her hands underneath his armpits, and then she gently eased him upwards so that he could lean his back against the bowsprit in a sitting position. It was the first time in days he'd been upright and his head swum a little as he struggled to support it on his neck and tried to ignore the dull ache in his belly. "There, you'll be able to see much better now."

His eyes searched the little boat; there she was, just visible past the curve of the sail, he could see her, Merryn, his Merryn; sitting in the rear of the boat one arm cradling the tiller. A smile crept onto his lips unbidden and her face lit up as their eyes met and she smiled back at him. Words were superfluous.

He was alive, alive despite it all. She was there, she still loved him, he could feel it. He sat there for a few minutes, just staring at her taking in every detail of her. Slowly he realised that this was the first time he had ever seen her in full daylight, and she was clothed.

Before very long his eyes grew heavy, and he drifted back into a contented slumber. All would be well now, he just knew it.

Chapter 39

As the dawns grey light lifted the dark shroud from the world once again, Finn awoke to find that both Merryn and Granny were awake and busy preparing a meagre breakfast. The little boat was rocking gently in a slight swell and the overcast sky gave the morning light a milky quality.

He craned his head around and looked out toward the southern horizon. He squinted as he tried to differentiate the low clouds from what appeared to be grey hills clustering on the edge of the watery world.

Merryn delivered a small bowl of thin grey sludge and a small wooden spoon with a smile. He smiled back and stifled a groan as he tried to ignore the aches and pains of his waking body and lever himself into a more upright position against the gunwale.

She hunkered down beside him and the tips of her toes touched his briefly sending a tickle up his shins, she kissed him delicately on the lips and he felt her mouth shift into a smile as she did so. "Did you sleep well?" She whispered.

Finn stared back blankly for a second, he caught himself staring and managed to mumble "Yes….. I slept very well thanks." He scooped up some of the sludge and smiled at her as he deposited it into his mouth. "Feels like sleeping's all I've done for days now, my head's all fuzzy, like it's been stuffed with thistle down. I should really try to fight it today, stay awake as long as possible. Hopefully the sea air should help clear my head."

A worried look crossed her face but she quickly covered it in a smile, hopefully before he noticed. "You obviously need the rest; you've been through so much. I really thought I'd lost you back there…….." The worried look returned to her face and he reached out to cup her tiny hand in his, which in truth wasn't all that much bigger.

Thordys shuffled back into place at the tiller. "Merryn, can you take up a little slack there?"

The girl quickly hopped up and pulled in a little rope and the sail abruptly ceased flapping in the breeze.

Finn turned towards the tiller. "I'm a little confused Granny; I notice we're heading south?"

Thordys pursed her lips and nodded "We are indeed. What of it?"

Finn stared at her but she appeared to be avoiding eye contact as she stared out past the prow. "You're heading back to Bruann aren't you? You know I can't go back home. I've been cast out; they almost killed me before I left. They probably would have done too, if it hadn't been for old Jack."

Thordys looked down at the boy and gave a small snort. "Home…. now there's a funny word…..There's no such thing as home, not for the likes of you and I boy. Admit it, you were always too restless for that wee place. You and me both really, although I think I managed to hide it much better than you ever did. Still hiding is a skill I've learned well over the years."

"Why are we heading back then? We could have stayed there in Holfstadir, the battle was won, Raghnall was defeated, things will be better now." He felt the frustration building, he had fought hard and his side had won; now he wasn't even there to reap the benefits of the victory.

Merryn sat back down quietly trying her hardest to go un-noticed.

Thordys fixed the boy with the hard look he knew well, it was the one he was on the receiving end of whenever he tried to get his own way. "What makes you so sure that things will be any different now that Raghnall is gone?"

"Harald is different, he's better; he was fighting for a cause, for his people. He has delivered the people from under Raghnall's yoke; the years of tyranny are over now. No one needs to hide any more!"

Thordys looked at the lad she'd raised. He was still so young and had so much to learn. She smiled in spite of herself and saw the flicker of anger that her smile caused flash across his eyes. "Fine words indeed. Look, I'm sure that this Harald is a fine man and I have no doubt that he has the very best of intentions; but let me assure you of this Finn; all men are the same deep down."

She quickly swallowed a mouthful of breakfast and went on, waving her spoon at no one in particular. "Do you think that Raghnall was so very different from your Harald in the beginning? I was there, I saw him for myself. He was a good man too back then, he had a cause and he only wanted the very best for his people, but things change. Not immediately but slowly, things change. The fear creeps in. The harder they try to hold on to all that power the easier it slips through their fingers, so they grip harder. It's like trying to grab a handful of sand. They become more ruthless, less trusting they see threats hiding in every shadow. All men are essentially the same; time and time again they repeat the mistakes of the men that went before. I've seen it happen more times that I'd care to remember." She stared out past the little boat, far out into the past lost in the memories of days long gone.

Finn dropped his eyes sullenly to the deck. "I saw you, you know? There on the battlefield, I saw you. I was lying there in Merryns arms and………. I saw."

Thordys met his eyes and gave a rye smile. "I thought you might have. Not many men have seen what you did. There are very few who have returned from the edge of things."

He looked up, tears building. "I would have gone with her you know? I'm sorry but I would have." He turned to Merryn, apology written on silent eyes.

With a glance Merryn took over the tiller and Thordys slipped over to the boy's side, she took his cheek gently in her hand and wiped away a tear with the tip of her thumb. "I know lad, I know. There was a small part of me that wanted to let you go with her. But it wasn't your time, not yet."

He looked up at the old woman as if seeing her for the first time. "You're not really my Granny are you?"

She smiled gently. "In my heart I am. I've loved you like the son I can never have. You took your first breath lying in my arms, all pink and wrinkled and so full of life. I needed you almost as much as you needed me back then. I lost my two best friends in all the world that day."

"Who are you then? Really?"

She softly stroked his cheek once more and sat upright, letting the years fall from her face like autumn leaves. "I am, or should I say I was, the first of the nine. Thordys Gildenhelm, shield-maiden, valkyrie and the eldest daughter of The All-father."

They stared, there were no words, Merryn felt a question forming but before it reached her lips it crumbled foolish and redundant. It was left by the wayside as her mind raced onward coming to terms with the truth of the situation.

Finn blinked to clear the salt tears, they were fogging his vision and he was not quite sure that he was seeing what he thought he was. It was the same person, there was no doubt about that, she was just considerably younger, well her face was at least, the eyes remained the same. Ancient eyes that had seen too much, they stared back at him, reassuring him in spite of his misgivings.

Thordys laughed; a short abrupt laugh a little too close to a bark. "Stop staring you two, you look like a couple of freshly landed haddock!"

Finn smiled, that was more like her. "So why exactly are we going back to Bruaan?"

Thordys took another mouthful of breakfast and continued the conversation as if nothing had changed. "Don't worry we're not staying long, you don't even have to set foot there if you don't want to. I left in a little bit of a hurry that's all, didn't have time to pack and I've forgotten a few bits and pieces I'd rather not leave behind. We can stop off as briefly as you like and then...............well, then we'll see."

Finn had more questions than he could count but he knew better than to ask them then and there. Granny or Thor.......whatever-her-name, didn't like to be interrogated. She did like to tell stories though and they wouldn't reach Bruaan till morning the next day at the earliest. "So what do I call you now then?"

She smiled at the lad. "Well most of my friends just call me Thora, but you my boy can stick with Granny, I've kind of got used to it over the years."

"Alright Granny, I think I'll take a wee turn at the helm, if that's alright?" He carefully levered himself up off the deck and shuffled his backside onto the bench at the helm taking his seat on the opposite side of the tiller from Merryn.

He curled his fingers around the pole and felt his fingers brush up against hers. She kept her hand there for a second and smiled at the lad before giving his hand a gentle squeeze. "Due south now, I'll clear up these breakfast things."

Chapter 40

Finn spent the rest of the morning at the tiller, it felt good to be doing something useful again, keeping the course true and the sail tight helped occupy his mind.

Merryn sat close by; she had played out a fishing line about a half hour ago and was being instructed on the subtle art by a very patient Granny. It felt odd calling her that now; she hardly looked old enough to warrant the name. He'd been trying to put an age on her and having changed his mind for the twentieth time in as many minutes he had settled on 30; or maybe 35 at the most.

He was staring again and she caught him. "You alright Finn? Careful you don't wear yourself out. I can take over the helm if you like?"

"Nah, I'm fine, just daydreaming, that's all."

"If you're sure then……" She glanced out past the bow again, checking the course. She thought he hadn't noticed, but he had. She had checked the course about six times now. She either didn't trust him or she doubted his ability to handle the little boat.

"Yes, I'm still heading due south, just like I was about an hour ago when you last checked! I know what I'm doing you know!"

Thordys smiled. "Yes I know, I know. I'm just a little worried that's all."

"Worried about what? Don't you trust me to do as I'm told?" He said trying hard to keep the frustration out of his voice.

"Of course I trust you. I know you better than you know yourself young man. I'm just wondering what kind of reception we'll get. I don't think either of us will exactly be welcomed with open arms."

Merryn watched her two companions bickering and tried to muffle a little giggle.

"What's so bloody funny?" Asked Finn.

She smiled. "It's just you two. The way you go on at each other, you're like an old married couple. A niggle here and a niggle there, have you always been like this?"

Thordys let out a chuckle of her own. "Only since he learned to speak."

"Yes, you probably got your own way entirely before then." He said stretching out to push at her shoulder with his bare foot.

Merryn gave the fishing line a little tug as she'd been shown. "I'm curious Thora, how is it that you found yourself raising a child?"

Finn was delighted; he'd been trying to think of a way to broach the subject all day. He struggled to stop the smile he felt creeping onto his face.

Thordys sat back against the gunwale. "Now that's a long story, still I suppose we have the time. Unless you two are too busy to listen?"

Merryn and Finn sat silent and watched her expectantly.

Thordys gazed out somewhere in the middle distance. "Alright then, well I suppose I should start at the beginning. As I mentioned earlier, I had been sent away by my father, the details don't really matter now I suppose, but obviously he was angry. Ha! Now there's an understatement! My sisters had done their best to argue on my behalf but when his mind is fixed on something there is nothing to be done to shift it. You'd have more luck asking the sun not to set." She sighed.

After a moment spent staring out at the dim and distant past she continued. "So anyway, I had been wandering Midgard for some time, I'd had a few adventures. It's quite a wonderful place down here really. I had travelled on foot, by horse and by ship for many years, I had loved, been loved, fought wars, watched men born and die, good and bad alike and I was growing a little weary; truth be told.

I was a short time after I'd left Raghnall and I had taken passage to the Southern Lands on a merchant's knarr; that's a large ship, broad in the beam and usually filled to the gunwales with cargo. After a week or so we made port in Aevanstoun, a grubby little cluster of hovels on the edge of a large forest. I had intended to say on board but as the crew offloaded their cargo, I saw that their next cargo was to be the produce of the local tannery. I couldn't quite bear the thought of a week at sea with the stench of badly tanned leather, so I grabbed my gear and set out on foot.

All roads out of Aevanstoun lead back inland and into the forest. Now when I say forest don't for a minute imagine some lush green forest of broadleaved oaks and noble beech trees, the forest there was a tightly packed morass of spindly pines with mean jagged branches. The canopy is so dense that it keeps both the sun and wind from coming anywhere near the forest floor. It's like travelling though perpetual night. The forest is the perfect breeding ground for every biting winged beastie you can imagine and some it's best you probably can't, the beasties that don't fly scuttle and they still bite.

I spent a couple of days trudging through that place, it still makes my skin crawl to think about it and believe it or not even after all these years I still have some souvenirs." She rolled back her sleeve and pointed out several small white dots on her forearm, scars from bites long healed.

"Eventually I came to the edge of the forest and found myself on the banks of a large lake; it was wonderful to feel the breeze in my hair and the warm sun on my skin again. I was weary and made camp right there on the lake-side, the fish there were fat, juicy and well fed on the insects that were blown into the water from the forest's edge. After my first decent night's sleep in days I struck out along the bank. The lake was huge and after two days of walking I had still not rounded the end. On the third day I saw a wisp of smoke rising from behind a small headland. I took to the forest edge and approached carefully, that land was unknown to me and I always did my best to avoid trouble. Well most of the time."

She turned and checked the course once more. Finn sighed. "I have it in hand, go on!"

"Where was I now……… Well the smoke was coming from a large round house; it was built on stilts out on top of the water. The floor of the house was a couple of feet above the top of the lake and there was a narrow walkway leading from the shore out to the doorway. The smoke I'd seen was coming from a gaping hole in the thatch roof which was still smouldering at the edges. When I got a little closer I could see that the woven sides of the house were smashed and broken, it was clear that something awful had happened there.

I kept watch for an hour or so from the shadows of the forest and when I was sure that the place was deserted I crept out. The mud on the bank had been churned by heavy feet and deposited along the walkway towards the building. I crossed the bridge and saw that what I had earlier taken for rocks breaking the waters surface were lifeless bodies, bloated and floating, limbs tangled in the wooden pilings.

I felt sticky blood grabbing at the soles of my boots as I entered the dark building. The only light inside was from the rent in the roof but it was obvious that the occupants of the house had met with a truly vicious end. The dwelling had been ransacked and their belongings lay broken and scattered on the floor.

I sat down on the remnants of what I took to be a bench or perhaps a bed, sickened and weary to my very bones. It was clear that whoever had lived there had been completely defenceless, most likely a small family of fisher-folk. They had probably built their house out there to avoid the bloody insects from the forest, pity they hadn't thought to build it a bit further out; it might have protected them from people too.

It was at that moment, while I was just sitting there, that I saw something move in the shadows. I was up, sword drawn and braced in an instant. *Show yourself before I separate your head from your neck*, I called. I heard a feint sob in reply and when I crept forward to investigate I found a small boy cowering behind a large basket. I guessed his age at about 5 or 6 years and he was caked in mud from the lakeside where he had obviously hidden. I still remember the tears streaming down his cheeks, his pale skin shining through the mud like tiny rivers."

She turned to the young man at the helm. "That was the first moment I set eyes on your father."

She clearly had a captive audience so she went on. "Well I put away my sword and with the help of a heel of loaf from my travelling pack I was able to coax the boy out from the shadows. I soon got him cleaned up and once I'd got some warm food inside him, he fell asleep with his head on my lap.

Things were a bit awkward at first, he didn't speak much and when he did it was in some strange tongue which was a mystery to me. But I couldn't leave him there; he'd have perished from hunger, so I found myself with a travelling companion.

We walked by day and set camp at night, and before long we came to the end of the lake. The lake emptied itself by way of a fast flowing river and once we'd followed that river for the best part of a week I found myself once more on the shores of the ocean. After a spell, maybe a fortnight or more, I'd come to realise that I couldn't continue wandering like I had been, not with a youngster in tow.

So I started looking for a place to stop for a while, as luck would have it Bruann was the only village I could find along that rocky shore. The locals were a bit wary at first. It's not every day that some strange woman walks into town, especially not accompanied by a young boy and with a sword strapped to her hip. I passed the boy off as my son and I made up some cock and bull story about the boys father being killed by raiders."

She smiled to herself. "That was back when Old Jack Spraggan was far from old, he was a very fine looking young man you know, and despite being recently wedded, he had a bit of a soft spot for me. Not that he ever acted upon it mind. He managed to persuade the ones that needed persuading and they agreed to take us in. Your father fitted in well there, they were fisher-folk, just like his parents had been, he thrived and to be honest so did I.

As the years passed by, without laying a finger on me; I began to hear the odd whisper about my appearance. It had never been an issue before as I'd never stayed in one place for long enough, so that's when I adopted this little *glamour*.

It's mostly in the eye of the beholder really and it gets easier the older you want to be. It started with a few crow's feet around my eyes and the odd grey hair. But as the years passed, little by little I made it more obvious, I made my movements a little more sluggish, I walked a little more slowly was slightly heavier on my feet, you get the gist.

Old people are almost invisible anyway; no one really pays any attention to them, not like they pay attention to a young maiden like you Merryn. If you were to walk through the town, any town, people would take in every subtle facet of you, how you hold your head, the slightest roll of your hips as you walk. Men and women alike, men for their blatantly obvious reasons and women; well they're just weighing up the competition.

So we stayed in Bruaan and became quite a cosy little family. Your father grew up, met your mother, wedded her and they both moved into the little cottage with me. You know the rest and you'll be sick of the sound of my voice by now in any case. I think it's time for something to eat. Any luck with that fishing line Merryn?"

Merryn looked along the line and gave it a small tug. "Nope, nothing yet."

"Oh well, keep at it. They might start biting as the sun goes down, I think there is a little bit of bread left. It's probably stale but It'll have to serve." And with that she clambered on all fours toward the bow of the boat.

Finn let out a little sail to catch the freshening wind. Granny's tale had left him with more questions than answers.

Chapter 41

They made landfall early the next day. As they were heading south past the jagged headland, Thordys tacked west, taking their course along the coastline towards Bruann. She found it strangely comforting to see the familiar heather covered hills and rocky coves, even the screeching seabirds seemed like old friends.

She waited until they were passing the small strand of beach about a league east of the village and then turned sharply towards shore. She left the sail full up, the boat picked up speed and they all braced themselves as the prow carved into the sandy beach and the small boat ground to a halt in the shallows.

Finn quickly lowered and stowed the sail with a little help from Merryn as Thordys hopped over the side and into the shallow water. Once they had dragged the boat a little higher onto the beach and shifted their provisions to a safe drier spot they stopped and all three sat down heavily on the sand.

Thordys began to pack a few scraps of food into an empty sack. "Right, I'll head up over the hill and walk into Bruann from the high road. I won't be long and it's probably safer if I go alone. I'm sure that neither of you have any objections?"

Finn tried to keep the relief he felt from his face. "Are you sure you'll be alright on your own?"

"Oh I'll be fine. They might be a little surprised to see me but it will be a very brief visit. They'll be all too glad of that." She sat up and swung the sack over her shoulder, "I'll be back before nightfall, you two might want to sort out somewhere for us to sleep tonight."

Finn and Merryn watched her walk off across the narrow beach and up the grassed slope; she seemed to gain a year with every step until the now very familiar old woman disappeared from view behind the hill.

Finn stood up and dusted the sand from his backside. "Well I suppose we'd better do as she says. The hollow underneath that crab-apple tree looks as good a place as any."

They gathered up the small collection of provisions and blankets and before too long they had laid out a cosy little camp for the night in the dappled shade of the crab-apple. Finn collected driftwood from the tide line for a fire and began to brew a little pot of tea from the herbs he'd found nearby.

They watched the tea brew in silence and then he poured a little of the tea into a small bowl and passed it to Merryn. They sat side by side cross-legged by the little fire sipping on the warm tea. "It's quite nice to be on dry land again, isn't it?"

She sipped and nodded. "Yes, although I was getting quite used to the boat. It feels a little odd now, when I close my eyes I feel as if I'm still rocking a little."

"I still can't believe that you followed me all that way. After everything, and what I said to you, I was horrible, you should have just........."

She smiled and shuffled up closer. "You were just upset that's all. I knew that deep down you didn't mean it. I could feel it in here." She took his hand and pressed it to her chest. "I could feel in here that you still loved me, just like I could feel that you were still alive all that time. When I saw you back there, in the battle, something inside me died a little."

He moved closer and kissed her softly tasting salt tears. He wrapped her in his arms and felt her sobs slowly subside as he kissed first her nose, then her wet cheeks and then lingered at her soft warm lips. He moved his hand up from her chest and cradled her head burying his fingers deep in the soft waves of her hair.

And so they found each other once more on that warm afternoon hidden from the world outside by the whispering leaves.

***

The path along the cliff-tops was dusty and warm, she was glad that she'd taken the small water skin with her as she stopped for a moment to slake her thirst. Bruaan was close now, she knew these hillsides well; in fact there was a nice little patch of ramsons quite close at hand. But that could wait. She swung the sack back over her shoulder and walked on.

As she topped the next rise she could see the outline of the rocky bay before her and she knew that Bruann lay hidden in the hollow just out of sight. There was a small boy tending some goats just off to her right, she most likely knew the lad but he was too far off for her to clearly distinguish his features.

She made it another six yards or so along the path when the boy, who'd clearly been day-dreaming up to that point, saw her approaching. He stopped idly swinging his crook, dropped it as if he'd suddenly realised that he was holding a venomous snake and ran off down towards the village. Good, she thought; that should bring the welcoming committee.

She was right of course, by the time she'd started making her way down the steep path to the village, she saw that a group of about twenty had gathered. They had clearly become less trusting while she'd been away, as she could see that at least four or five of the group carried cudgels of some description.

As she drew nearer a male voice hailed her. "Ho there! State your business!"

She recognised Billy Ogg's voice immediately and shouted back. "My business is none of yours, Billy Ogg!"

There was a murmur of dissent from the group but she continued towards them unperturbed. She stopped when she was within a matter of yards from the group and still well outside cudgel range. They were all male and apart from Jack Spraggan who wore the barest hint of a smile none of them looked particularly pleased to see her.

Jack spoke up. "I'm pleased to see that you're well but we didn't expect to see you here again Thora, especially approaching from the landward side of things."

She smiled, secretly enjoying the wary looks she was receiving from Billy Ogg and his friends. "I didn't expect to be back here either Jack. I see you've been busy putting things right." She cast her eye in the general direction of the freshly repaired cottages and then let her gaze rest accusingly upon the cottage that she and Finn had called home. It remained as it had been, black and broken, like a cavity in a health smile.

Jack sighed. "We're getting there slowly but surely. But you didn't come all this way to inspect the repairs did you?"

"No, you're right I didn't. I wouldn't have come back at all, it's just my leaving was a little hurried, as you'll no doubt remember and I've left a few bits and pieces behind. If you'll allow me to gather my things I'll be on my way again and you can all forget that you ever knew me."

Jack was about to reply, when Billy Ogg broke in. "What makes you think we'd let the likes of you back into *our* village?"

She smiled. "Ah, I see the less enlightened members of the village have appointed themselves a spokesman." Then she let a little menace creep into her voice. "Listen Billy, and listen good, I'm trying to be nice here; asking permission to collect my things. These things are mine and mine alone. Trust me, if you knew the nature of the things I'm here to collect you'd be glad to let me have them and see the back of me. Now don't make me ask again or I might forget to be quite so nice."

Billy shuffled his feet, he weighed the stout cudgel in his hands for a second and then though the better of it. "Let her take her stuff and be dammed! Bloody witch!" He turned on his heels and most of the rest of the welcoming committee followed suit.

Jack turned to walk back down into the village leaving a noticeable gap between himself and the others, and she fell in step alongside him on the path. "Finn told me what you did for him Jack." She whispered. "You have my thanks; the boy would never have survived without you."

Jack kept his eyes down watching the path ahead; she noticed that he leaned a little heavier on his stick these days. "It was nothing Thora, you'd have done as much and more if it had been one of mine."

"Aye perhaps your right Jack, but I thank you in any case."

"You'll be needing access to the cavern I assume?" He said turning towards her a little. "I did notice your old chest when I was last down there."

She nodded. "I trust it's not been touched."

"All of us elders know better than to go anywhere near that chest Thora. You know that."

***

Merryn lay there staring off at nothing in particular, his chest rising and falling under the weight of her head.

She had longed to be with him like this, ever since he'd first woken out there on the boat, but she'd restrained herself. She had felt so self conscious of her feelings out there under the watchful eye of Thora. Although she now knew the truth of the matter, Thora still felt very much like his grandmother and you couldn't kiss a boy properly in front of his grandmother.

She still couldn't quite believe that he had survived his injuries, he should be dead by rights; she knew that. She was quite sure that he'd been dead when she'd held him. She remembered the weight of his limp body and shuddered a little despite herself, raising goose-flesh along her arms.

Still he was here now and that was all that mattered really. She calmed herself and absentmindedly drew her fingers along the raised scar that was forming under the knotted yarn on his chest. He grumbled a little in his sleep and she quickly withdrew her fingertips.

He was still so weary, his exertions had left him drained and he had fallen asleep quicker than she'd thought was possible. So she lay there listening to the regular thump of his heart and not for the first time in the past few days her thoughts turned to the future.

What was in store for them both? She still wasn't entirely sure.

She had always been so sure of so many things, headstrong according to her father; who would know. That had probably always been the best way to describe her.

So she began to list the things that she was still sure of.

She loved Finn. She could not imagine a future that didn't involve him. She had come so close to loosing him forever that she knew she could not face the prospect again.

She loved her home. Her mother, her father, her family, friends and all that *home* meant to her. She knew that and she knew that some small facet of her heart that wasn't given to Finn, longed for home, it drew her back there.

She was *seilkind*, asking her to turn her back on that and all that it meant would be like asking her to stop breathing. She may manage to do so for a short time, but the endeavour was ultimately doomed to failure. She was who she was. She was also what she was. Was it possible for anyone to change that?

She would find a way to make it work. Perhaps his idea of finding a place, some small island maybe, far across the sea, but close enough to Tir-nan-og that she could come and go as she pleased was a good one. It would be a compromise, but wasn't that the very essence of life? Compromise.

Yes they'd make it work, somehow. Her family would just have to accept the *landling* boy; she'd convince them, she'd make them see that there was no other way.

Unconsciously she had reached out with her bare foot and now found that it rested upon the small bundle that was her seal-skin. She felt the familiar warmth of the soft fur on her skin and its calming effect. Yes she would make it work.

Before long she joined Finn and slipped into slumber. They lay there entwined in the dappled light as the sun crept steadily to the west; safe, warm and oblivious to the arrival of the dark raven now perched on the top-most branch of the crab-apple tree.

Chapter 42

Thordys slowly climbed the steep path out of Bruann, her feet scuffed over familiar rocks and unbidden her mind began to wander the past and all the times good and bad that she had spent there in the village.

She passed the smooth stone where Finn as a young boy had slipped in his haste to get to the top. She could still see him sitting there; knee skinned, dropped tears making dark spots on the sandstone. It was the first but by no means the last of his hurts she'd mend.

She shifted the sack on her shoulder and trudged on. The chest was not the lightest of burdens but she wouldn't have attempted to move its precious contents without the protection of the dense wooden box. She didn't have far to go and the road would level out soon.

When she got to the top of the hill, she stopped for a moment, laid down her baggage and looked back over the village hands on hips. All was as it always had been, from the very first moment she'd set eyes on the place so little had changed. She felt sure that if she returned in another hundred years it would all still be just the same. She made a silent promise to herself that she would do just that.

She watched as the last of the boats was dragged out of the water up onto the small strip of beach. Then the chattering women arrived, baskets braced on their hips to collect the days catch. It was such a lovely image, played out as it was in the dying afternoon light.

She gathered up the sack once more and turned her back on the village as she trudged along the path, her lengthening shadow going on ahead, as the sun descended toward the western hills.

The walk along the hill-tops was uneventful and she reached the rise above the beach just as the first few stars of evening were beginning to show themselves up above. She saw a feint wisp of smoke rising from under the shade of the stunted crab-apple tree and smiled at the thought of the two youngsters camped underneath. She felt sure that they would have passed a pleasant afternoon in her absence.

Young love was such a wonderful thing after all.

She quite deliberately ignored the Raven perched on the squat buckthorn bush as she passed.

"Kraa!" it called, managing to sound just as put-out as it felt.

She stopped and turned; anger flaring in her eyes. "Give me one good reason I should speak to you? Where were you last week when I, no when *we* could have done with a little help?"

The Raven did its best to look ashamed, not an easy task when you've only black eyes, black beak and black feathers to work with. "Kraa!" it said by way of apology.

She gave her shoulders a little shrug, grudgingly. "Yes I know he keeps you very busy, I can appreciate that. But you really let me down: and I thought we were friends?"

She turned to go. "I'll see you again soon no doubt. You can tell him I'm still dreadfully sorry and all that."

The Raven watched her go; head cocked to one side for a few seconds before it took to the wing and disappeared over the hill.

When she got to the tree she saw that Finn was busy roasting fish over the hot coals at the side of the fire, Merryn was picking her way through a bowl full of greens that they'd gathered. "You've been busy I see." She said as she bent to gently lay down the sack and its precious contents.

The two youngsters looked up and smiled, it was growing dark but she was sure that they were both blushing just a little. "You had a successful trip too I see." Said Finn; nodding towards the dark shape on the ground.

She sat down crossing her legs under her. "Yes it went very well, but we'll get to that later, I'm starved."

Once they had eaten the best meal they'd had for days, Finn's attention returned to the dark bundle that Thordys had brought back from the village. She saw him staring and smiled a little, she was going to enjoy this.

He looked up from the bundle and met her eyes. "So what was so important then?"

She pursed her lips, saying nothing and shifting onto her knees she pulled the sack towards her. She folded back the rough material and drew the dark russet box from inside, laying it carefully on top of the empty sack.

She sat back on her heels and watched the light from the small camp-fire flicker on the metal bindings of the chest for a moment.

Finn and Merryn sat expectantly and watched as she fished out the small key and slid it into the lock hidden in the mouth of the ornate metal wolf. The light click of the lock mechanism was barely heard over the crackle of the campfire.

She withdrew the key and leaving the lid closed she looked up at her captive audience. "This box contains many things that are precious to me. Some I own, some I'm ashamed to say I have stolen and some of them I have in my possession merely for safekeeping."

She lifted the lid and smiled at the familiar glow as she made a silent inventory of the contents. All was as it should be.

She reached in with both hands and carefully drew out the large dark sphere. The dim light flared at the edges of the gilt silver continents as she gently moved it away from the chest. The sphere seemed a little too large to have ever fitted inside the box but they said nothing and watched silently as she gently laid it onto a blanket.

The next item to be taken from the box was the golden masked helmet that seemed strangely familiar to Finn. The reason for its familiarity lingered at the outer fringes of memory, close but not quite within his grasp. Once this was laid carefully beside the sphere Thordys smiled at the expectant looks on their faces and she reached into the chest once more.

This time she rooted around inside the box and eventually drew out a dark bundle around a foot in length. She leaned over and softly laid the package in front of the lad. "This, my dearest Finn, is yours."

He looked up from the object, confusion plain on his face.

Thordys smiled. "You don't recognise it do you? But I'm sure that young Merryn here has a very good idea what it is."

Finn turned towards the girl and was surprised to see the delight dancing in her eyes alongside the firelight. She reached out her hand and gently touched the dark bundle, feeling the warm velvet-like texture she knew so well. "It's a seal-skin!" She said trying to suppress the giggle she found bubbling up from her throat.

Finn reached out for the skin and gently stroked the smooth warmth of it. His finger-tips tingled and he felt a calm he had never known before trickle into his body. The familiar tension he had lived with all his life but never quite noticed, left him and he drew a deep breath as he realised that for the first time in his short life he felt whole. He lifted the skin onto his lap and looked up questioningly.

Thordys smiled. "As I said some of the things I have purely for safekeeping. This skin is yours my boy, it was born with you; I should know I was there. I don't think I really understood the nature of the thing, but having spent so long with young Merryn here I think I am beginning to realise that I should never have kept it from you. I was wrong and I am more deeply sorry than I could ever explain."

Finn sat silently his eyes fixed on the dark bundle.

She went on. "Merryn, when I told you that you weren't the first Selkie I had known; I was telling the truth. Finn's mother was the first and the only other. She was a good woman, she loved your father Finn and she loved you however briefly, from the moment she saw you. She was my friend. When it was her time, she wouldn't allow any of the other women from the village to help with the birthing, so it was just her and I alone."

The tears welled in the corner of her eyes at the memory of it all. "I was not experienced enough back then, when it began to go wrong I panicked, I begged her to let me get help but she would have none of it. She knew that if any of the local women saw you being born a selkie it would be the end of it, so she gave herself up for you. I tried everything I could but there was just so much blood, she was holding you in her arms as she slipped away."

She reached out and placed a gentle hand on the lad's shoulder. He raised his head and she saw that he too was crying. "This should have been your mother's gift to you, but I didn't understand. I hid it away, kept it from you. I thought I was protecting you. That was my last promise to her, to always protect you."

***

The moonlight glistened on the water, illuminating the bubbling tips of the small waves lapping the sandy shore. The sea was calm; reflecting the myriad stars like a black mirror, it was impossible to see where the sea met the sky and the world seemed wrapped in a dark glittering blanket.

The maid and the lad stood there at the waters edge unashamedly naked as the day they were born. Both held dark skins draped like soft velvet cloaks over their arms. They looked so alike standing there, their pale skin glowing in the soft moonlight.

Thordys smiled, although in truth she was once again close to tears. "I think it's time."

The lad turned toward her and she tried not to stare at the scars marking his young body, the boy had been through so much. Starlight glistened on the tears building in the corners of his dark eyes and he smiled at her. "How do you say goodbye Granny?"

She smiled back and wrapped him in her arms one last time. "You don't my boy, you say farewell. We'll meet again, someday, I feel it."

He returned the hug and kissed her softly on the cheek as he pulled away. "Where will you go now?"

Thordys wiped her wet eyes with the back of her hand and gave a wry smile. "Believe it or not, I'm long overdue a visit to an old acquaintance, a dragon actually. Like I said; some of my bits and pieces are not mine by rights." She gave a small shrug.

Merryn placed her hand on his shoulder. "Are you ready Finn?"

He nodded and they both took a few steps into the water, stopping when the small waves lapped at their knees.

Merryn turned and blew her a small kiss. Then they both drew the dark skins faintly glimmering, over their shoulders and dived forward into the sea.

If her eyes had been just a little better or the moon just a little bit brighter, she might have seen two black heads, bobbing on the mirrored surface, as the dark eyes of the seal gazed back at the lonely figure on the beach.

Printed in Great Britain
by Amazon.co.uk, Ltd.,
Marston Gate.